Three Times Blessed

Other **Belles of Timber Creek** Books
TWICE LOVED

And Coming Soon
ONE TRUE LOVE

Three Times Blessed

Belles of Timber Creek

Lori Copeland

AVON

INSPIRE

An Imprint of HarperCollins*Publishers*

THREE TIMES BLESSED. Copyright © 2009 by Copeland, Inc. All rights reserved. Printed in the United States of America. No part of this book may be used or reproduced in any manner whatsoever without written permission except in the case of brief quotations embodied in critical articles and reviews. For information address HarperCollins Publishers, 10 East 53rd Street, New York, NY 10022.

Scripture taken from *The Message*. Copyright 1993, 1994, 1995, 1996, 2000, 2001, 2002. Used by permission of NavPress Publishing Group.

ISBN-13: 978-1-6152-3291-8

As silver in a crucible and gold in a pan,
so our lives are assayed by God.
Proverbs 17:3 (*The Message*)

Prologue

"Copper! Where are you!" Audrey Pride slammed the front door and raced through the parlor. Copper appeared in the back doorway. "What?"

"Our prayers have been answered!" Audrey waved the telegraph wire that had just been delivered by horseback.

Copper's eyes lit. "We have the jobs!"

"Well—just me, for now, but I'm sure Beeder's Cove will reach the same decision any day now."

Clasping each other's arms, the two women danced around the kitchen. Audrey had always believed in the power of prayer, but God had worked even more swiftly than she'd dared hope. Why, they'd only been back from Thunder Ridge scant weeks, and already she had secured Blackberry Hill's teaching position. The news was simply too good to be true. The school board had indicated it might be months before they reopened school, but the proof of vigilant prayer was in her hand, a telegraph from Blackberry

Hill informing her that she was to come right away, that they planned to open school that fall, and much was to be done in preparation.

Copper paused. "I'll come with you."

"Of course you'll come with me, you goose!" Audrey reached for another tight hug. "I couldn't move without you. You can stay with Willow, and by fall I just know that Beeder's Cove will summon you."

Copper hugged back tightly. "We've been through too much to part ways now."

"Way too much," Audrey agreed, thinking back to the hours of fighting on the battlefront together. She, Willow Madison, and Copper had helped defend Timber Creek from the Yanks, but they'd lost. The town was mostly burned-out shells now. A small rural population still existed, but one by one the families were leaving in search of new homesteads. The war was over, and now Copper, Willow, and she would be reunited, even if Willow was planning to marry Silas Sterling and remain in Thunder Ridge, Texas. Blackberry Hill was a scant few miles down the road, and Beeder's Cove the same small distance to the south.

At least the three women would be together again.

Willow's letters had begged for Audrey and Copper to leave Timber Creek and move to Thunder Ridge. Judge Madison had even invited them to stay with him. He had a big old house, but he suffered from ill health.

The two women looked at each other and screamed in unison.

"We're really going!"

Audrey broke into action. "We really are! With my teaching position I can support the both of us, and we won't be a burden to Willow and the judge. We'll pack tonight, and leave first thing in the morning."

Within the hour, they'd packed the wagon and made ready.

Approaching hoofbeats awoke both women before dawn. A rider appeared on their doorstep, and Audrey hurried to slide the thick bolt. Since the war, no town was safe from marauding bands of displaced soldiers and Indians, and because the male population of Timber Creek was practically nil, the town was most susceptible to foul play. The rider wordlessly handed her a wire.

Her heart sank. Maybe Blackberry Hill had changed its mind. Maybe they wouldn't be opening a school this fall after all. Disappointment rose like bile to the back of her throat.

Yawning, Copper appeared behind her, tying the sash of her robe. "Who is it?"

Audrey read the name on the missive and suddenly broke into a wide grin. "Unless I miss my guess, your prayers have just been answered." She handed her friend a wire sent from Beeder's Cove. They both had jobs.

Life was about to get a whole lot better.

Chapter 1

Thunder boomed, jarring the ground. Audrey rose from the seat and sawed back on the reins as the horse bolted. "Hold on!" Copper sat beside her, clutching the bench and shrieking. Drat this downpour! When they'd left Timber Creek three days ago, she'd intended to make a grand but refined entrance into town.

"Audrey Pride! You slow this wagon down this instant!" Copper demanded.

"Just hold on. Thunder Ridge is coming up." Copper was anxious, while she, Audrey, took pride in fortitude. My goodness, if she came apart with every little unexpected bend in the road—or violent storm—she'd be nothing but shattered flesh. Her father's legacy had been fortitude, and he'd taught his daughter well. If a thing was worth having, time was unimportant if in the end you acquired your goal. *A man's wisdom gives him patience* . . . Proverbs, wasn't it?

The buckboard glanced off something solid and jolted

hard, nearly pitching the women out. Audrey regained her grip on the reins and fought to keep the horse under control in the blinding rain. "What'd we hit?" she called above the thunder volleys.

"How should I know? Everything's a blur and I'm drenched to the core!" *Oh please, God, not the water tower. The town was suffering from a dreadful drought, and water was a precious commodity.*

It never rained in Thunder Ridge. That's what Willow claimed in every letter. Well, if this wasn't rain, Audrey would like to know what it was.

Only scant weeks ago she'd spent time here with Willow and her stricken uncle. At the time it had been so dry they were rationing water, not storing it. The wagon burst into town, horse galloping full ahead.

"We're going to die," Copper moaned. "Life's over."

"Oh hush." Audrey stood and sawed back on the reins, slowing the frightened mare.

A strong male hand latched on to the bridle. Copper swooned, lying halfway across Audrey's lap and the wagon bench. When the wagon bucked to a stop, Audrey realized Eli Gray had taken control of the rig. Their gazes touched, then skipped apart. Goose bumps—and not the ones caused by rain, stood out on her flesh. *Eli.* But if the black scowl on his face was any indication of welcome, she might as well turn around and go home.

Quickly adjusting her bonnet, she recovered what was left of her composure. "Eli! How nice to see you again!" She reached out to him. His hand remained on the bridle. The snub didn't surprise her.

"Is anyone hurt?"

She turned to check on Copper, who had not stirred. Her friend's usually rosy complexion was white as a January snowbank. Her gaze traveled back to where they'd come from, only to see a toppled tower. Oh my goodness. They had hit the town's water supply after all.

Rain fell in sheets as Willow Madison raced toward the wagon, shouting her name. Tucker Gray trailed in her wake. "Audrey! Copper? Oh my goodness. Is anyone hurt?" As she arrived breathlessly, Willow's gaze searched Audrey's.

Accepting Eli's gentlemanly hand, which was finally outstretched, Audrey stepped lightly from the wagon. "I'm fine, but Copper might need some smelling salts."

Bystanders turned to accommodate the request as Audrey stepped into Willow's waiting arms for a hug that felt like coming home. Oh, how she'd missed Willow's uplifting smile. "Oh, it's so good to see you again!"

"I had no idea you were coming until Silas told me not more than an hour ago about Blackberry Hill's news. Why didn't you write and tell me!"

"Everything happened so quickly. First the wire arrived saying that Blackberry Hill has decided to reopen school, and then on its heel, the wire confirming that Beeder's Cove needed Copper's services right away. We threw everything we owned into the wagon, closed our seamstress business—which admittedly was paltry, at best, and were on our way within hours. We knew we'd be here before a letter could reach you."

Audrey turned back to Copper, who was struggling to sit up, her cheeks starting to show pink.

Copper stirred, lifting her head. "Where . . . what?"

"You're all right," Audrey soothed. "See? We made it just fine."

Copper's eyes widened. "Are we dead?"

Sighing, Audrey murmured, "Dead? Really, Copper. Look around you. Does this look like Paradise to you?"

Copper's eyes roamed her surroundings. Audrey traced her gaze to water standing in puddles, running in streams. Actually, the town looked . . . soggy. The sawmill was only half rebuilt. Rain-soaked, wide-eyed strangers peered at them. And the two Gray cousins, Tucker and Eli, looked as stern as she'd ever seen them look.

"No, I suppose not." Copper straightened her bonnet and tucked a few strands of wet hair back from her forehead.

Caleb, cousin to Tucker and Eli, arrived. He jumped from his horse and removed his hat, his eyes fixed on Audrey. "Miss Pride! What are you doing back?"

At the sound of his voice Audrey turned, but his gaze was fixed on the chaotic scene. "Caleb! How nice to see you again."

Grinning, he turned and took her extended hand. "I didn't expect you back so soon. To what do we owe the pleasure?"

"I'm going to be teaching in Blackberry Hill this fall."

"Is that a fact?" His grin widened, and his eyes strayed back to Copper. "Well, praise the Lord. What happened?"

"Accident," Audrey murmured, pulling her cape closer as the rain beat on her shoulders. Heat spread across her cheeks. How could she have hit the water tower? "Thunder spooked the horse." Willow might have inadvertently burned the sawmill. But, if Uncle Judge Wallace hadn't asked his niece to bring kerosene, and the thunder hadn't spooked her horse, why the whole incident wouldn't have happened. Yet Audrey had now destroyed the town's water supply. Caleb turned back from the damaged tower to her.

She lifted her shoulders. "Quite a coincidence? Willow, then me, disrupting so much?"

"Quite." His gaze shifted to Eli and Tucker. Eli shrugged. "The wagon must have hit that weak support bar on the tower. Although I can't imagine how the horse would have missed . . ."

Copper shook her curls and interrupted, her fingers pressed to her temples. "I have a splitting headache."

Willow helped her down from the seat. "Let's get you to the judge's house and into dry clothing."

Tucker stepped closer to support Copper's slight weight. "Would you like me to carry you, Miss Wilson?"

"No thank you. I can walk." Copper straightened, fingered her hair into place, and the three headed to Uncle Wallace's house, an ugly green structure that sat on the hill overlooking the mill.

Audrey waited, uncertain about what she should do with the wagon. Should she follow Willow or wait for someone to escort her? Her gaze pivoted to Eli.

A tall man dressed in denims and a plaid shirt pushed his way to the front of the crowd, trying to draw her attention. "Miss Pride?"

She turned. "Yes?"

"Oliver Jackson—we met a few weeks back? Head of Blackberry Hill school board?"

"Oh yes! Mr. Jackson." Audrey reached to shake his hand. Her rescuer. If it were not for the teaching job she'd still be in Timber Creek, sewing on an occasional button or patch for a passerby. How nice of the committee to send a representative.

Oliver shook his head. "I'm sorry, Miss Pride. I feared you might not get the second wire in time."

"Wire? We received one from Beeder's Cove. Is that what you mean?"

He shook his head, casting his eyes to the ground. "We earnestly thought we'd be able to reopen the school right away, but it seems our bookkeeper's excitement exceeded our finances." He looked up. "It will be *next* fall before we can reopen the school."

Audrey's jaw dropped.

Shaking his head, he solemnly confessed. "I understand your dismay, and we're prepared to pay your expenses back to Timber Creek." He removed his hat, revealing a crop of snow-white hair rimming a bald head. "We're most sorry, ma'am. We sent a second telegram as soon as we recognized our mistake."

That missive would have been delivered to a now-deserted shack in Timber Creek. She and Copper had left so quickly the wire wouldn't have had time to reach them. Eyes to the ground, the man threaded his way back through the crowd.

Audrey's head spun. No job? Independence drained away. She glanced to see Eli and Caleb standing to the side, listening to the exchange. She managed a weak smile.

What would she do? Return to Timber Creek? Without Copper? She couldn't bear the thought.

An elderly lady stepped up. "Pardon, dear, but I overheard your conversation, and I just wanted to say that I hear the undertaker is looking for an assistant."

"Undertaker?"

"Kirkland Burying."

"Kirkland Burying? That's the undertaker's name?"

The woman nodded and smiled as if she wasn't aware of the irony. "Place belongs to Hank and Marion Burying, but their older son, Kirkland, runs it. The Buryings have been in the business as long as anyone can recall. Now Kirkland's off buying supplies, but he'll be back directly. Early next week, I'd say. You can go on down and have a talk with the boy. Work might not suit you, but it'd pay your bills and let you sleep better at night."

Audrey shifted, trying to absorb the full impact of the news. She had no means of support. Copper would be teaching in Beeder's Cove, Willow would be here in Thunder Ridge, and Audrey couldn't think about returning to Timber Creek alone. Willow and Copper were the only family she had, and she couldn't be apart from them. Not now, not when it felt as if her world had just fallen apart.

But she didn't know a thing about burying, except it involved dead bodies.

Caleb's voice interrupted her thoughts. "Eli will take your wagon to the judge's house."

"Thank you." Audrey fell into step, still trying to absorb the news. Well, the situation called for patience. She didn't have a job at the moment, but come next fall she would. All she had to do was find something to tide her over, allow her a smidgen of independence. A smile touched the corners of her mouth when she saw Eli reach for the horse's reins. Yes, patience, in this case, could be helpful. The unforeseen delay would allow her time to attract this particular man's attention. And attract she would. She'd favored Eli over any of the Gray cousins from the day they'd first met. Perhaps God had sensed that the man had grieved long enough.

But could she work with dead folks? She supposed she could perform whatever service the undertaker required. They sure wouldn't be likely to talk back. She shook the thought aside and tried not to concentrate on the long-term implications of her fears. She could do anything if it kept her with Willow and Copper, and Eli Gray within eyesight.

Casting a final glance at the mill site, Audrey trailed Caleb up the hill where the judge's home sat. What was it the Good Book warned, "Don't worry about tomorrow, today had its share of trouble"? Not an exact quote, but the same sentiment.

All she had to do was keep reasonably independent until the teaching position became available; pride said she must earn her keep. And she would, but in the meantime she intended to pursue this fine man who was now leading her horse up the hill. She might not attract his attention now, not today, or tomorrow, or maybe a year from now, but eventually he would have to notice her. She understood his need to overcome his loss; she'd lost mother, father, and an invalid brother a few years back, so grief wasn't foreign to her. Mr. Gray needed time, but eventually he would be able to put the past aside. She felt it in her bones, and when she felt something in her bones it was a certainty.

Mind made up, she dismissed the unsettling turn of events and followed Eli up the hill.

Chapter 2

⁓

Audrey caught up and plodded beside him, her wet shoes squishing with every step. The rain turned from downpour to a fine mist. At least now she could walk upright instead of fighting a blowing curtain of water. She glanced up at him, thinking it was kind of him to offer his services—but then he hadn't. Caleb had offered for him.

He glanced back at her. "It's a good thing there aren't more of you Timber Creek women. Wouldn't be anything left of the town. You're taking it apart piece by piece."

She swiped a rain-soaked fringe of hair out of her eyes and gave him a look he couldn't miss. "Purely accident, of course. Do you think I'd deliberately hit a water tower?"

His shook his head. "I can't say, ma'am. Most folks would have avoided it."

"First of all, I'm not a ma'am—" She ducked, but a wet branch slapped her and dropped what felt like a full bucket of water in her face and down her neck. *Land sakes!* She'd never experienced such a drenching. "And secondly, no one in their right mind would intentionally hit an object that large."

"If you say so."

Patience? She was going to need a two-by-four to get this man's attention. "I thought it never rained here!"

"I guess you broke the drought," he called. "Most welcome it is too. Every bucket and pan in town is set out to catch the water."

Even though he didn't say it, Audrey knew he was thinking about the toppled water supply. Thanks to her, the town no longer had a source to hold the precious liquid. She was beginning to understand how Willow must have felt when she inadvertently spilled the kerosene and set the sawmill on fire. Humiliated. And furious. Why would Thunder Ridge build something as important as a water tower so close to the road in the first place? Any sensible person would know to build it back from the road. 'Course the horse was going so fast, who knew whether they were even on the road at that point?

They reached the stable, and Eli led the horse inside, out of the rain. Audrey followed, thinking what a pitiful picture she made. Water dripped from her clothes and hair, forming a good-sized puddle. A white leghorn hen high-stepped toward her and dipped its head to drink thirstily. She tossed her wet hair aside with one finger. She had always taken pains with her appearance, not overly fussy but sure to look presentable. What must Eli Gray think of her now?

She shivered when a chilly breeze blew from the open door. No doubt she would catch her death standing there in damp clothing.

Eli devoted his attention to the horse, socializing apparently forgotten. Audrey reached to pet Willow's mare that had served them so well during the war. "Hello, ole girl. Remember me?"

The horse nuzzled her hand.

Eli paused, his eyes on the friendly exchange. "Guess you two go way back?"

"Yes, during the war we found her in a field one day, with no apparent owner. We took her home, and she's been a godsend in our lives."

His eyes motioned to a stack of empty feed sacks. "Hand me one. The mare needs to be wiped down."

Audrey stepped away from the stall. "I can care for my horse." She didn't want him thinking that she was a helpless woman.

"Just hand me one, and sit down on that bucket before you faint."

"I don't faint."

"No?" His gaze fixed on her. "Most women I know keel over at the slightest provocation."

"I'm not 'most' women." She handed him a dry feed sack. "And Willow and Copper aren't either."

Cool blue eyes assessed her. "How long do you plan to stay in Thunder Ridge this time?"

Audrey sank down on the bucket, fingers working a pleat into the fabric of her soaked skirt. "I'm not sure—I'll need to find work." She glanced at him. "You overheard my conversation with Mr. Jackson?"

"Sorry—voices carry."

"Yes, I am most disappointed."

How could she break the news to Willow? In Blackberry Hill, she would have had a room. Now she was homeless. Destitute. Everything she owned was packed in a satchel and getting soaked sitting in the back of that wretched wagon.

She started. How could she have forgotten her bags? "Our things! We left them in the wagon."

"I'll fetch them in a minute."

She got up. "You don't have to. I can get them myself." Before he could object, she slipped out the door. A fine mist sprayed her face. She waded around standing puddles to unload the satchels. Everything else would have to wait until the rain stopped.

Eli didn't look up when she stumbled over the hen as she came back through the door, a bag in each hand. A rooster came at her, pecking at her heels. She dropped the bags beside an empty stall, nudging the nuisance away with her foot. She'd boil that rude little fowl for supper.

"Here! Git!" Eli scattered the fowl. "So, what are you going to do now?"

Other than eat that rooster? She didn't know.

She sat down, sighing. "Willow invited me to stay with her and the judge but I don't want to impose. I'll look for work right away."

He poured oats into a feed box and placed it in the stall and then tossed a handful of grain to the chickens. Audrey shot the fowl a warning look and then smiled when Eli turned in her direction.

"Not a lot of work in these parts. I suppose if you were a man, we could put you on at the mill. We'll need workers, and with the water tower to rebuild we'll need even more, but I can't picture you doing hard labor."

She allotted a tolerant smile. "Nor can I, Mr. Gray—at least not climbing on mill roofs and toting shingles, but perhaps I could clean houses or get a job at the general store. There must be something available."

"What about the Burying Parlor? Heard Gertie mention the job to you."

"Yes, she did. I haven't had time to consider the prospect."

"What's your friend's plan?" He picked up a lead rope and draped it over the stall door, avoiding eye contact.

Jealousy pricked her. Copper? Had Copper romantically caught his eye—well, of course he'd noticed her. She was hard to miss with all that red hair and flawless complexion, but had he really noticed her? In the way Audrey hoped to attract his favor?

She took in his broad shoulders stretching the soaked fabric of his shirt. She quickly looked away. When had she become so scandalous? Decent women didn't notice such things. Flustered, she said the first thing that popped into mind.

"You'll be delighted to know that Beeder's Cove has hired her for the new teaching position."

"Really?" He glanced up. "When did this come about?"

"Recently—the day my wire from Blackberry Hill arrived." She grinned. "Shall I give her your regards?"

Color crept up his neck. "That's not necessary. I'll see her around."

Audrey was aware of the fire in her own cheeks getting warmer. Well, at least he didn't appear smitten with Copper. She mentally added a checkmark in her favor. But in keeping with friendship, she added. "Copper's a lovely woman."

He tossed a blanket over a stall. "She's one fine lady."

She frowned. So he had noticed her.

"A bit willful for my taste." He adjusted the bill of his hat. "No offense."

She relaxed. "None taken." Copper could argue with a stump. She switched subjects. "Do you know anything about the Burying Parlor?"

He paused. "I try not to go near the place. I had my fill of the dead during the war. Never got very close to bodies, but I knew they were there. It'll be fine with me if I never see another."

She thought back to Timber Creek and the fighting the women had endured there. "War is horrible, isn't it?"

"Be glad you didn't see any actual battle."

She tensed, slanting him a look. "I saw plenty of fighting. I can fire a gun as well or better than you can."

He braced one hand on the stable wall, looking down at her. "If you say so."

"I'll have you understand I'm an excellent markswoman. I rarely miss. I'll challenge you to a duel when the rain lets up. See who the best shot is."

His brows knitted in disbelief. "You best retract your offer. I might take you up on it."

She matched his smirk. "Never. It matters little to me who's the best shot, just as long as we don't shoot each other. Give me the chance to prove my claim."

His gaze lightly skimmed her. "I don't have time for contests. But you asked about the Burying Parlor. Are you seriously thinking about taking the job?"

She lifted a shoulder. "I'm not certain. I don't fancy the idea, but I may have little choice in the matter."

"Think you can handle dead folks?"

She met him look for look. "If I must."

He chuckled. "You're as feisty as your friend."

"I'm nothing like Copper—not that that would be a

bad thing. And truthfully, I don't know if I can handle the dead."

"But you're considering it?"

"A woman in my position can't be choosy."

Thunder rocked the building and sent her flying off the bucket with an involuntary scream. Before she even realized it, she clutched Eli's arm as if he were a lifeline. Her body was trembling, probably from the shock of the wagon accident, the thoughts of dead people, and the chill of wet clothing. For a moment she feared that she really would faint. He slipped his left arm around her, holding her like a frightened child until the thunderous echoes faded.

She straightened and moved away, cheeks burning as she struggled to gain her composure. "Sorry. I don't know what came over me."

"You'll get used to the noise. It happens a lot around here."

"I'll not be caught unaware again." She straightened her hair. "The thunder took me by surprise, that's all."

But that wasn't all. The fear still haunted her as much as she'd prayed for God to take it away. It was the war battles; the stench of gunpowder, the screams, and the hopelessness of not knowing if they would make it out alive.

But they had.

She forced a smile. "I better go inside and change into dry clothing."

When she stepped from the building, thunder unleashed another deluge of cold rain. She forged through the blast of wind until a firm hand grasped her arm, and she looked up to find Eli walking beside her.

"Hold on to me. I'll get you to the house!"

The unrelenting downpour and brute force wind dashed

any desire for independence. She clung to him, grateful for his assistance. They waded through puddles, not even trying to go around them. She could barely see the outlines of the house. A sea of mud stretched before her. Audrey plowed into it, one foot sliding forward. She grabbed his arm in a desperate attempt to keep from falling. Knocked off balance, his booted feet slid out from under him. She heard him yell as they went down together in the soft, squishy morass.

Gasping, she sank into the cold sludge. Beside her Eli thrashed, trying and failing to stand up. He sat flat down in the mire. Then he was back on his feet again as she pushed to her knees, attempting to gain traction. He loomed over her, and she raised apprehensive eyes to meet his, aware that she had caused the humiliating mishap.

Mud smeared his features and coated his jacket and pants. For a moment he stared at her, as if riveted to an offensive sight. Then one corner of his mouth quirked in a grin.

"If your momma could only see you now."

She stared at him, jaw agape, then, to her surprise, a chuckle formed deep in her chest, bubbling to the surface. He reached down to help her up, and they clung to each other, laughing, as thunder and lightning rumbled overhead.

Lifting her face to the rain, she shouted, "If we stand here long enough, the rain will wash us clean!"

He slid one arm around her waist, bracing against the gale. "I believe I'd rather have the comfort of Wallace's kitchen. And hot coffee."

"Hot coffee sounds wonderful." And the feel of his arm around her was even more stimulating than coffee. Suddenly the day had been salvaged.

Chapter 3

Willow opened the back door before Eli had a chance to knock, shielding her eyes from the blowing rain. "Oh dear, Audrey! I was so worried about you." Her friend's eyes skimmed Audrey's appearance. "What happened?"

"I fell in the mud." Audrey brushed ineffectively at her soiled skirt and stepped into the kitchen.

Tucker cocked a brow at Eli. "Aren't you a little old to be playing in the mud?"

Eli glanced at the assembled company sitting at the table. "I'd talk. You look like a drowned rat."

Water was starting to pool beneath Audrey's feet. The cook stove gave off a measure of heat to the rainy dampness. On her earlier visit, she'd noticed a well-stocked woodpile, and Willow had confided that the Gray cousins daily replenished the stack closest to the door.

Eli nodded. "Ladies, I apologize for my appearance. I'd best get on home and clean up."

Willow playfully shook her finger at him. "You'll do no such thing. I'll find you some dry clothes, and you can wash in the second floor dressing room. Tucker and Caleb can bring up water."

Eli looked as if he might protest, but Willow was already halfway out of the room. "Audrey, your room is on the third floor next to Copper. I'll fetch one of the dresses you sent me when I bring your water."

"What about Copper? How is she?" Audrey called to Willow's retreating back.

"She's fast asleep. I don't believe the accident will have any lasting effect. She washed up, and I put her into a warm gown. She was asleep the minute her head hit the pillow."

Audrey nodded. "Tomorrow she should see the doctor, just in case."

"That's already been decided. Now let's get you out of those wet garments."

Until that moment, Audrey hadn't realized how badly she wanted to be rid of the muddy clothing. She climbed the stairs to her room, undaunted by the third floor bedroom. She'd gotten used to the climb on her last visit.

Shortly, Willow reappeared with a pitcher of water and clean clothing, and then excused herself to take care of the men.

Audrey filled the china bowl sitting on the washstand, then stripped to her undergarments. A bar of sweet-smelling soap sat beside the pitcher. She sniffed the delicate fragrance. Honeysuckle. She must acquire Willow's art of distilling flowers and plants and transferring the delicate scents to soap and creams. Thirty minutes later she descended the stairs, revived because of the good scrub and dry clothing.

She reached the bottom of the stairs and looked up. Three stories. Sakes alive. What had the judge been thinking?

The home was most inconvenient, and painted such an ugly shade of green. She'd been too busy fighting wind and rain earlier to pay attention to outward appearances this time, but she remembered the color all too clearly.

When she entered the kitchen Caleb, Tucker, and Eli were seated at the table. For a moment her gaze caught Eli's, but he looked away.

His reticence had returned.

Willow hovered over the mill owner, pouring coffee, her hand brushing Tucker's broad shoulder. The attraction between the two was so apparent that Audrey felt a twinge of envy. How could Willow think of marrying Silas Sterling— a man who was decades older than she? Yet her friend's heart was set on the match, and no matter how she and Copper argued against the sacrificial plan, Willow remained firm. She would marry the wealthy Silas so that Audrey, Copper, and Judge Madison would be cared for. But the plan was so pointless. Audrey would take care of herself. The idea of being dependent on anyone else was unthinkable.

Sighing, she began to wash dishes. She'd worked hard to gain her teaching credentials, and her pupils were almost like her own family. She gave her heart to every class, and when the school year ended it took weeks to emotionally let go of the children. Only then could she look forward to a new batch.

She studied the cousins from the corner of her eye. Of the three men, Caleb was the most handsome and outgoing, but there was something about Eli that made her tingle—she longed to erase that hurt that lingered in the depths of his eyes. Perhaps her feelings rose from the fact that he was a single father with a charming little boy to raise. A child needed both mother and father, and yet it wasn't the maternal instinct that drew her. It was he. Dark, mystifying. He.

Close to dark, the cousins rose to leave. Rain splashed the windowpanes, but all three men declared they wouldn't melt. The dry spell had lasted for so long, nobody was sure what to expect from the heavy downpour.

Lightning forked the sky as Eli paused in the doorway. "I'll return Wallace's clothes tomorrow."

Willow patted his arm. "Don't worry about it. Return them whenever it's convenient. The judge won't be wearing them anytime soon." She shook her head. "Weeks have passed, and the judge hasn't shown any improvement. He just lies upstairs in his second floor bedroom, not interested in anything. He used to stay busy, keeping an eye on the town, but he's just an invalid now. His speech is incoherent, and he barely eats a thing. I'm so worried about him."

Audrey's gaze moved to Tucker's hand tightly clasping Willow's. She smiled and swayed toward him, and he dropped a kiss on the top of her head. Audrey frowned. Maybe more had changed than Willow had confided in her letters. If she was set on marrying Silas Sterling, why was she holding Tucker Gray's hand? And more to the point, why was he dropping kisses on her? When Audrey had left last month, they had been firing verbal cannonballs at each other.

Willow returned to the kitchen when the door closed behind the men. "Oh, *dear* Audrey. I'm so thrilled you're back. I've missed you so much."

Audrey made a face. "I doubt if the townspeople think it's such a blessing after I destroyed the water tower."

Willow laughed. "Well, they forgave me for demolishing the mill, and I'm sure they'll survive this latest catastrophe." She refilled her cup and sat down at the table. "Now, let's catch up on what's been happening."

The kitchen door opened and Copper appeared, yawning.

Willow started. "What are you doing out of bed? I thought you were asleep for the night."

"I slept a bit. Is there fresh coffee?"

Audrey popped out of her chair. "I'll get you a cup." She poured the steaming liquid and laced it heavily with cream.

Copper sat down at the table, red hair blazing in the lamplight, eyes sparkling.

Audrey laid the cup in front of Copper, then turned on Willow. "Willow Madison. What is going on? I thought you were determined to marry Silas Sterling, but you and Tucker Gray seem awfully cozy tonight."

Willow lifted her shoulders, grinning. "Marrying Silas was the plan, of course, but when it came time to accept his proposal, I couldn't do it."

Copper stifled another yawn. "I knew you couldn't go through with it. What changed your mind?"

"The good Lord and common sense. Suddenly I knew marrying Silas would be a travesty to him—he deserves more than a marriage of convenience—plus the fact that I finally conceded that I'm hopelessly in love with Tucker Gray."

"What?" the others spouted in unison.

Nodding, Willow sighed. "Just today, I told Silas that I love Tucker, and it wouldn't be fair to marry him when I knew I could never love any man the way I love Tucker."

Copper's hand flew up to cover her mouth. "He must be crushed. He seems like such a pleasant man."

"He is a most wonderful man, but he had already realized I didn't love him, and he was kind about my decision. And he offered pay off the judge's house so there'll be no more financial worries."

"He would do that? After you refused his hand in marriage?"

"I told you. In addition to being a good man, he's most generous with his incredible wealth. And he and the judge have been longtime friends. I immediately told Tucker what I'd done."

Copper eased forward, suddenly all ears. "What did he say?"

"He said, and I quote, 'Will you marry me?' And it took me a full second to agree."

The girls screamed.

"When did this all happen?"

"Just a few minutes before you arrived."

When they finally calmed, Copper spoke. "I'm so thrilled for you." She toyed with a spoon. "We were very concerned, of course, about your intentions to marry without love. It was so like you, dear Willow, to want to sacrifice yourself for us, but it is now unnecessary. I'll be teaching in Beeder's Cove, and according to the wire I received, rooming with the Widow Potts."

"I've heard good things about her," Willow said. "And you're fortunate not to be rooming with a large family. It will be much more peaceful and quiet."

"You're right, of course, and I feel very fortunate to have such a good position."

Willow glanced at Audrey. "What about you?"

Audrey shook her head. "Unfortunately, a Blackberry Hill school board official informed me earlier that the town jumped the gun a bit, and they won't be reopening their school this year. He said he'd sent a wire informing me of the mistake, but I guess it's sitting in Timber Creek."

"What?" Copper half rose.

"It's true," Audrey admitted. "Mr. Jackson saw our arrival and let me know the news. They offered to pay my way back to Timber Creek, but I don't want to go back there alone."

"What crushing news for you." Willow sighed. "But you needn't worry. You can stay here for as long as you want. It will be wonderful having you around, and when Tucker and I get married you can have the whole third floor. I would love it, and since Silas is paying off the mortgage, no one will have to worry about being thrown out in the street. I should have known, with Silas's nature, he would be too good to me and Tucker."

Willow's offer was endearing. She'd always been compassionate and quick to help others, but Audrey really didn't look forward to sharing a house with newlyweds. She would find something that would allow her to be independent as soon as possible.

Copper leaned forward. "Silas is really going to pay off the mortgage?"

Willow nodded. "No one was more surprised than I. There seem to be no limits to the man's generosity."

Sighing, Audrey confided, "There is one place I might find employment. I understand the funeral parlor needs an assistant."

Copper choked on a mouthful of coffee. Willow reached over and pounded her on the back until she stopped coughing. Tears streamed from her eyes as she gasped for breath. When she could finally speak, she stared reproachfully at Audrey. "Joking about something like that is irreverent. Shame on you."

"I'm not joking. The parlor needs help. I need a job. It's not what I would choose, but I need something to do until Blackberry Hill reopens school."

"But, Audrey, think! A funeral parlor? Dead bodies? How could you bear to do such a thing?"

"You touched dead bodies in the war, Copper, what's the difference?"

"I don't know, but it just seems like there is a difference. Surely there's other available work. What about working as a seamstress? If there had been anyone left in Timber Creek we could have had a good business."

Willow shook her head. "I've heard that our town seamstress, Annie Jones, had to close months ago from lack of business."

Audrey glanced up. "Do you know the Burying family?"

"Their name is Burying?" Copper exclaimed.

Willow laughed. "It is a strange name for the type of business they run but completely fitting. Hank is a very curious man, and his son, Kirkland, even odder. But nice. They're a cordial family."

Audrey turned wary at Willow's tone. "Curious in what way?"

"Peculiar," Willow admitted. "Very bizarre at times— actually, I'd say extremely eccentric."

Audrey sagged against her chair back. Maybe applying for

the position wasn't a good idea. She was already apprehensive about working in a funeral parlor. Working with the deceased and an eccentric proprietor might be more than she could manage.

"I'm sure you'll get along famously," Willow said. "The family is well thought of in Thunder Ridge. The aging parents own the business, but Kirkland actually runs it. They build caskets too. I believe it's rather profitable."

Profitable or not, Audrey knew it was her only option for now. "I can get along with anyone if I have to. I'll stop by and talk to this Kirkland once he's back in town." She searched for a change of subject. "But enough about unpleasant business. We haven't heard your wedding plans yet."

"Oh, the wedding!" Willow's eyes lit with excitement. "We haven't had time to make plans. It's all so new to us."

Copper grinned. "Are we bridesmaids?"

"Of course. We'll decide on gowns the moment we set a date."

"Make it soon," Copper advised. "Don't give him an opportunity to change his mind."

"Not a chance," Willow said. "Like it or not, Tucker Gray is stuck with me for life."

"What a romantic sentiment," Audrey mused. "Stuck for life. The rest of your lives. It has such a romantic permanence about it."

"Indeed it does." Willow glanced at the wall clock. "My goodness, I had no idea it was so late. You've both had a stressful day. We need to get to bed."

"On the third floor," Copper moaned. "Tell me again whatever possessed the judge to build a house like this?"

"I know the climb is wearisome." Willow carried the cups

to the sink. "But there is one thing to say for the upstairs, you feel as if you're on top of the world when you're up there. The view is almost worth the climb."

Copper shoved back from the table. "Well, since we do have to climb, let's get started. My bed is going to feel extra comfortable tonight."

Later, when the others had closed their doors, Audrey stood by the window in her darkened bedroom, staring out at the lightning and listening to the peals of thunder.

Could she apply for that job at the funeral home? She told herself that she could, but it would be difficult. Yet, if she could get the work, it would allow her a viable reason to remain in Thunder Ridge. Her thoughts skipped back to the afternoon and the brief moment she'd heard Eli's laughter. Well, he'd proved that he could laugh.

Perhaps that was a sign from God that she should do whatever needed to be done to reach her main goal. That being— marriage to Eli Gray? She smiled. Of course. Marriage to Eli Gray. This afternoon he had proved that barriers could be broken, if only momentarily.

She bowed her head. *God, help me to make the right decision. I'm increasingly discovering that my ways aren't your ways, but if there's the slightest chance that I might obtain my desire to capture the heart of Eli Gray, then allow me the fortitude to do what I must.*

If God responded, she missed it amid all the thunder and lightning.

Chapter 4

Sullen, rolling thunder woke Audrey. Rain lashed the windowpanes, and Judge Madison's old house vibrated with the newest storm. Nothing in Thunder Ridge went half done. It either rained like pouring water from a spout, or the weather was so dry the grasshoppers begged for mercy.

Crawling off the mattress, she stifled a groan. Every muscle in her body ached. Yesterday had been a trial, but today she was determined to look on the bright side. God was in control, wasn't he? If she didn't understand her present predicament, surely he did. When Kirkland Burying returned, she'd make herself apply for the assistant position. No doubt the community had a need for the service, and if tending the deceased would pay for her keep, she could do whatever was required.

She paused at her bedroom window and scanned the dreary landscape. The millpond was almost bank full. Logs jammed the small body of water. If there was much more rain it would overflow across the road. From her window it looked like most of the roads were almost impassable already, except maybe with a boat.

The smell of frying meat drifted up the stairway. She moved away from the window and gave a final glance in the mirror before she descended the stairway, suddenly very hungry.

When she walked into the warm kitchen, Copper was at the stove stirring oatmeal. The heat from the cook stove was sweltering.

Outside, rain drummed a steady beat on recently parched ground, and she was reminded of a song her mother used to sing about little raindrop soldiers. The refrain danced through her mind with an old familiarity.

Their little drums go rat-a-tat-tat, their little feet go pitter-pat.

She smiled at the reminiscence, and pilfered a piece of bacon. "I see you're not suffering any ill effects from the accident. Can I help with anything?"

Copper indicated a stack of plates. "You can set the table if you like. Willow is upstairs feeding Wallace. We'll eat when she comes down."

Audrey arranged the plates and silverware. "Sorry I overslept. You should have awakened me."

"You had a hard day yesterday. I had a feeling you needed the rest."

Willow entered the room carrying a tray. "Oh, there you are, Audrey. How do you feel?"

"Sore and tired," she admitted, "but I suppose I'll live. I see it's still raining."

"Hasn't let up all night." Willow sat the tray by the sink.

"It's hard to remember how hard we prayed for rain. Seems the good Lord is sending abundance."

Copper laughed. "Be careful what you ask for. The Bible says God gives full measure, tamped down and running over."

"I've already had more than I want. If it keeps this up we'll float away, like a bilious green ark without the animals." She untied her apron and sat down. "Uncle Wallace eats so little these days. He's so frail. He barely weighs more than I do."

"Would he sip some broth?" Copper asked. "I could simmer a little meat with some onions and garlic."

"He might," Willow mused. "It would be worth a try, if you don't mind."

"I'll get it started right after breakfast." Copper dished up the oatmeal and placed the bowl on the table. "There's bacon and toast if you want."

"None for me," Willow said, and Audrey echoed the refusal.

When the women were seated around the table, Willow bowed her head and asked the blessing. While they ate they caught up on everything that had happened since their last visit. A knock at the door sent Willow scurrying to answer. Audrey could hear her talking, and a man's voice responding. Moments later she entered the kitchen with Eli. Audrey's heart skipped a beat.

He removed his jacket, hanging it in the corner to drip. "Morning, ladies. Fine weather for ducks."

Audrey reached for another cup. "What are you doing out so early?"

He handed Willow a bundle of clothing. "Brought Wallace's clothes home. I tried to keep them dry, but as hard as it's raining, they're almost as wet as I am. Tell Wallace I said much obliged for the loan."

Willow took the soggy offering. "I'm just happy we found something to fit you. Are you working at the mill today?"

Audrey filled his cup, and after some coaxing, he pulled out a chair and sat down, clearly uncomfortable with the company. "Can't. The ground's a mess out there. Men can't get to work, and even if they could, everything is water-logged. We've been trying to turn the water away from the mill. So far we've succeeded, but I don't know how long we can hold out if it doesn't let up soon." He took a sip of coffee. "Wallace okay this morning?"

Willow sighed. "Still lethargic. I believe his mind is slipping. He called me Claudine."

Audrey bent over Eli's shoulder to set fresh cream on the table. The brief contact sent chills down her spine. He smelled woodsy, clean, so unlike some of the mill workers who obviously considered soap one of women's frivolities.

"How long ago was that stroke?"

"Early July."

Eli raised an eyebrow. "His wife's been dead for some time, but I guess it's natural to be confused where the mind's concerned. These things take time to pull out of, and some never do."

"He still misses Claudine dreadfully. They were insepar-able, you know." Willow stepped to the window and lifted the curtain. "Have you seen Tucker today?"

"He's at the mill, mooning over you." He flashed an ornery grin.

"Oh—silly."

"No, you've got that man as lovesick as an old coon hound."

"Good." Willow grinned and turned back to the sink full of dishes.

"It has to be hard for the judge," Audrey picked up the thread of conversation, holding Eli as long as possible. "I wish we could do something to make him more comfortable."

"He sleeps most of the time." Willow dunked an iron skillet into the dishpan of sudsy water. "He doesn't seem to be in pain."

Audrey finally made eye contact, but Eli became absorbed in the cream pitcher. He drained his cup and shoved his chair back. "I've got to get to the mill. Caleb and Tucker are filling sandbags."

"Why don't you come for supper tonight?" Audrey couldn't believe she was so bold. "Bring Caleb and Tucker."

She glanced at Willow's stunned expression.

"I'll cook," she added.

"Thanks, but the sandbagging will keep us busy. We'll work through the night."

He left, and Copper closed the door behind him. She turned to eye Audrey, who felt heat suffuse her cheeks. "Well, they have to eat."

Willow and Copper snickered.

"Audrey loves Eli," Copper teased.

"Audrey *doesn't* love her friends at the moment, and she's going upstairs now."

Copper shrugged. "Oh, stay and help dust. I promise I won't say another word about him."

"Him who?" Audrey tossed back. Her plans were her

plans, and until they materialized she had no reason to share her intentions with these two and have them tease her mercilessly.

"Him anybody," Copper said. "You choose."

While Willow put light bread to rise, Copper and Audrey dusted the various figurines and pieces of glassware cluttering the parlor tables.

Copper paused with feather duster in hand. "You know, there's enough stuff here to start a store. Willow should go into business."

"True, but that would hurt Wallace. These are all Claudine's treasures."

Copper made a face. "I was teasing, of course, but you have to admit there's an enormous amount of clutter here. Wallace must have spent a fortune on all this glass and knick-knacks."

Willow's voice floated from the kitchen. "Ladies, we have company!"

The women trooped to the kitchen to find Widow Gleeson holding a copy of *Godey's Lady's Book*. The widow stood in the doorway, smiling, a man's black rain cape draped over her shoulders. Stout boots protected her feet from the puddles, and a straw hat that had seen better days covered her head. "Just heard about Tucker and Willow's wedding, and I thought you ladies might enjoy looking through the book."

"We'd love it, Mrs. Gleeson. Thank you so much for your thoughtfulness."

"No trouble a' tall. I was on my way to the mercantile anyway." She nodded toward Audrey and Copper. "The rain is wonderful, isn't it?"

"Wonderful," both women agreed.

"I'll be on my way."

When the door closed, Willow carried the book to the table while Copper discarded the duster. "Good! You find something you like, and I promise Audrey and I will have it sewn in no time."

The women pored over the pages, discussing the intrinsic worth of each style. Finally they settled on one they all favored. The dress had a fitted, fully lined bodice with long sleeves, and lace trim at the waist, around the wrists, and on the bib collar.

"Now, for the hard part," Audrey said. "Where do we find the needed material? No one sells decent yard goods in Thunder Ridge."

Willow frowned. "You're right, the general store only sells essentials, and I wouldn't touch anything in my aunt's sewing room. Uncle Wallace wants Claudine's personal effects kept intact, as if he's expecting her to walk through the door any moment. But I spotted some trunks in the attic when I was up there one day. I didn't investigate them, but given Aunt Claudine's habit of keeping everything, including scraps of thread, there just might be something up there that we can use."

Copper sprang to her feet. "Let's go see! It'll be fun."

Willow brought candles, and they climbed the steep, winding staircase to the attic.

Rain beat against the dirty windows as they entered the storage space. Gloomy skies dimmed the outside light, so they lifted their candles, moving them back and forth to search each part of the musty room. Willow paused before a large camel-backed trunk. "Let's see what's in here."

The first garment Copper pulled out was a blue poplin

dress with leg-of-mutton sleeves. "Claudine had good taste in clothing, if not houses."

Audrey modeled a Huntley bonnet, a black velvet cap decorated with plumes; and Willow draped a black satin cape, a palatine, trimmed with apricot-colored satin and black lace, over her shoulders. "I never dreamed Aunt Claudine was so fashionable. When I met her she had put on quite a bit of weight. These gowns are small."

After digging through several of the trunks, but finding nothing suitable for a wedding dress, Audrey opened a small chest shoved back in a corner. "Look, Willow! How perfect." She held up a dress of creamy white satin. The fitted bodice had rows of delicate lace. The sleeves were narrower than leg-of-mutton but not tight enough to be called form-fitted. "Do you suppose it's Claudine's wedding gown?"

"There's no way to know, but it is lovely." She fingered the exquisite fabric. "Perfectly lovely."

"Oh, Willow," Copper gasped. "It's even prettier than the one in the book."

Willow took the dress and held it up to her. "What do you think?"

"A little long, but that can be easily remedied." Copper stepped back, experienced eyes focused on the garment. "A little tuck here, one there, and it will fit you beautifully."

"I don't know." Willow frowned. "This must be Aunt Claudine's. I'd have to ask permission to wear it, and I don't want to upset Uncle Wallace."

"Let's take the gown downstairs," Copper suggested. "Then when you feel the time is right you can tell him you found it, and ask permission to be married in it. I'll bet he'll consider it an honor."

Audrey had been searching the trunk, gently folding articles of clothing. Her hand touched something solid. She shifted a dark green velvet jacket to find a photo album. Copper was still rambling on about the find, but Audrey's attention turned to yellowed pages, fascinated by images of people. Next to the last page she paused, sucking in a breath.

"Willow, look at this. Here's the dress."

Copper peered over her shoulder, "Oh, land's sake, it is. Who are these people?" A proud groom and a tall beauty stared out from the yellowed pages.

Audrey read the spidery script written underneath. "It's Wallace and Claudine. This must be their wedding picture. Wasn't she pretty?"

"And Wallace," Copper exclaimed. "Quite dashing."

Willow peered over her shoulder. "They made an elegant couple. They look so happy."

"Surely Wallace will allow you to be married in the gown," Copper decided. "Have you told him you aren't going to marry Silas?"

"I've not had enough nerve to tell him. He was so determined we marry that I can't bear to disappoint him."

"You know, Willow, despite the fact I was dead set against your plan, in retrospect, Wallace was trying to make certain you'd be well looked after when he was gone. He meant well."

"I know he did, and his eyes lit when I told him Silas intends to pay off the house note—"

"You told him about Silas paying the note but not your change in wedding plans?" Copper gasped.

"Well . . . I was approaching the subject, but he was

tiring and . . . I'm sure Uncle Wallace will understand. I'm just a coward, and I'm hoping he'll improve and he'll see the wisdom in my good fortune to find a man that I really love."

Audrey modeled a jacket in front of the mirror. "Do you want me to tell him? Sometimes disappointing news is easier to hear when told by a second party."

"No, of course not. I'll tell him. Just not today."

A drop of rain fell from the ceiling, striking Audrey's forehead. She gasped, and Willow tilted her head back, gazing up. "Drats. The roof is leaking."

Audrey wiped rain away. "If one little drop is all it leaks in a rain like this one, we'll be all right."

The women straightened the attic and returned to the downstairs, stopping off at Willow's room to hang the dress in the closet. She lovingly stroked the satin fabric, and Audrey knew that she was thinking of how she would appear to Tucker on their wedding day.

After supper Copper wanted to bake a cake. Sugar was running low, so Audrey gladly ran the errand. The tiny general store was mostly occupied by men wearing boots and slickers when she arrived. They sat around the potbellied stove that threw out so much heat the store felt like a sweltering wet wool blanket.

She purchased a pound of sugar and turned to leave when she bumped into Eli carrying a small brown bag. Their gazes locked, and she realized his excuse for not coming to supper had been manufactured. Still, she summoned a naive smile. "Copper wants to make a cake and we were low on sugar. I volunteered to fetch some for her."

Color crept up his ears. He lifted the bag. "Had a hankering for jelly beans."

She bit back the impulse to invite him for cake, but that would be too awkward since he'd already refused her supper invitation. "How's the sandbagging coming along?"

"Making progress." He held the door open for her to walk out in front of him. Falling into step, they walked toward the sawmill and the judge's house. "Rain's nice, but it could let up a little."

"Yes. Very wet."

Wet. Honestly, Audrey. He'll think you're a simpleton.

She caught sight of a portly boy splashing in a big puddle. The child was covered in mud, head to foot. With every uninhibited leap, he sent the water high enough to drench his head and shoulders. "Look at that child. He'll ruin those fine boots."

Frowning, Eli paused. "That's Horace Padget, Jr., the banker's son. I wonder if Cordelia knows he's outside."

Audrey had seen the child around, and Willow had mentioned the Padgets only last evening. They appeared to be a selfish, self-centered lot. "The boy's mother?"

"His jailer. She keeps that boy on a tight leash. My boy, Tate, plays with him, but truthfully, I'd rather he didn't. The child needs a switching."

"Oh . . . is that necessary?" She didn't hold with switchings unless absolutely necessary.

"Cordelia protects him like a cranky hawk."

"Only child?"

He nodded. "God is merciful."

As they watched, Horace slipped and landed facedown in

a mud hole. He lumbered to his feet, squalling at the top of his lungs.

Wincing, Eli said. "Got a good pair of lungs, doesn't he?"

Audrey's first instinct was to comfort the boy. "Is he hurt?"

"No, he's just mad." He stalked over and bent to pull the boy out of the puddle.

Junior wiped his eyes, glaring up at Eli. "You pushed me."

"I wasn't even close to you."

"I'm going to tell Ma. You'll be in big trouble."

"I'm scared." He wiped mud out of Junior's eyes. "You aren't supposed to stomp in puddles, are you?"

He sniffed. "What's a puddle?"

"Mud puddle." He gestured to the standing water. "What you've been playing in."

"I ain't ever"—Junior sniffed—"sawed one."

"Haven't seen one," Audrey corrected from the sidelines.

Junior glared at her. "Who's that?"

"Someone who needs to get out of the rain." Eli gripped the boy's shoulder. "You've seen a mud puddle before, but you were pretty young. Come on. We'll take you home."

Audrey watched as Eli marched the child out of the standing water. What with the lack of rain over the years, perhaps the child was enthralled by the new sight.

Horace looked like he wanted to object, but after a glance at Audrey and apparently seeing no support there, he ducked his head and walked between the couple.

In an attempt to keep a straight face, Audrey focused on the house up ahead, perched on a high bluff. Built in the Victorian style, the structure was intimidating, to say the least, with wide gables and wraparound porches.

They scaled the brick-lined path, and the front door flew

open. A tall, thin woman with her dark hair pulled back in a formidable pompadour obscured the doorway. "Hor . . . race! Oh my poor baby. What's happened?"

"He had an accident," Eli began, but Junior interrupted.

"He pushed me down, Ma! In a big ole, dirty, wet hole."

"Pushed you?" Cordelia's hawkish eyes whipped to pin Eli and Audrey. "Is this true? Why would you do such a thing to an innocent child?"

"No, you don't understand," Audrey began, but Cordelia rolled right over her.

"I can't believe an adult would do something so childish." She yanked Horace behind her skirts. "You get off this property right now, or I'll set the dogs on you, Eli Gray! The very idea, pushing a helpless child—and you keep that son of yours away from my Horace. He's a bad influence."

She slammed the door in their faces.

Eli shook his head. "Helpless? That boy is about as helpless as a prairie rattler."

A dog howled from behind the house.

He reached for Audrey's arm. "Let's get out of here before she makes good on her threat. She's got big dogs."

They hurried down the brick path, their boots slipping on the uneven ground. Audrey resisted the urge to look back, determined not to let Eli witness her fear.

Eli, walking ahead, called over his shoulder, "I didn't push that boy."

"I know."

"I tried to help him."

"I witnessed every moment."

"You'd think she'd have been grateful."

"You'd think."

He kicked a limb out of the path. "I don't see how Horace puts up with Cordelia. She's meaner than any two women put together."

"I suppose only God understands her."

He paused, and tipped his head to let the water run off his brim. "I'll bet he gets a mite bent out of shape dealing with her." He looked up, breaking into a grin. "What are you wearing?"

"What?" Audrey reached up, and with a sinking sensation she realized she was wearing Wallace's old hat.

"The hat."

"Oh." She curtsied. "The latest Paris fashion. If you must know, I'm a slave to fashion."

He took a step back, his eyes skimming her drenched appearance. "Yes. I can see."

Heat tinged her cheeks, and she shimmied around him. "I'm about to drown." She'd like nothing more than to stand and chat with him all day, rain or no rain, but she supposed there was such a thing as appearances. She couldn't appear too eager.

The last thing she wanted was to scare the man deeper into his shell.

Chapter 5

Audrey lifted her eyes to the sky, hoping to see a thinning of the clouds hovering over Thunder Ridge, but the dark haze was just as black and ominous as ever. Turning, she went inside the judge's house, pausing long enough to remove her wet cape before she entered the kitchen.

The cozy room smelled of baking bread. Copper sat at the kitchen table, hand propped on her chin, perusing a book. "Was that Eli with you? Why didn't he come in?"

Audrey smiled. Why indeed? Not that she hadn't thought to ask, but after his previous refusal, she didn't want to be turned down again.

"Well," Copper mused. "If you married him you wouldn't have to teach school."

Audrey hung her cape to dry. "I don't recall his asking me."

Copper shrugged. "Perhaps you should work on that."

Audrey mussed the top of her friend's hair as she

walked by. "I'm not husband hunting." She had absolutely no intention of telling Copper her plan. It was a most scandalous undertaking, and the dark, hurting man who refused to look her way was totally naive of her objective. No point putting ideas in Copper's nosy head. Eli deliberately avoided women, and she had no intention of allowing Copper to embarrass the man by hurrying Audrey's strategy along.

Willow entered the kitchen, frowning. "I just checked the attic and the roof's leaking like a sieve. I'm taking some pans and buckets up there to catch the drips."

"I'll help. You won't have to make so many trips if we share the work."

Copper abandoned the book and began to gather an armload of pans, while Audrey hooked the bails on several buckets. "How many do we need?"

"As many as Abraham's descendants." Willow pulled more pans from the cupboards. "I can't believe how many drips there are. As soon as it dries out we'll have to see about patching the holes."

The women carried as many pans and buckets as they could hold on the first trip, setting them under the leaks. Raindrops plinked the metal containers.

Audrey descended the narrow stairway to get a couple of mops. She and Copper wiped up puddles deeply pooled on the attic floor.

Copper peered up at the ceiling. "I think we've covered them all."

A new trickle formed as they watched. Copper jumped aside as a second drop followed the first. "Drats. There's another one. Do we have any more pans?"

"I'll go look." Audrey returned to the kitchen and rummaged through the pantry and storage room closet, retrieving a couple of extra chamber pots.

Willow was on her knees, wiping up water when she returned. "What's that you have?"

Audrey held up the containers. "It's all I could find. We barely have enough pans left for cooking use. These will work."

"How disgusting, Audrey." Cringing, Copper reached for a pot and set it under the newest leak.

"Disgusting or not, I'll leave the extra one up here. No doubt we'll need it too before we're finished."

Willow straightened, pressing a hand to the small of her back. "That's all we can do right now. Don't breathe a word of this to Uncle Wallace. He doesn't need to be worrying about a roof. I'll take care of the crisis, some way."

They returned to the kitchen and started chores.

Audrey was starting to realize that every day in Thunder Ridge brought new problems. Most likely half the town had leaky roofs. Many of the residents wouldn't have bothered keeping their roofs in good repair since the area had suffered drought for so many years, and others didn't have the funds for needed repairs.

A knock sounded on the back door, and she turned to answer. Tate Gray stood in the doorway, holding a frog. She took a step back. The frog didn't frighten her, but she couldn't say she liked the slimy little creatures.

"Yes. Tate?" The boy was drenched from head to foot. She wondered if his grandmother knew he was out without a slicker.

"I got a present for you." He handed Audrey the frog, bending a bit to peer between her and the doorsill. "You wouldn't have any cookies, would you?"

"Oh . . . no, I'm sorry. We don't." She bit back a grin. "Have you had your supper?"

He nodded. "But I got this hankering for sweets, and Grandma didn't feel like baking today."

By now Willow and Copper had joined her at the doorway. Willow smiled. "I have some nice blackberry jam—would that do?—on a slice of bread."

His face brightened. "That would do just fine, ma'am."

Draping her arm around the lad, Willow led him to the table, and Audrey closed the door. She glanced at Willow and smiled. When Willow and Tucker married, the child would be family, a nice thought on a cold, rainy day.

Later that evening Willow sank into a chair and sighed. "What a day. The only good thing that's happened is Tate's visit. I'll have to make sure the cookie tin is filled from now on."

Copper reached for a spoon. "Now that you're all going to be family, you'll have a lot of baking to do."

Leaning back, Willow closed her eyes. "I can barely wait."

Audrey was surprised to feel the prick of envy. She was prepared to wait for Eli, but seeing Willow so happy and content made her want to speed up the process. But love didn't happen overnight, and she wanted nothing less than Eli's whole heart. She added a dollop of cream to her cup, thinking about the eligible prospects. There weren't many in Thunder Ridge. She'd set her cap for Eli, but what about Copper? The three of them had been hoping for marriage for longer than she could remember, but what with the war taking away so many of the young men . . . "Copper, why don't you pursue Caleb? He's a wonderful marriage prospect."

Copper dropped her fork on the saucer and propped her elbows on the table. "Pursue Caleb? No, he's nice enough, handsome, and perfectly charming. He has the prettiest eyes, and he's enjoyable to be around, but there just aren't any sparks between us."

"Ladies." Willow cautioned. "Sparks are nice, but I'm with Audrey. I'd rather hoped that you—or one of you—would fall in love with Caleb and settle in Thunder Ridge. I don't want us to be separated again."

Audrey glanced up to find both women's gazes pinned on her. *Please don't let them mention Eli.* She couldn't lie, and she wasn't adept at misleading, but she certainly didn't want to tell them about her developing feelings for the man.

"Caleb would make a fine husband," Willow said, her gaze now focused on both young women. "You could do worse."

Copper pursed her lips. "Listen to her, Audrey. The two of you would get along famously together. You make a striking couple."

"Please. Caleb isn't romantically interested in me. Someday, when the right woman comes along, he'll marry quickly. What about Meredith Johnson? Now that Tucker's engaged to you, Willow, Meredith will surely set her cap for either Caleb or Eli." Audrey paused. She hadn't considered that possibility. Perhaps she would have to be more aggressive than she liked.

"Meredith Johnson is too flighty for either Caleb or Eli," Willow objected with a frown.

"You're just jealous because Tucker courted her." Copper smirked. "She's actually very pretty."

Audrey didn't think so. She'd seen the young woman from Blackberry Hill at social functions during her last visit, and she agreed with Willow. Caleb needed a more mature mate.

Audrey shook her head. "All right, enough with the matchmaking. Willow, how's Wallace this evening?" Her visits to the judge had been brief. He was always asleep, or if his eyes were open he didn't seem to recognize her.

Willow lifted thin shoulders. "He's not interested in anything. Tucker's been so busy trying to mop up at the mill that he hasn't been able to stop by for their daily visit and Bible reading. The judge misses those sessions."

Audrey drained her cup. "I'll be happy to read the Bible to the judge anytime he wants."

"I'd be delighted to do the same," Copper offered.

"You're so kind. My biggest concern is that I don't have enough money to fix the roof. I don't want to bother Tucker about it, because there's nothing he can do at the moment, and it would just be another bill facing him." She sighed. "Maybe it would have been better if Silas hadn't agreed to pay off the mortgage. That way the bank could just have this big old leaky barn."

"Never let your uncle hear you say that. He's a man of his word, and he gave his word he would repay the loan. Did he ever know about the foreclosure threat?" Copper asked.

"No, and I don't intend to ever tell him. He loves this old relic. He and Claudine were so happy here together. While we all agree it's a decidedly inconvenient place to live, and that horrible shade of green is enough to make a body ill, he thinks it's a slice of heaven."

"It's sad," Audrey agreed. "I'm as poor as a church mouse, or I would help. Perhaps if I get the parlor job . . ."

"If you decided to sell the house once the judge passes, where would you and Tucker live?" Audrey brushed crumbs off the tablecloth. More to the point, what would she do? She couldn't expect Tucker and Willow to provide for her, but unless the Burying Parlor took her on, she'd have little choice.

Willow reached to take her hand. "Don't worry. Tucker will provide for all three of us, if necessary."

"Does he have a spacious home?"

Willow hesitated. "Well, no. Actually, it's a one-room cabin, but we'll manage. Eli has a wonderful house, fairly spacious, but his mother and Tate live with him. Mrs. Gray is sixty-five and ailing. She has her hands full with Tate. But don't worry, we may not have a mansion, but we'll manage."

Audrey would settle for a dry roof over her head. *Lord, don't think I'm not grateful. I am, and if taking the funeral parlor position will keep me independent, I do so heartily.*

Alone in her bedroom later, Audrey turned down the bed and laid out her nightgown before she blew out the candle and stood at the window watching the violent display of barbed lightning streak an angry sky. The flood held one ray of blessing: If lightning struck anything, every building in town would be too wet to burn.

She sank to her knees, propping her arms on the window-sill. What would she do if Willow and Tucker couldn't afford to keep this house, and she didn't get the parlor position? Tucker had heavy financial responsibilities with the mill. The payroll and new equipment to keep the business running would be expensive. Could he scrape together enough manpower and discarded shingles to put a new roof on this old relic?

So many questions and so few answers. At this point, Audrey wasn't sure she'd have a roof over her head much longer. Willow would take care of her as long as she could, but the time might come that she couldn't. Then where would Audrey go?

Chapter 6

Early Sunday morning, Audrey waded through mud to feed the stock. The judge had a milk cow, chickens, and an old pig, and now the horse had been added. Rain and thunder charged the air, the barrage endless. Finishing the stable chores, she hurried back to the dry house.

Stomping mud off her boots, she turned the door handle and entered the kitchen, shaking water off the judge's old hat. Arms crossed, Willow stood staring morosely out the window at the watery deluge.

"Why aren't you dressed for services?"

"You and Copper go on to church. I don't want to leave Wallace alone this morning. He was so confused when I took him his breakfast."

"No, I'll stay. You go on," Audrey insisted. "Folks enjoy your music so much."

Willow spent enough time in this house looking after the ailing judge, and the congregation would be greatly disappointed if she didn't show up to play the new organ Silas Sterling had so generously donated. "You and Tucker need time together. I don't mind the least sitting with the judge." A missed opportunity to see Eli, but perhaps Willow would invite him to dinner.

Copper came into the room, positioning a hair comb. "Both of you go. I'll stay home with the judge."

Willow let the curtain drop back into place. "I don't want either of you to stay home because of me, but I admit, I would dearly love to play this morning, and a couple of hours with Tucker without worrying about leaky roofs and Uncle Wallace would be heaven."

Copper sighed. "Then go. I'll fix one of those nice fryers running around the yard. My hair frizzes something awful in this weather. Bring Tucker and Caleb back to dinner with you."

"And Eli," Audrey echoed.

When the two women turned to look at her, she shrugged. "It wouldn't be polite not to invite him and his son."

A heavy knock sounded at the front door, and Willow turned to answer. Audrey heard voices, and Willow came back trailed by Deet Jackson, one of the retired mill workers.

"Morning, ladies." His gaze swept the kitchen, apparently looking for a place to hang his dripping hat. "Think it'll rain?"

Audrey smiled at the humor attempt and took the hat from him and hung it on the back of a chair close to the oven heat.

Willow smiled. "What brings you out this morning, Deet?"

"It's Sunday." Deet hefted the coffeepot and filled a cup. "Thought you ladies might want to attend church."

Willow's face lit expectantly. "We do, but there's Uncle Wallace."

"That's why I'm here. I'll be right glad to stay with Wallace."

"Oh, Deet, that's nice of you, but I don't want to be a bother."

Audrey lifted a brow when Willow whirled, heading upstairs to change dresses before the conversation ended.

Deet shuffled to the coffeepot. "Nothing wrong with bothering your friends once in a while, and me and the judge go way back. Now, I ain't taking no for an answer. You ladies skedaddle. Go put those pretty frocks on while I sit and enjoy my coffee. Service starts in thirty minutes, and I'll be expecting lunch afterwards."

Deet was more than six feet tall, with a mop of silvery gray curls that needed a good combing, and more likely than not that was a tobacco chaw in the left side of his mouth. Audrey accepted and followed Copper upstairs.

Later, the women gathered back in the kitchen. Audrey noticed none wore her Sunday best. They were garbed in everyday calico and sturdy boots. No fancy slippers or frilly lace for this worship service. Delicate footwear would be ruined before they took a dozen steps in the reddish mire waiting outside the door.

Deet nodded his approval. "Dressed for the weather. Mighty smart. I heard the church roof is holding, no leaks yet. That's more than you can say for three-fourths of the houses in town. Got a real mess on our hands, we do."

"My hair looks like a rat's nest," Copper groused.

Audrey tied her bonnet tightly. "Your hair looks fine. And when have you ever encountered a frizzy rat's nest?"

"By the time we get to church, you'll see one, I guarantee."

Willow opened the door. "No one will notice. We'll be late, and the congregation will undoubtedly be focused on our tardiness."

* * *

Audrey stepped into the gloomy church vestibule and shook rain from her cloak. A mouse scurried past her, and she stepped to the side. A scant few had braved the dreadful weather to worship God, and those scant few were mostly sitting in the back pews.

Cordelia and Horace Padget swept past moments before the singing began. Cordelia's eyes met Audrey's for a frosty moment. She tilted her chin and tightened her lips, and her features corkscrewed as though she'd caught a distinctly obnoxious odor. The woman had an air about her. An uppity stance.

Horace nodded, and Junior stuck out his tongue.

Audrey's hand itched to administer a swift swat on the youngster's backside. Right here in the house of the Lord. Spare the rod, spoil the child. Proverbs. Yet she'd never struck anyone in her life and she certainly didn't intend to start with Cordelia's son. Poor Willow. The fire, the finger pointing associated with the accident, looking after her ailing uncle's needs. Audrey was certain she'd had no time to think about teaching this fall, nor prepare for the event. She glanced at Junior. And that child would be in her classroom. Would events settle down so Willow could concentrate on what she was here for: to be the new teacher? She wondered.

Junior crushed a woman's foot, and the woman let out a responsive groan.

Six long, excruciating hours.

Eli and Tate arrived, drenched to the bone. Father and son stood in the doorway while Eli's eyes scanned the empty pews. Tate spied Audrey sitting on the aisle and ran to greet her. His face was shining in welcome. "Miss Pride!"

She hugged him, luxuriating in the child's amicable greeting. He leaned to whisper, "You got those cookies baked?"

"Not yet, but soon, I promise."

Eli paused beside her pew, and she glanced up to meet his guarded eyes. For a moment she thought she saw recognition in their depths, but then he reached for Tate's hand. "Come on, son. Services are about to begin."

"No!" The boy wiggled closer to Audrey.

She sent the child a warning look, but he ignored the silent signal. "I want to sit with Miss Pride." He sprang up to squeeze between Audrey and the aisle armrest and settled on the bench.

Eli frowned and motioned for them all to scoot over and he sat down beside his son. He appeared considerably discomfited by the circumstance. Audrey forced her eyes to the pulpit. Copper elbowed her, grinning. She tolerantly closed her eyes, praying for strength. If Copper were ever to guess just how much she liked this man, her plan would go down in flames. Eli would be frightened off like a scared rooster.

Willow slid behind the organ keyboard as the song leader approached the podium. "Shall we sing, 'Showers of Blessing'?"

Germaine Howard spoke up from the all-men's choir. "We've been blessed about enough. Ain't there any songs in that book about dry ground?"

The song leader's face colored. "Well . . . ah . . . does anyone have a more appropriate offering?"

A second man spoke. "How about 'Dem bones, dem bones, dem dry bones—'"

Willow cleared her throat. "Excellent suggestion, Mr. Rice, but I don't have the music. Shall we try page forty-seven?"

The congregation rose to their feet and joined in the singing, bolstering the men's voices. Caleb and Tucker stood tall and handsome in the choir, as did Eli, who had left his seat to join them. He stood behind a portly gentleman in the tenor section, and Audrey fancied she could hear his harmony above all the others. When the song service ended, Eli returned to the pew and Tate. Judging by his dark expression, he'd about as soon sit on a cactus in the far corner than have the church members catch him sitting almost beside a woman.

Reverend Cordell approached the podium and opened his Bible. "Let us pray."

Audrey focused as he asked God's blessing on the congregation, on the church, and then his prayers seemed to deepen spiritually as he offered up a heartfelt thank-you for the rain, and then even more pleading for it to end. Hearty amens echoed through the small sanctuary. Audrey's included.

During preaching, she couldn't keep from sneaking a glance at Eli, only to find him looking at her. Heat tinged her cheeks, and she directed her attention to Reverend Cordell for the remainder of the service.

After church, the congregation filed out into a cloudburst. Most trudged off on foot, avoiding miniature lakes of standing water.

Tate grabbed Audrey's hand. "I want to go with you."

Eli squashed the thought. "Tate. That's not possible."

"Oh, Eli, come to dinner with us." Willow, arm through Tucker's, grinned at the child. "We're having fried chicken. We haven't had a good visit in ever so long." Glancing up at Tucker, she said, "And of course, you're invited."

"I'd better be." He returned her grin.

Caleb pulled his collar closer in the driving downpour. "Is your eyesight bad? What about me?"

Copper caught Audrey's eyes and playfully mimicked, *What about me?* Audrey glanced away. "You're invited too, Caleb."

His grin widened. "Why, thank you, Miss Pride. How can a man refuse a warm and heartfelt invitation like that? I'd be most happy to come."

"Sorry, Willow, but Tate and I can't make it." Eli said stiffly. "Maybe another time. Ma will be waiting dinner for us."

Audrey mentally sighed as he led a fussy Tate away. Eli Gray could stand a good lesson on manners. She firmed her lips and pulled her cloak more tightly over her shoulders.

When the small group reached the house, Deet stood at the window and peered through the frosty pane. "What a mess. Roads are washed out, and felled trees and brush are beginning to clog the river."

Audrey shook out her cape, hung it to dry, and then set plates and silverware on the table. The men, other than Deet, settled in the front parlor. Deet settled at the dinner table.

"Bunch of us men gotta go clean out the river after dinner."

"Sounds risky. Tucker isn't going, is he?"

"Yep. He's the one that set it up."

Audrey's hands paused. "Maybe we shouldn't mention it to Willow. Just let Tucker tell her." Willow was a worrier, and there was no reason to upset her. Man's work was often dangerous.

"It could be treacherous," Deet agreed. "But we aim to be

careful." He tucked his napkin under his chin. "Eli able to get to services today?"

Audrey thought back to the excruciating preaching hour. She'd never been more uncomfortable or more conscious of a man's anxiety than she had been during that service. "He and Tate were there." She started on the potatoes and made swift work of the task.

"He and the boy not coming to dinner?"

"He was invited, but he declined the invitation."

"Fine man."

"He is at that." She peeled the last potato and tossed it into the pot, her mind reliving Eli's coolness this morning. He was going to be a hard one to attract.

"Shame about his wife dying while he was off fighting the war."

Audrey turned to look at him, distracted. "Who?"

"Eli."

She nodded. "That must have been a terrible experience."

Willow breezed into the kitchen, dumping canned corn into a pan. She glanced at Deet perched at the table. "Dinner will be a while, Deet. Hope you don't mind."

"Don't mind at all. I'll jest sit here and visit."

The old man leaned back in his chair. "Funny how those three boys are all so different. If Tucker had lost a wife, now, he'd get upset, but he'd get over it. He'd know he didn't have a choice. Caleb, now, he'd turn it over to God, do his grieving, and keep on trusting. Eli, he's different. Always been more sensitive. Things bother him. Keeps his problems bottled up inside."

Audrey set the pan of potatoes on the stove to boil. "How so?"

"Well, Eli, now, he blames himself. Feels he let Genevieve down. Felt like he should have been here when she had the young'un, and he wasn't."

"He was fighting for freedom. He was a long way from here," Audrey argued.

"That's the way you and I see it. Eli, now, he sees it differently. In his mind he let her down."

"Do you think he'll ever get over it?" Willow entered the conversation.

"Can't say. Maybe if the right woman comes along and tears down those brick walls he's built around his heart." His shrewd eyes bored into Audrey. "I figure she'd have her work cut out for her, though. Bringing that one around will be a right smart chore. It'll take one of those Proverbs 31 women, for sure."

Audrey winced. Well, she wasn't a saint. Far from it, but with enough time, hopefully she could chip away his defense.

She sat quietly through dinner, eating and ignoring the chatter going on around her. Not a word was mentioned about the men's planned afternoon work clearing the river. Audrey kept quiet. If Tucker didn't want to worry Willow, then she had no right to intervene. Sometimes she wondered if men ever longed to rid themselves of their expected and sometimes hazardous roles.

By late afternoon, the men had gone and the weather had worn thin with Copper, who was never known for her patience. "If this blessed rain doesn't stop I'll never get to Beeder's Cove. School is supposed to start in a week, and here I am stranded in Thunder Ridge."

"You're such a fusspot. If it's raining this hard in Beeder's

Cove, and word is that it is, you wouldn't be able to do anything except sit in the kitchen with the Widow Potts and drink tea." Willow got up to close the damper on the stove.

"I'd rather be here with you than stuck there, but I'm anxious to start the new position."

A muffled explosion rattled the windowpanes and interrupted the conversation. Audrey started and whirled to look out the window. After a continued silence, she twisted around to face the women. "The men must have blown the logjam."

"I hope no one was hurt," Willow said.

Copper patted her hand. "Don't worry. I've been praying for Tucker's safety."

Willow frowned. "Tucker? Why? He's home, isn't he?"

"Uh . . ." Audrey glanced at Copper.

Slamming her palm on the table, Willow flared. "What!"

Audrey winced. "Well, I didn't want to say anything for fear you'd react this way, but Tucker, Caleb, Eli, and some other men are clearing debris out of the river. It's blocking the water flow."

"Great day in the morning." Willow turned ashen. "He didn't mention a word to me. I thought they were all in the barn."

"Maybe he didn't want to worry you," Audrey defended. "He didn't want you to be concerned."

"Didn't want me to be concerned? Of course I'm concerned. I love the man!"

It occurred to her that Eli had occupied most of her thoughts this afternoon. Had she been worried about his safety?

Copper gave a philosophical smile. "Ah, love. We sure are obsessive about those who are most important to us. The best thing we can do this wretched afternoon is to rest. If anything goes wrong, someone will let us know. Until then, it would be a waste of time to pace the floor and fret ourselves into frenzy. Let's nap."

"Nap? With Tucker standing waist-deep in roiling water? Are you addled?" Willow sprang to her feet. "Audrey, are you coming?"

Copper's jaw dropped. "You're going out there?"

"Of course I'm going out there. I have to see if he's all right." Willow reached for her cape.

Sleep eluded Audrey. Though she wanted to go with Willow, her concern would be too obvious, so she remained with Copper, but she couldn't nap. While Copper and the judge snoozed upstairs, she draped a piece of tarpaulin around her shoulders to keep out the rain and went for a walk.

She turned a corner and ran smack into Eli. He caught her shoulders to steady her. Their gazes locked, and she swallowed. "You're all right."

"Beg pardon?"

"You're all right. Willow . . . she was concerned about Tucker—and you, of course."

"Concerned? Why would she be concerned?"

"Oh, you know women. Clearing the river and all . . ."

"It's clear for the time being." He looked up. "It's starting to come down harder. You best get inside."

They fell into step and hurried toward the judge's house. Audrey assumed Eli was heading home.

They hadn't gone far before Audrey paused and pointed. "Junior's at it again."

Horace Junior was stomping a puddle dry. Off to the side sat a large black dog, watching. Suddenly the dog bounded to its feet, tail wagging, and raced toward Junior.

"The dog's going to knock him down," Eli predicted. "And we'll get blamed."

"Get away, you dog, you!" Junior yelled. "Go on, scat!"

The dog hit the water and Junior screamed, arms flailing. Barks and shrill screeches filled the air as he fell flat on his back. Eli gave a sharp whistle and waved his arms. "Go on, scat!"

The dog bounded out of the water and stood watching, tail wagging, and tongue hanging out. Eli grabbed Horace Junior by the collar and hauled him to his feet. "Why don't you stay home and out of trouble?"

Junior wiped water from his eyes. "It's boring there."

"But why play where you know you're not supposed to?"

"Because I want to. Ma won't let me go anywhere, and you won't let Tate play in the cellar today."

"You tell your ma I pushed you again, and I'll dust your britches."

The boy smirked. "I'm not afraid of you. You can't touch me. Ma said so."

"One more fib and you'll find out how hard I can touch the seat of your britches." He collared him onto the path.

Audrey trailed behind him and the boy as they trudged toward the Padgets' back door.

Cordelia flung open the door and glared at Eli. "What is it now?" Her eyes scanned the muddy child.

Junior opened his mouth and then glanced at Eli. For a

long minute he was silent, and then he said, "A big, bad dog knocked me in a mud puddle."

She gasped. "You were attacked by a beastly animal?"

Removing his hat in the driving downpour, Eli explained. "It wasn't beastly. It was a dog. The animal wanted to play."

Junior's mother's lips thinned to a tight line. "Your dog?"

"Never saw the dog before. It was a mutt."

She eyed him. "I'm grateful, of course, but I do wish you and that boy of yours would stop encouraging Junior to be such a ruffian." She pulled the child inside and firmly closed the door.

With a resigned sigh, Eli put his hat on. "Encourage him? Encourage him? That woman is a—"

"She is, indeed," Audrey said before he made an unkindly comparison.

"The next time I see that boy in trouble, I'll let him be."

"You won't do that."

The muscle in his jaw twitched before he recovered. "I won't. But it's mighty tempting. That child is going to grow up and work in his daddy's bank someday. Downright scary, isn't it?"

They reached the judge's house and paused. Audrey smiled. "Would you care to come in?"

"Thanks, I need to get home."

"Surely. Some other time?"

He didn't respond.

He left on his way, and she went inside the house.

Chapter 7

Audrey rummaged through her slim supply of dresses, searching for the proper attire. What did one wear to apply for a mortuary position? Black. She didn't have a black dress; the navy blue would have to suffice.

Not that she meant to overpower Kirkland Burying, but she had to have that job if she wanted to stay in town. It was almost impossible to appear professional when one looked like a drowned cat, but she had to make the effort.

When she came down to breakfast, Willow smiled sympathetically. "I know you really don't want to do this, but if it will help your chances, I'll be praying."

"I appreciate it." Audrey picked up the pitcher and poured milk into a glass. "I'm not eager to work in a funeral parlor. I'm a teacher, but until a teaching position opens up, I still have to eat and provide a roof over my head, and I will not impose on you and Wallace one minute more than is absolutely necessary."

Willow expertly flipped a pancake. "You know we're happy to have you, although I do know your independent streak. I'd feel the same if I were in your situation, but Audrey, please don't be in a hurry to move out. I enjoy having you here so much. Having you and Copper around makes it easier to deal with Uncle's illness. Even with Tucker's love and care, I get awfully lonely sometimes."

Audrey stopped to slip her arm around Willow's slim shoulders. "I know you do. But one of these days you'll be married, and it will be better then. I'm not your responsibility, and I definitely don't want to be around when you and Tucker set up housekeeping. That's not even a consideration, even if you do manage to scrape together enough money to repair the roof and live here instead of in Tucker's one-room cabin."

Willow grinned. "I'm not looking forward to living in the cabin either, but really I don't care what kind of place we share as long as I can be with Tucker. I never dreamed that falling in love could be like this. How I pray that you and Copper will find someone as wonderful."

Audrey laughed. "Well, no doubt we'd like that too, but I'm sure no matter who we find, you won't think he measures up to Tucker."

Willow slid a plate of pancakes and sausage patties in front of her. "Probably not. When I think of how much at odds we were for the longest time, it's nothing short of a miracle that we're together now."

After breakfast, Audrey went upstairs to fetch her cape. She took one last look in the mirror, wishing against all odds that she would look half as nice when she reached the funeral parlor. Even with rain protection she would be soaked through before she reached her destination.

She paused at the kitchen door to say good-bye to Willow and Copper, who was now seated at the table eating breakfast. Willow came over to give her a hug. "If this is God's will, it will work out all right."

Copper made a moue of distaste. "You're really going to go through with this? I can't believe you'd work in a funeral parlor. It's really mind-reeling."

"Well perhaps, dear one, you'll be forced to do something you dislike."

Copper cut a piece of sausage, eyeing her. "We have choices."

"Not always."

"Perhaps the burying business wouldn't be so bad." Willow was still trying to reassure her. "I'm sure it will be much better than you expect. After all, people come to pay their respects to their loved ones, and you'll have an opportunity to serve in a way you'd never have otherwise. It can't be all that bad."

Copper shivered. "Well, it's not for me. However, I do wish you well, Audrey love. You must know, though, that I'm praying God has something more suitable in store for you."

"That would be nice," Audrey agreed. "However, until God sends something different my way, I have no choice except to talk to Mr. Burying about employment."

She left before Copper could argue. It seemed to her they should be less vocal and more supportive. A blast of wind-driven rain staggered her as she stepped off Wallace's front stoop. She hoisted the tarp, bowed her head, and plowed through the lake of water that formed the yard.

Five minutes later, she paused outside the sturdy frame

building, eyeing what she hoped would be her place of employment. White, two-story, with an attractive front porch. A small, discreet sign, white with black letters, identified the establishment as *Burying Funeral Parlor.* Audrey swallowed, glanced up and down the street, and then forced her feet up the brick steps.

The porch roof sheltered her from the rain, and she lowered the tarp and shook off the water. She wet her lips and breathed a sigh before pushing open the door and stepping inside. A tall, thin man wielding a feather duster turned to face her. She stopped, not sure what to do next.

The man approached. "Kirkland Burying at your disposal. What may I do for you?" His voice had a hollow sound, like someone standing at the bottom of a well. Deep, dark, sunken eyes stared into hers. His complexion was pale, as if he didn't spend much time out of doors, unlike the ruddy features of the Gray cousins. The hand he extended was slender, with long, tapered fingers that felt cool to the touch.

She forced a smile. "My name is Audrey Pride, and I understand you are in need of an assistant. I'm here to inquire about the position."

"Ah. I see."

No, he didn't, but she waited. Finally he cleared his throat. "Mmm, yes. You have prior experience?"

"None—other than I've buried a few on the battlefield."

"On the battlefield."

She nodded. "I fought in the war."

"Indeed."

"Does that count?"

"Depends on which side you fought."

"Oh—the South."

"Well then, let me give you a tour of the home. The up-stairs is my private living quarters, of course, and as a rule is off limits."

As a rule? Were there exceptions? He lived here? Above the funeral parlor? Would she actually be working in the man's house? Copper would really be appalled when she heard this.

Kirkland motioned toward the front of the room to a platform extending out about four feet from the wall. "The semi-final resting place."

"The final being . . . ?"

"The grave, of course."

"Oh. Of course." Audrey stared. She tried to picture a casket fitting into that space, with the lintel framing it, lend-ing dignity to the deceased. At either end stood floor lamps about five feet tall, with brass bases and stained glass shades. Wooden chairs were arranged in rows, facing the viewing area. The floor was of wide oak planks, and dusty, wine-colored drapes framed the windows. She sniffed, breathing in the musty scent. If she got the job, the first thing she would do was give the place a good cleaning.

"And now if you'll follow me." Kirkland led her through alcoves, foyers, and hallways, past a small office, and into a back room outfitted with three sturdy tables. "Preparation room." His voice took on a formal tone. "I will bathe the men's bodies, of course. You will take care of the women."

Take care of them. Bathe the bodies. Audrey swallowed. "By myself?" The question came out as a squeak, and she cleared her throat and tried again. "Alone? I mean—I'll do it by myself?"

"Of course. Nothing to it. The bodies get a little stiff at first, but then they loosen up. It's difficult getting the clothing on. Dead weight." He brayed a laugh. When she remained silent, he prodded. "Dead weight. Get it?"

She stared at him, bewildered. He shook his head, and a pitying expression crossed his face. "That was a joke. You do have a sense of humor, do you not? It helps in this business."

"Oh yes. I can see where it might." *My stars*. Willow was right. The man was definitely odd. She obediently followed him to a small walnut table holding jars of creams.

Kirkland indicated the ointments. "Face paint. You do know how to use it, I assume?"

"Certainly." Not that she'd had much experience with such things. It was nothing ladies were supposed to do, and her life had held little opportunity for such frivolous habits. It had been all she could do since the war to hold body and soul together.

Kirkland was speaking. "Just a touch, you know. A faint blush, a dusting of powder, a smidgen of color around the eyes. Subtle nuances. Very subtle. Often I'm told people look better when I'm through with them than they did when they were alive."

Audrey closed her eyes and breathed a faint prayer. Bathe and dress dead bodies? Paint them? And she'd have to fix their hair. It had been easier to think about this in the judge's kitchen. Here in the building where the work was actually done, it all seemed so overwhelming . . . and final.

"Do people hold services here? In Timber Creek the last rites were held in their homes."

Kirkland sniffed. "Oh my yes, for the most part. Of course there are those who can't afford our services and prefer to have the deceased in their homes. They prepare the loved one themselves, but people with discriminating tastes prefer the services of the Burying Funeral Parlor. There is no comparison in the quality, of course."

"Of course." Snob appeal was alive and well in Thunder Ridge. Audrey paused, head cocked slightly, listening. For some time she had been aware of a tapping noise. "What is that?"

Kirkland raised his eyebrows. "What is what?"

"That noise. Like hammers."

"Oh that." Kirkland shrugged. "I employ a couple of men to build caskets. It's far too cost prohibitive to have them brought in, and it's a profitable sideline for us."

"The casket."

He nodded. "The casket. Don't be afraid to voice the word. It will be of grave concern to our customer." He brayed. "Get it? Of grave concern?"

She managed a tolerant smile. "Got it."

Evidently there was more to leaving the earth than she'd previously thought. Comb the hair, rub on a little face paint, and that would be it. Even though others had tried to prepare her, she had harbored a secret hope that the bodies would come washed and dressed. She tried to picture herself wrestling with a cold, lifeless corpse, but the image wouldn't form.

Could she do this? The alternative course filled her with dread. Live with Tucker and Willow, and them newlyweds? She couldn't do that. Somehow she had to be independent, and Kirkland Burying and his fancy funeral parlor was her only hope. She gathered her courage. "When can I start work?"

"Tomorrow? We don't have anything scheduled right now, but that will give you time to learn the burying business." He watched her. "Get it? The Burying business?"

"Got it. Tomorrow then. What time?"

"Eight o'clock. I suppose we should discuss compensation."

Definitely they should. If she must do this kind of work, she expected some rather nice compensation. Why else would she subject herself to Burying humor?

Get it?

He sighed heavily, lips pursed, as if in pain. "The position pays fifty cents a week plus two dollars a client."

Audrey's heart constricted. Not a fortune, to be sure, but she could manage. God was surely smiling on her.

"Very well, I'll be here at eight o'clock prompt."

She left the funeral parlor in a blinding downpour. *It never rains in Thunder Ridge.* Willow's litany in her former letters rang in her ears. What a joke. She stepped in a puddle, splashing mud over the hem of her best dress. She could probably have worn her everyday calico with the same results. She quickened her steps. All she wanted now was to get back to the house and change out of these wet clothes.

With her head bent against the wind and the tarp held in front of her, she found it difficult to see where she was going. She struck something fairly solid and heard a muffled grunt. Pulling the tarp aside, she stared up into the eyes of Eli Gray.

He frowned at her. "Miss Pride. You do seem to favor rain, don't you?"

"No . . . I just applied for a position at the funeral parlor."

Eli shook his head, his gaze wandering to the dreary-looking establishment. "Is that a position worthy of a lady?"

Audrey braced against the cold rain. "It's worthy of this lady. I fought a war, remember?"

His expression softened. "I understand, but I still wonder if there isn't a better choice."

She tried to smile but the rain took her breath. "I begin work tomorrow morning."

He took her arm, and she experienced a jolt. How very odd that his touch could set up such a reaction so soon. Oh, she knew this was her man, but she'd rather thought this sort of electricity the novels touted would come later. Much later. He led her around standing water, and she shamelessly huddled against him. "I thought it never rained in Thunder Ridge."

He smiled down at her. "Well, that's what we used to say, but seems things are changing around here."

"Well, you know what they say. Change is good."

"Who says that?"

She shrugged. "Folks who don't mind change, I suppose."

He took the tarp and walked beside her, shielding her from the worst of the blowing downpour. When they reached the judge's house, she stopped and turned to face him. "Will you come in?"

For a moment he hesitated, and then his expression turned aloof. "Not today." He handed her the covering, his hand lingering for a moment on hers, then he turned and walked off. She watched him go, heaving a mental sigh.

It appeared Eli Gray's walls held firm, even in the rain.

Chapter 8

❧

"You did what?" Audrey's hands shot to her hips, and she glared at Copper. "Why did you do that?" After a perfectly wretched morning, Copper had just increased the misery.

"I thought you'd be pleased. He's such fun, Audrey. Why not invite him to supper? I invited Tucker and Eli too, but neither could come, though Tucker wanted to."

And Eli didn't. Copper might as well say it. "You've made it very clear you have no personal interest in Caleb. Why invite him to supper if the other men can't come?"

"I'm not interested in Caleb—romantically."

"Nor am I."

"I'm just trying to be hospitable."

Copper's expression turned as bland as buttermilk, but Audrey wasn't fooled. She was up to her old matchmaking tricks, and it wasn't going to work. She heaved a sigh. "Don't try to pair me off with him. End of discussion."

"I don't understand why you're so distressed. I do believe you're protesting too much, Audrey Pride. Are you sure you aren't the least bit attracted to Caleb Gray? He's a very attractive man, and eligible."

"Then you may have him. And don't expect me to help with supper." Turning on her heel, Audrey headed for the stairs and her room. If she stayed a moment longer she would surely say more than she intended. If this rain didn't stop and Copper didn't go on her way to Beeder's Cove, she was going to lose her mind!

In her room, Audrey flung herself on the bed, lying flat on her back and staring at the ceiling. Why did life have to be so complicated? *Lord, forgive my ill-temper. You've already done more for me than I deserve, and I'm grateful. Thank you for the job; I'll do the very best I can, but please silence Copper . . . in a compassionate way.*

A commotion outside the window drew her. She slid off the mattress and stood behind the curtain, peering out as Willow and Copper dashed through the rain, chasing a fat Rhode Island Red pullet around the yard. Apparently they were going to have chicken again, if they could catch the main dish.

Copper finally cornered the pullet in an open shed and emerged holding the fowl by the legs. Willow had the dishpan ready, and Copper laid the chicken over the chopping block and raised the ax. It took three tries before she finally managed to kill the ill-fated bird. Willow brought a teakettle of boiling water to scald the carcass, and the women gingerly began to pluck off the wet feathers.

Turning away, Audrey decided she wouldn't eat that night. Copper wanted guests? Then she could entertain.

*　*　*

That evening, Copper answered the door and ushered Caleb inside. Relenting, Audrey came downstairs because she was hungry. If she skipped supper, she'd only be scouring the kitchen later for something to tide her over until breakfast. She took a second look at Caleb as she passed the foyer. The man was resplendent tonight, dressed in a blue shirt and black trousers. Every hair was in place, overshadowing his usual appearance of locks tumbling over his forehead in an unruly mass of curls. He removed the canvas rain cape and grinned at her.

"Evening, Audrey. First time I've seen you dry since the night you arrived."

She smiled. "I know. It feels downright strange to wear dry clothing. I'm starting to mildew."

Willow urged the guest into the kitchen, where the table sagged beneath its load of baked chicken and dressing, gravy, and mashed potatoes. Audrey began to fill cups.

"Sure wish Tucker and Eli could have come." Willow bent to take a pan of bread out of the oven.

"Tucker was a mite envious of me, but he had a meeting with a potential customer."

"Yes, so he said when he stopped by earlier."

"Are you afraid he's off to see Meredith Johnson?" he teased.

Willow closed the oven door. "Not in the least. Meredith knows her life would be worthless if she messes with my man."

Once everyone was seated, Caleb asked the blessing, thanking God for the bountiful feast, and in a deep baritone, mentioning that others might be in need of showers, and the citizens of Thunder Ridge were ready to share.

Succulent chicken and the scent of fragrant sage dressing filled the kitchen. Willow and Copper had outdone themselves tonight. Beet pickles glowed ruby-red in a cut-glass bowl. Caleb speared one with his fork, and held it up, admiring it.

"First time I've had beet pickles since the war."

"Betsy Pike sent them so they're bound to be good," Willow said.

Audrey had met Betsy on her last visit and taken to the newly widowed woman. Her husband, Leonidias, passed quite suddenly, leaving Betsy alone to care for her ailing mother, and she could no longer make the short trip from Blackberry Hill to Thunder Ridge to help cook and clean for Wallace.

Willow passed a bowl of potatoes to Caleb. "Save room for dessert. Copper made dried apple pies."

"Love those." Caleb flashed a smile in Copper's direction.

Audrey watched closely for any sign of sparks, but none was apparent. Sighing, she picked up her fork. Why would her interest lie in the one Gray cousin who wouldn't give her the time of day, when here was Caleb, underfoot and available?

Talk turned to the rain and how well the town was coping. Caleb cut a bite of chicken. "If the river keeps rising, the mill will be under water before long."

Willow paused, her fork in mid-air. "Poor Tucker. Yet another financial blow. I'm grateful Uncle Wallace's house is on high ground. So far we've been safe from floodwaters."

Audrey noticed that she made no mention of the overflowing attic pans and chamber pots, which they would have to empty again before going to bed. Tucker would have to know about the leaky roof soon, but Willow was as independent as the day was long, and she'd not bother him with one more worry. Audrey knew if anyone told Caleb, he would pass the information along to Tucker in an attempt to help.

"The cemetery has us a little worried." Caleb buttered a roll. "The road's washed out. Can't get anyone down there now. If no one dies until the water goes down we won't have a worry, otherwise we'll be in a fix." He turned to give Audrey a mischievous smile. "Speaking of which, I heard you're going to be working with Kirkland."

Nodding, Audrey took a bite of green beans, picturing the strange man in her mind. Copper's eyes turned accusingly on Audrey, and she affected a mock shudder. "Can't we talk about something more agreeable? Let's talk about pleasant subjects."

Audrey calmly took a bite of potatoes. "Let's talk about Copper's hen-killing ability."

Copper shot her a dry look. "Let's not."

Caleb didn't seem to notice the exchange. "Dying and burying are a normal part of life."

"Yet we do our best to avoid the entire process," Audrey noted.

"Well, I'm not partial to the idea, but not because I think the deceased are something to avoid or that I fear them. Like you women, I've had enough of death to last me for a spell."

"Enough talk of death and dying. Is everyone ready for pie now?"

"I am." Caleb pushed his plate aside. "Looking forward to it, as a matter of fact." He winked at Copper.

"Copper makes excellent pies," Audrey said. "She certainly knows her way around a kitchen."

Her friend bent to remove Tucker's empty supper plate. "Don't listen to her. My pies are nothing compared to Audrey's wild plum cobbler. Her crust is as light as an angel's kiss." Copper smirked at Audrey from behind Caleb's back.

Oh, don't start, Copper. Two could play this game. Audrey lightly dabbed her mouth with a napkin. "It's sweet of you to say so, but nothing can compare to Copper's rabbit stew. She uses just the right blend of herbs and spices."

Copper's brow lifted in battle, and her lips firmed. "Ah, but you should try Audrey's biscuits, flaky on the inside, delicately browned on the outside." She banged Caleb's empty plate near the sink. "Pure perfection—with just a hint of butter, and a spoonful of honey."

"Well!" Audrey set her water glass down firmly. "You haven't lived until you've tasted Copper's Lord Baltimore cake. She'll have to bake you one. Soon."

"Cherry pie! I defy anyone to show me a better cherry pie than Audrey's," Copper challenged.

"Fried chicken!"

"Yams! Have you tasted Audrey's yams? Unbelievable!"

Blinking, his forkful of pie held halfway to his mouth, Caleb's eyes pivoted from one woman to the other, seemingly trying to keep up with the bizarre exchange. Audrey realized the tone of their voices held more than a little hostility. She glanced at Willow, whose expression cured her of any desire to continue the game. In their zeal to club each other with compliments, they had gone too far.

Willow quietly rose and walked to the stove. "Actually they are both fine cooks. Would anyone like more coffee?"

Audrey picked up her fork and took a bite of pie. A glance

at Copper showed her doing the same. An uncomfortable silence settled around the table.

Willow returned to sit down, eyes watchful, clearly daring the two women to erupt into another round of one-upmanship.

Caleb glanced at Audrey. "Then you took the job at the Burying Parlor."

"This morning."

"Well, I suppose you don't have much choice, but sure doesn't seem like work you'd take to, honestly."

"Why do you say that?"

He swallowed a sip of coffee before answering. "From your earlier tone, I don't think you're cut out for that sort of work. Don't seem proper for a woman to be dressing dead bodies."

Copper's fork clattered to the plate. "Do what?"

"Dress bodies."

The woman paled. "You can't be serious?"

He nodded.

She turned to Audrey. "You can't do that. I won't allow it. There must be work elsewhere."

Audrey blotted her lips with a linen napkin. "If you'll excuse me, I'm rather tired. I believe I'll retire early."

"But you don't have to do this," her friend argued.

Caleb shook his head. "You have friends to help you. Give it time. Something will turn up."

Audrey focused on him. "The Burying Parlor is all that's available. You just said I don't have much choice."

Caleb's eyes held hers for a moment, and then he nodded. "You're right. I apologize. I'll not mention the subject again."

Willow cleared her throat. "What about parlor games? Is anyone interested?"

"I am." Copper shoved her chair back and stood up. "What shall we play?"

"Something nice and quiet. I don't want to disturb Uncle Wallace. Stay, Audrey. It's still early."

Audrey wanted nothing more than to go to bed and put the evening to rest. This entire day had been taxing, and she'd had enough. Without Eli, she had no desire to stay.

"I know." Copper clapped her hands. "Let's have a spelling bee."

"We can't have a spelling bee," Audrey objected. "There are only four of us. Who will give out the words?"

"Wait." Willow dug a couple of dictionaries out of a crowded bookcase. "Copper and I will give the two of you a word to spell, and then you can give us one."

Audrey sighed, something she'd done a lot of lately. Rain pounded the roof as Caleb lined up chairs, two on each side, facing each other. Copper thumbed through their dictionary.

"All right, Caleb, here's your first word. *Pluvious.*"

"P-l-u- . . . Are you sure that's a real word? What does it mean?"

Copper smirked. "Rainy."

Caleb nodded. "Well, that's appropriate. Let's see P-l-u-v-i-o-u-s. *Pluvious.*"

"Correct. Your turn."

"And you've got a good one coming." Caleb turned the worn pages. "*Poetaster.*"

Willow's left brow lifted. "Meaning what?"

Audrey shifted in her chair and crossed her arms. *Poetaster.* She should have excused herself earlier.

He gave a hint. "A writer of bad poetry."

Copper laughed. "You take that one, Willow. I'll wait for the next."

"Spelled just like it sounds," Caleb said. "*Poet-aster.*"

Willow closed her eyes, and then spelled it correctly. "*Poetaster.*"

Copper spelled *reliquary,* a small box. Then it was Audrey's turn. She had been only half listening to the easy banter going on around her, still annoyed at her friends for arranging the evening.

Turning to her, Copper grinned mischievously. "*Sententious.* Saying much in a few words."

"C-o-p-p-e-r," Audrey spelled. "Saying little in many words."

Copper glared. "Incorrect."

Audrey drew a deep breath. "S-e-n- . . . t-e- . . . Say it again."

"*Sententious.*"

"S-e-n-t-e-n-s-h-u-s."

Copper giggled. "Wrong. You're a schoolteacher and you can't spell?"

Caleb sobered. "I always figured teachers were the smartest folks alive."

"Audrey." Willow shook her head in disapproval. "That was fairly easy."

"I'm sorry. I wasn't paying attention."

The words came out sharper than she intended, but she didn't care. Willow's chiding was the last straw. She hadn't wanted to play this idiotic game anyway.

Caleb dug out his pocket watch and squinted at the time. "It's late. I'd better head on home. Thank you, ladies, for a delightful meal, and a lovely evening. Don't know when I've had such a good time."

Willow took his proffered hand. "We'll have to do it again, sometime soon. Perhaps Tucker and Eli can come too."

"Excellent idea. They'd appreciate a good meal, and the charming company." He shook Copper's hand and then Audrey's. When he smiled down at her, she grinned, repentant, and clasped his hand with both of hers.

"I'm sorry I was so distracted tonight."

"I'd say you have good reason to be. Maybe the sun will come out tomorrow, and we'll all feel better."

Before checking the attic water pails, Willow paused in front of Wallace's door and quietly checked on him. The three women then parted to their bedrooms. Audrey and Copper shared a warm hug, apologizing for their sparring natures, and said good night.

In the privacy of her room, Audrey slumped to the bed. Her mood tonight had been atrocious. Was it because Willow and Copper were trying to initiate a relationship between her and Caleb, one she clearly didn't want?

Or because she was forced to work in a funeral parlor in order to retain her independence? Both were reason enough, but still she would have to apologize for her behavior. Poor Caleb. He must think woe was the man who landed either her or Copper.

And he would be entirely correct.

Chapter 9

⌒

Audrey woke with a sense of dread. Today she started work at the Burying Funeral Parlor. Working with Kirkland Burying. Just the thought made her want to pull the covers over her head and hide but she couldn't.

She slid out of bed and moved to the window. Rain. Wouldn't the sun shine on Thunder Ridge again? She sniffed. The house was beginning to smell of mold—and something else she couldn't identify. Thunder Ridge needed sunshine and fresh air. Fresh, dry air.

The scent of frying sausage and freshly brewed coffee rose to meet her as she descended the stairs.

Copper paused from arranging plates and silverware on the table. "Good morning. You look very becoming." Obviously the behavior they'd both exhibited last night was forgotten.

Audrey glanced down at the gray poplin dress with white collar and cuffs. "You don't think it's too somber?"

"No, very appropriate." Copper cocked her head to one

side, thoughtful. "After all, one can hardly look frivolous when working at a funeral parlor. It might not set well with the clients."

"The clients are dead."

Copper shook her head. "I was referring to the family, of course."

Willow filled three cups and carried them to the table. "You better dress warmly. You'll be sopping wet before you reach the parlor."

"I know." Audrey sat down at the table. "Hardly seems worthwhile to wear anything very nice, but one must make the effort."

They held hands as Willow asked the blessing. Audrey raised her head to find Copper staring at her. "What?"

"I just wish you didn't have to do this. Really, Audrey. If you don't want to impose on Willow, you could always come to Beeder's Cove with me. I'm sure the widow would let you share my room."

Audrey shook her head. "You'll have enough to worry about with your new job, and a new town. I'll be just fine. And with what Kirkland is paying me I'll be able to visit you often."

"Well, we'll be praying for you, won't we, Willow." Copper broke a biscuit in half and buttered it. "With God's help we can work our way through this." She shot a rebellious glance at the rain-streaked window. "It would be easier if the sun shone once in a while. I declare, Willow. When I think of all the letters we got from you complaining about the endless drought, it hardly seems believable we're getting so much moisture now."

Audrey blotted her lips with the linen napkin and rose to her feet. "I have to be going. I'll be home for dinner, if that's all right. In the future, I'll take a biscuit and piece of meat and eat at the parlor."

"I expect you to eat dinner with us," Willow said. "We'll have it ready whenever you get here. Be careful."

"I'll get the slicker." Copper hurried to the pantry where the capes and rain gear hung. She returned with the item in hand. "Oh, Audrey. You need something for your head."

"I have Wallace's hat. It will do fine."

She stepped out into driving rain. Head ducked, she waded across the water-soaked yard. The hour was still early, and not many stirred about. Most folks had more sense than to be out in this weather. She slogged on, recalling Caleb's worries. No one could hold a funeral in weather like this, so she would be spared the expected duties today—unless someone had passed overnight. Kirkland had mentioned there weren't a lot of deaths in the area, but the parlor served all three towns: Beeder's Cove, Blackberry Hill, and Thunder Ridge.

The funeral home came into sight and she scurried toward the establishment, anxious to get out of the weather. She was sweating like a horse under the canvas slicker.

The porch offered part shelter. Her heart skipped a beat as she pushed open the door and stepped inside the dank foyer. Silence. Deep, dark silence greeted her. She shivered, nerves on edge.

"Hello there."

The somber voice was hollow and unexpected. Audrey choked back a scream and turned to meet her employer. "I didn't see you."

He nodded. "I'm easy to overlook."

Her mind raced. With a mighty effort she pulled her

thoughts together. At least he was breathing. That was in his favor.

Kirkland rubbed his hands together. "Now, what shall we have you do first?"

Audrey frantically searched for some familiar task to begin with. "Well . . . I could clean."

"Clean?"

"Yes. Sweep floors, wash inside windows, that sort of thing." She warmed to the idea. "Grieving families deserve a spotless place to say good-bye to their loved one."

He nodded, thoughtful. "I believe you're right. Clean. Of course. Where would you like to start?"

"Here." Perhaps she should make that clear that she would not approach his private quarters. "I wouldn't dream of intruding on your living space."

He frowned. "They could use a good turning out."

"I don't believe that would be appropriate."

He pursed his lips, and she could almost see his thought process. Finally he nodded, and she sensed his regret. "Not today, at least, but when you are caught up we'll readdress the issue."

She would take a long time to get caught up. "Show me where to find cleaning supplies, and I'll get busy."

He led her to a small closet in the back room. "All we have is in here."

She eyed a worn broom, a ragged mop, and a dried, cracked bar of lye soap. Not much indeed. However, it would do. "I'll need a water bucket and some dusting cloths."

"I believe I can locate those. I'll bring them into the viewing room. You can start there."

She nodded.

Moving to the viewing room, she dragged a sturdy chair over to the window and began removing the curtains. A cloud of dust greeted her. She sneezed. Violently. Again. Good gracious. Apparently the curtains hadn't been cleaned in years. An entire family of spiders lurked within the grimy folds. She let the heavy velvet fall to the floor in a crumpled heap.

Kirkland brought an empty bucket and a handful of cloths. "I believe these will be sufficient."

"And the water?" Audrey asked. Water should be the least of her worries.

"Oh yes. Water." After a moment when she thought he would refuse and ask her to fetch it herself, he picked up the bucket and left.

She turned back to the task at hand with a rueful glance at her good gray poplin dress. She should have worn something more suited to cleaning.

Kirkland returned with the bucket half filled with water and immediately left, probably thinking she'd put him to work. Gathering an armful of dusty drapes, she carried them to a back room. After violently shaking them to dislodge as much dust as possible, she stretched them over the tables and went back to the viewing room to wash windows.

She had finished rehanging the curtains and had swept and mopped when the door opened and a small, birdlike woman entered. Audrey twitched her cuffs into place and straightened her shoulders. "May I help you?"

The woman eyed her, her gaze running up and down. "Hello dear. I'm Marion Burying. Kirkland's mother?" The woman's voice was thin and reedlike, matching her appearance.

"Oh yes. I'm Audrey Pride." This tiny figure was the mother of long, tall, Kirkland? It hardly seemed physically possible.

"You're the new assistant." Her features pulled into one giant wrinkle with a smile. "You are just as lovely as Kirkland says."

Audrey felt heat flood her cheeks. "I've . . . been doing some heavy cleaning."

Mother Kirkland glanced around the room, nodding. "The old place needs it. When I could, I cleaned often, but that's been many years ago." Her expression suddenly turned calculating. "Kirkland is looking for a wife."

Nodding, Audrey wasn't sure how to answer.

"He's a good worker. Good provider."

Audrey fixed her eyes to the old woman's features, trying to manage an appropriate response. "Yes . . ."

"Don't want anyone taking advantage of his good looks just to secure her future, you understand that. He'd make some lucky girl a good husband, but I'd want him to have a woman who would take care of him in his old age. You understand?" Her eyes searched Audrey's, skipping here and there. "You look like a sturdy, healthy young woman. Nice wide hips for birthing."

Audrey's friendly smile remained in place but her mind raced. Surely the woman wasn't suggesting that Audrey was here in search of a husband. "Beg your pardon?"

Marion smiled, patting the new assistant's hand. "You could provide a man with lots of heirs."

Audrey grasped the back of a chair so tightly her knuckles turned white. Blood drained from her face, and she fought the urge to flee. Swallowing, she groped for words. "Uh . . . I'd best get back to work. Must earn my salary, you know."

She started to turn away, but Marion grasped her arm and emphasized, "A very good provider. His wife would want for nothing. Hank and I are getting old—we won't be around always to look after him."

Meeting a mother's pleading gaze, Audrey realized how a bird must feel when confronted by a cat. A large cat. If she didn't need this job so fiercely, she'd walk out.

Marion patted her arm, each pat like a small enforcing blow. "Think on it now. A woman could do worse, but don't be swayed by his charm and money alone. When Kirkland marries, it will be for life."

Audrey drew herself up, shoulders back, head high. In what she hoped was a convincing voice, she proceeded to try to dash Mrs. Burying's hope. "I'm sure there are many women in Thunder Ridge who recognize your son's sterling qualities. However, I'm afraid I must decline. I'm not in a position to marry at this time."

The woman squinted at her. "You're married?"

"No." She couldn't lie. She wanted to, but she couldn't.

Marion winked. "Then our conversation has not been in vain. Have a wonderful day, Miss Pride. I'll be around most every day to check on you."

She fluttered toward the door as Audrey's gaze followed her with dismay.

Marry Kirkland Burying?

Mr. Burying had failed to mention that particular obligation.

Chapter 10

O ther than her encounter with Marion, Audrey left the mortuary feeling quite good about her first morning. She, Audrey Pride, had just completed half a day's work and come out well. Of course she would eventually have to handle deceased saints—or in some cases, the eternally doomed. Would they look different? Would some have a perpetual smile on their lips or would smoke rise from others?

Audrey! She mentally shook herself.

Of course one couldn't determine someone's eternal destination by gawking at a dead body. And she resolved to never gawk. Now that she had committed to the job, she would give it all the love and reverence required. She'd earned her keep today.

Rain splashed down her back, but apparently she was adapting because it didn't bother her as much as it had when she arrived in Thunder Ridge. She was getting used to everything being damp and clingy. The smell of mold and must, the eternal showers, the blasts of thunder and lightning flares were becoming commonplace.

Tate Gray approached from the opposite direction. For once the little boy didn't flash a winning smile and offer a high-spirited greeting. Instead he fixed his stare on his boots, apparently intending to ignore her. Surely she hadn't done anything to offend the child . . . oh, the cookies. She hadn't gotten around to baking the boy's requested cookies. As they drew closer, she reached out and touched the child's shoulder. "Tate? Aren't you going to speak?"

He glanced up at her and then looked away. "Hello."

She knelt. "Is there anything wrong?" The usually high-spirited child was anything but his boisterous self today. She sincerely hoped that one of the town bullies hadn't been picking on him again.

He shrugged.

"Well, something seems to be amiss. Aren't we friends?" Maybe a little coaxing would bring the boy around. The incessant rain seemed to bog down everyone's spirits.

He glanced up. "We are?"

"Most definitely. Now why don't you tell me what's bothering you. Perhaps I can help."

He frowned, resembling his father so much it touched her heart. "I'm not supposed to bother you."

"Bother me?" Now why would he say such a thing? She bent to take his hand. "You could never bother me. I like for you to talk to me, come visit. I still intend to bake those cookies for you."

"Really?" His expression lightened. "You don't think I'm a pest?"

"A smart boy like you a pest? Never. Why would you think such a thing?" Though she feared she knew the source. Eli. Apparently he'd warned Tate to stay away from her. She'd have a good talk with him about this matter.

Tate grinned. "I'm smart?"

"You are. You already know how to cipher. I heard you the other day when you were playing with Horace, Jr."

The boy's head drooped. "Yeah, Horace and me was supposed to play in the cellar today, but his ma caught us and sent me packing. I'm supposed to stay away from him too."

Too? Then her assumptions were correct. Eli didn't want him near her. Audrey sighed. And Cordelia had ordered this innocent child to stay away from Horace, Jr. "Who suggested that you were a pest?"

"Eli." Tate's expression was open and innocent. "He said I wasn't to bother you, that you had too much to do and I'd just be in the way."

Audrey had a strong urge to go find Eli Gray and give him a good swat upside the head. It was one thing for him to avoid her, but to suggest she didn't value this child's trust and companionship was going too far. Stemming her anger, she said softly, "You're never in my way, but Tate, Eli is your father and you shouldn't call him by his first name."

"Why not? That's his name, and ever'body else calls him Eli."

"Because it's not respectful. He's your father."

"What'd you want me to call him?"

"Oh . . . how about Father?"

He shook his head. "Don't want to. That sounds sissy."

"Well then how about Daddy?"

The boy shook his head.

"Dad? Pa?" Audrey searched for every known salutation.

"Pa?" Tate's features turned serious. "That's what Harry Bellows calls his pa."

"It's a very proper name."

"Pa." The boy tested the name on his tongue. "You think he'd dust my britches if I called him that?"

Straightening, Audrey took a deep breath, stilling her impatience. Why had this man let his child refer to him by his given name all these years? "I'm quite sure he will be pleased." And if he wasn't, he'd have to deal with her.

"All right then, I'll call him Pa. He'll be surprised, won't he?"

Quite. But she kept her thoughts to herself. "Where were you going? Do you have a reason to be out in this rain?"

He shook his head. "Nope. Not got nary a reason."

"Then why are you out in this deluge?" The boy needed someone to look after him, and obviously Mrs. Gray was too ill to keep up with the six-year-old.

He shook his head. "Just wandering around." They fell into step and began walking. When they turned a corner and came face-to-face with Eli, Tate paused. Surprise flickered across the father's face, and then he turned a stern eye on his son.

"I've been looking for you. Don't you know better than to be out in the rain?"

"I like the rain. Like to splash in puddles." As if to illustrate his statement he stomped his boot in a nearby hole. Muddy water flew. Audrey caught most of it full in the face. Surprised and shocked, she gasped.

"Tate!" Eli roared.

Boys. Audrey removed a hankie from her purse and

mopped up. Undoubtedly Eli must have his hands full with his rambunctious son. Precious as Tate was, he could be trying. She offered a forgiving smile. "Didn't you like to play in puddles when you were his age?"

For a moment she thought he would return her warm greeting, but his attention settled on his son. "Go on home and get into dry clothes."

To his credit, the child didn't put up a fuss.

Audrey extended her cape. "Walk with me, and we can try to stay dry. Or not get any wetter, anyway." Without waiting for his answer, she handed Eli the slicker, drawing Tate beneath the shelter. He smiled up at her, a heartbreakingly sweet, little-boy grin. Eli would answer to her if he ever again warned this child not to bother her.

Eli took the shelter but his expression remained stern.

Tate splashed through another puddle. "I like walking in the rain, don't you, Miss Pride?"

"Sometimes. Today is nice," she agreed. "At least it isn't thundering. I'm still not fond of the noise."

"I like it," Tate declared. "Sounds like fireworks. Do you like fireworks, Miss Pride? I think they're wonderful."

"I like them, but I like to know when to expect the fireworks to explode. The thunder catches me unaware. It can be quite nerve shattering." She glanced at Eli, who remained silent.

"Pa doesn't like fireworks, do you, Pa? He says they remind him of the war." Tate grinned at her as he tested the new name.

She patted his head, hoping her smile let him know how proud of him she was. It wouldn't have surprised her if he had forgotten their talk on proper salutations.

Eli shot him a stunned glance, but remained quiet. Audrey smothered a grin. He must be wondering why Tate had suddenly called him by his rightful title.

Audrey's hand brushed Eli's arm as she reached to keep Tate under the slicker. *Brazen*, she silently reprimanded. Yet she couldn't deny that she enjoyed walking beside his tall frame, brashly aware of his maleness. Perhaps too aware. She carefully controlled her expression, determined not to let him guess her thoughts.

Stealing a glance, she was surprised to meet his eyes. For an instant something warm and intimate flickered between them, and then his expression shuttered closed.

When they reached the judge's house, Eli relinquished the covering. She shook her head. "No, you keep it. You and Tate need shelter. You can bring it back later."

He hesitated. Tate grabbed his hand. "Miss Pride won't care if we come back and see her. She says I don't bother her at all. I'm smart. She likes to talk to me."

Eli glanced down at his son, and Audrey held her breath. Frowning, he handed the slicker to her. "No, son. It's thoughtful of Miss Pride to offer, but we can get along fine without it."

Audrey watched as the two turned and walked off in the rain. Eli's hand rested on Tate's shoulder, propelling him along. The boy looked back at her, and she smiled. He waved. There was no doubt that Eli was the boy's father. They walked with the same uneven stride.

"Bye, Miss Pride. I'll be seeing you again, soon."

"I'll look forward to it." Audrey gave him one last glance and went inside. As she moved toward the kitchen she could hear Copper's excited voice.

Her friend turned to greet her. "Oh, there you are. Wait until you hear the news."

"What news is that?" She hoped it was something good. As far as she was concerned, it was time something positive happened.

Tucker, Caleb, and Willow were seated at the table with Copper. They smiled, giving Copper the floor. Audrey moved over to stand in front of the stove, hoping the heat would dry the skirt of her dress a bit before she sat down in one of Wallace's nice oak chairs.

"I've been to Beeder's Cove." Copper grinned triumphantly. "What do you think of that?"

"How did you get there?" Audrey demanded. "I thought the roads were washed out."

"They are, but only for a short distance out of town, and then it's passable on foot. The heaviest of rain appears to be concentrated in our area. Caleb was kind enough to take me by boat, and then we walked the rest of the way. We just got back."

"That's wonderful—I trust you had a nice visit?"

"Fabulous. The schoolhouse is only temporary, of course, until the town can erect a permanent structure. The room is adequate. I'm to start with thirteen pupils, and I can't wait. The school board seemed agreeable to all of my requests, and the parents I met were friendly and welcoming."

Reaching for a towel, Audrey began to dry her hair. "At least something good has come of our move. I'm happy for you." And she was. Of course she was. Copper was very dear to her, and it was wonderful that everything was coming up roses for her. But it hurt that her plans lay in ruins. Who knew when Blackberry Hill would reopen its school, and until then she was stuck at the Burying Parlor.

"Did you meet the Widow Potts?"

Copper nodded. "I did, and she is most genteel. Her house is well maintained, with beautiful furniture and accessories, and I'm to have a room of my own. It's delightful. Lace curtains, a braided bedside rug, and even a desk and chair for my use. I couldn't ask for more."

"I'm sure you'll be very happy there." Audrey did her best to sound excited, but an attack of self-pity struck and struck hard.

Tucker and Caleb stayed for dinner. Audrey gave a quick thought to Eli and Tate, dining with the ailing Mrs. Gray. Was the woman able to cook? Could she be trusted with the care of a lively little boy like Tate? She'd never met Mrs. Gray, but she had formed a mental picture of a delicate, ailing woman striving to make a home for her son and grandson. She'd probably welcome a younger woman's help, one who could take the load off her shoulders.

Audrey gave herself a mental shake. If Eli ever fell in love again, it would surely not be with her. That much was beginning to be apparent. For all her "patience," she couldn't make a dent in his armor. The man went out of his way to avoid any meaningful contact.

Tucker asked the blessing, and Willow passed a plate of pork chops. The biscuits were light and flaky; the gravy hot and flavorful, but for Audrey the meal had lost its luster. She was happy for Copper. But she wanted a school too. She was a teacher, not an undertaker.

Copper handed her a steaming bowl. "How was your first morning of work?"

Caleb paused in the act of buttering a biscuit. "You went to work today?"

She nodded.

Tucker grinned. "How'd you get along with Kirkland?"

"Just fine. He seems to know what he's doing, and since it's the only funeral parlor around, I'm sure he does a steady business." She didn't mention Marion. She didn't want to think about Marion. That problem would have to be dealt with eventually, but the first day of employment didn't seem like the time to irritate your employer.

"Did you . . . ?" Copper paused. "Oh, Audrey, say you didn't. I can't bear to think of you doing that."

"No, I cleaned today, and Kirkland said they had very few buryings. That's why he can afford to pay me so handsomely for each . . . client."

"The pay is good?" Tucker forked a couple of chops.

"Two dollars each."

Caleb let out a low whistle. "That's mighty good wages."

"Yes, but I'll only make that on clients. Otherwise, the job pays fifty cents a week. I'm sure it won't be all that bad. After all, we saw worse in the war."

"But we didn't clean them up," Copper pointed out. "We just rolled them into the holes and Asa covered them up with dirt."

"Copper, that is absolutely disgusting. The Burying Parlor is a bit more civilized. I'm sure I'll be perfectly fine." Audrey cut a bite of meat and chewed it with deliberation, hoping someone would change the subject.

Tucker frowned. "When have you ever put on face paint? No respectable woman uses such artificial beauty aids."

Willow spoke up. "Of course Audrey has never worn face paint, but how difficult can it be? I'm sure she'll do just fine."

The face paint didn't worry her, but Mother Burying was going to keep her awake nights.

Chapter 11

A ray of sun filtered through roiling clouds when Copper opened the back door to admit the three Gray cousins the following morning. The unexpected, but welcome brightness startled her, but before she could close the door, black clouds had overtaken the light.

When the three men entered the kitchen, the room suddenly felt much smaller with their statuesque frames taking up all the space. Audrey, who had been in the process of taking a pan of biscuits from the oven, paused, one hand pressed against her throat. From the men's sober expressions, it was obvious the early morning visit was anything but social.

"What is it? Has there been a mill accident?" Willow asked.

Tucker shook his head. "Got a wagon train stranded on the outskirts of town. They're headed to Colorado Springs, and sickness has broken out."

"It's no wonder with this weather." Audrey grabbed the pan with a hot pad. "Can we help?"

"We can help—question is, do we want to?" Caleb's slicker dripped rain on the floor. "The outbreak looks to be real serious."

"How serious?" Copper demanded. "You mean like cholera bad?"

"Don't know exactly how bad it is or how bad it will get," Eli admitted. "Doc Smith and Jolie are down there now trying to help."

Jolie. The Acadian woman who lived on the outskirts of Thunder Ridge. Audrey remembered her from her prior visit. Folks who feared a doctor, or couldn't afford one, went to her for herbs and potions. She'd been quite helpful when Willow had burned the sawmill. Willow had needed immediate attention, and the town doctor had been out of town.

Eli cleared his throat, meeting Audrey's gaze for the first time. "Would it be all right if I brought Tate over here? I don't want him around that wagon train, and Ma isn't always able to keep him in line. Until I know what's wrong with those people, I don't want him exposed to the sickness. Can you help a few days?"

"Of course, bring him right away and I'll take care of him." Audrey paused. "Oh, I forgot." Her heart sank. For once he had acknowledged her, and now she must refuse. "I have to go to the parlor. Copper, will you be here?"

"Of course. I'll be happy to watch him." Copper flashed a helpful smile, and relief crossed Eli's features.

"Much obliged. I'll go fetch him. And I sure do thank you, Copper, for taking him in."

But she *would* have, Audrey wanted to say, but didn't. She had a job.

"It's no trouble," Willow assured him. "Bring your mother too. We'd enjoy the company."

He declined. "If you'll just see to the boy . . ."

Audrey intervened. "Of course we'll help. I'll complete my work at the parlor and come home as soon as possible. I'll probably be back before Tate gets here."

Eli left, and Tucker flashed Willow a stern glance. "Are you sure about this? He's a handful. Do you have time to keep an eye on him and Wallace too?"

Copper held up a restraining hand. "Excuse me? I believe I offered to take care of Tate. Willow won't have to lift a hand. I'm a teacher, remember? I'm sure I can entertain one little boy without any trouble."

"Don't worry, Tucker." Willow returned to the sink. "Copper and Tate will get along nicely. He can stay here in the kitchen and help bake."

"It's easy to see you don't know our little Tate," Caleb said. "If you can get him to sit for five minutes, you'll be working a miracle. The boy has ants in his pants."

Audrey heaved a sigh. She was standing right there, and they were ignoring her. Yes, she had to work, but she and Tate were friends. She'd promised to bake cookies; this would be the perfect time.

By evening, Eli delivered the child. "I'm going to stay with you, Miss Pride!"

"No, son." Eli said. "You're going to be in Copper's care. Audrey has work to attend to." He glanced at Copper. "I'd hoped to get him here sooner but something came up."

Tate stuck out his lower lip and frowned. "I want Miss Pride."

Eli's tone sharpened. "Miss Wilson will look after you. You mind what she says. And I don't want any back talk."

Tate puffed up like a spotted toad. Obviously he wasn't happy with the situation or his father's tone.

Audrey knelt in front of him. "I'll speak to Copper and we'll bake those cookies—"

"Don't be coddling him, Miss Pride."

Audrey rose to face him, rebuke on the tip of her tongue. She amended her response.

"Perhaps your father will let you stay for supper tonight, and you can help set the table." Surely he would allow the child food. "Would that be all right?"

Tate brightened. "Just us two?"

"Just the two of us," Audrey promised. She slanted a look at Eli. "If your father doesn't object, he's invited to eat with us."

Eli frowned, but one look at Tate and it was apparent to everyone present that if he wanted his son to cooperate, he'd have to give in on this one. "I suppose. But you mind your manners, and don't give Miss Wilson any trouble. She's taking care of you, not Miss Pride. You hear me, Tate?"

"I hear you, Eli." Tate gave him back frown for frown.

Audrey sighed. Seemed they were back to first names. She'd work with the boy again tonight about the proper way to address his father. Right now was not the time to get into semantics with Eli standing there looking like a thundercloud.

With a backward glance at Audrey, Eli turned and left.

Copper appeared, smiling a welcome at Tate. "How about you and me sitting down here at the table and drawing a picture?"

"I don't want to draw pictures."

Audrey placed a hand on Tate's shoulder. "I expect you to

be nice and treat Copper with respect. If you don't, then we won't be able to have our time together tonight."

Tate sent her a rebellious look, but then he sighed. "All right. Where's the pencil?"

Audrey nodded her approval.

Tate grinned. "If I'm extra nice will you play two games tonight?"

She smiled. "We'll see. In the meantime, you and Copper have fun."

She might as well go back to the funeral home and clean the back room. Eli had made it clear that Copper was in charge. If she was here she'd only mother the boy.

As she let herself out of the back door, her thoughts turned to the stranded wagon train. The rigs were covered with canvas but they wouldn't be totally waterproof. Between the rain and the illness the travelers must be miserable. Lights glowed behind the windows of the funeral home when she approached. Leaving the slicker on the porch, Audrey entered the foyer.

Kirkland approached. "Oh . . . I'm glad you've returned. You've heard the news."

Audrey smiled. "What news?"

His eye lit with uncharacteristic fervor. "The wagon train. Wonders of wonders, we've got bodies to prepare. Three, and possibly more to come!"

Her knees momentarily buckled. The room tilted. The wagon train. Illness. The implication of the men's prior conversation impacted her. "Three?" The number came out in a feeble squeak.

"All from the wagon train. Three passed during the night, and others have fallen ill. We're going to be very busy."

Audrey reached for a chair to support her weight. "Why so many deaths?"

Kirkland shook his head. "Some sort of malady has befallen the group. The cause isn't important. The issue is that we have work to do. A lot of work. Come now, we must get busy. More could come at any time. Large party—over thirty families traveling."

Audrey swallowed. *Malady. Deadly illness. Large party.* "But if they're contagious?" Which had been Eli's fear. Something like this had been known to impact whole communities.

"Miss Pride. Are you interested in employment or medical issues?" He lifted both hands and clapped a couple of snappy beats. "Come now. Work awaits us! It matters not how the client passed on. It's our job to make them presentable. Now stop asking questions, and get busy. Your client is in room one."

"My client?"

"Yes, the body you are to prepare. *Client* sounds so much more genteel than *corpse*, don't you agree?"

"Oh—agreed." Much more genteel.

And dead.

"Fine. Right through there. Claude will bring you what you need." He disappeared, and Audrey tried to assimilate the shocking turn of events. A body. She was expected to prepare a body for burial on her second day at work? With no prior instructions or training? She had no idea what the process would involve, and Kirkland Burying was going to be of limited help. Claude could advise her, although his main task was building Burying caskets. Her eyes traveled the dim foyer. She couldn't stand there forever, so taking a deep breath, she walked to room one where her first client waited her.

A woman lay stretched on the table. Her dress was wet and mud-stained, her long hair stuck to her back. Her face was pinched and white, as though she had been ill a long time, but it was her hands that caught Audrey's eyes. Calloused, dry, cracked skin; nails ragged with dirt underneath—the hands of a woman who'd worked hard all her life. She was young, maybe not many years older than Audrey. A single worn gold band encircled her ring finger.

The door opened and Audrey whirled, hand to her heart. Claude entered, carrying a large basin of hot water and a bar of lye soap. A towel and washcloth hung over his arm.

"Here you go, Miss Pride. You need anything else, just call and I'll fetch it."

Nodding, Audrey didn't trust her voice. She was two breaths away from hysterics. The moment Claude left she went in search of Kirkland. This was insane. She needed instructions. She knew nothing about what was expected of her. She knocked gently on his office door, afraid to enter. What if he was working on a male victim?

She took a step back. She was beginning to understand why everyone was so opposed to her working here. She wasn't thrilled about it herself.

Kirkland came to the door. "Yes? What is it?"

"What am I supposed to do?"

"With what?"

"With my . . . client?"

"Why, bathe her, of course. Dress her and arrange her hair and face paint."

Of course. She would need to be cleansed and made presentable. "Certainly. I can do that." Audrey backed away from the door, and Kirkland closed it before she could ask the second question: *Then what?*

She went back to stare at the young woman. *Oh Lord, help me do this.* But then she didn't have a choice if she wanted to keep her job. She reached for a pair of scissors and approached the table. Her husband had brought clean garments.

Working carefully for the next hour, she cut off the dress and the coarse pantaloons. The bleached muslin undergarments came off easily, but she had trouble with the chemise. Finally the discarded bits of clothing lay in a muddy heap on the floor beside the table. The corpse lay before her, vulnerable in death. Her heart softened. The girl was a nursing mother. Her breasts were swollen with milk. Somewhere, someone was wet nursing this mother's child. She felt tears gathering in her eyes.

She dipped the washcloth in water and began to gently clean the lifeless limbs, trying to close her mind to what her hands were doing. Audrey took a deep breath and tightened her hold on the woman, struggling to lift the body to wash her back. But a muffled crash from outside the room startled her and her hands slipped, and somehow she ended up on the table on top of her client. For one awful moment, Audrey looked death squarely in the eye.

Groaning, she scrambled off the table and nervously patted the woman's hand. "Sorry. Please forgive me. I'm new at this."

Silence met her apology.

Drawing a deep breath, Audrey began again. She was not suited for this work. She had just apologized to a dead woman. She reached for the washcloth when a new thought struck her. If this woman had been a Christian, she could very well be sitting up in heaven watching Audrey manhandle the wretched clay that had once housed her soul. The thought unnerved her. She cast a nervous glance upward, vowing to be more careful this time.

The slender, pale body was finally bathed and ready for the clothes that had been left. She lifted the dress, rose-pink calico with ruffles at the throat. The stitches were small and even, excellent workmanship. She wondered if the woman had sewn the garment, wondered what she had been like in life. Wondered if they would have liked each other. Where was her husband now? Heartsick, grieving? Or just sick, like others who'd fallen victim to the malady? It occurred to her for the first time what a truly sad situation this was. Death was never easy to accept. All this time she'd been concentrating on herself, forgetting that a short time ago this woman had been busy with her life, nursing her baby. Living. She edged the dress over the form and fastened the tiny buttons at the back.

Next she picked up a brush and began working on the hair, arranging the still-damp tresses in a soft mass atop her head. She should speak to the husband. Was this how his wife fashioned her hair, or did she allow the thick, lustrous curls to hang loose and unencumbered?

She reached for the face paint and recalled Kirkland's warning to be subtle. Just enough to restore life back into her face. Gently, with a feather touch, she applied the artifice. The face looked even younger now, with a sweet expression. Audrey stood beside the table, unable to believe the transformation. Her client looked to be at perfect peace.

Reaching to take the still hand, Audrey whispered. "You look beautiful. Rest in God's love."

She left the room to summon Claude.

Claude and Jim, fellow employee, brought in a fresh, new casket. The scent of pine filled the room. They gently placed the body inside and carried it to the parlor. After lowering the casket to a narrow table positioned between the stained glass lamps, they left. Audrey sniffed delicately. The lamps, which were beautiful with the light shining through them, smelled faintly of kerosene. Candles should replace the fuel. She'd suggest it to Kirkland.

The door opened, and a man, perhaps in his early thirties, entered. He approached the casket, the brim of his sodden hat crumpled in his hand, face working. Audrey stepped back as he stared down at the woman lying cold and still. Finally he looked up and met her eyes, tears rolling down his cheeks. "She looks real nice." His voice was husky with grief.

Audrey nodded, unshed tears forming a lump in her throat.

The man held out his hand and she took it, wincing as he gripped hard. "I'm beholden to you, ma'am. It won't be so hard to remember her this way instead of so sick and helpless." His voice broke, and he swiped at the tears shining on his cheeks. He moved back to the casket to stare at the body.

Audrey didn't want to intrude on his grief, but the nursing child haunted her. "Is the baby well?"

Without turning, he nodded, his shoulders heaving with grief. "A son."

"I'll pray that God will keep his hand on the child."

As Audrey watched, he reached out a calloused finger and brushed his wife's cheek. "Good-bye, Nellie. I'll miss you something fierce." His shoulders shook as he turned and walked toward the door.

"Wait."

He stopped and looked back.

"Would you like a lock of her hair?" Audrey silently chastised herself for asking, but his expression softened.

"Why, yes, ma'am. I'd like that a lot."

She used scissors to clip a long strand of the chestnut-brown hair and handed it to him.

"Is this how Nellie wore her hair? Would you like for me to change anything?"

He stepped back to gaze at the lifeless form for so long, she wondered if he intended to answer her. Then he said quietly. "She looks like the day I married her. She came from Boston, you know. Her folks didn't want her to marry me, but she went against their wishes. I wonder if this is God's punishment."

"I don't know much about those things," Audrey admitted softly. "But I do know God promises us he always has our best in mind, whether we can see it or not."

He wound the clipped lock of hair around his forefinger, and then removed the coil and tucked it in his shirt pocket. "Thank you kindly, ma'am, for all your goodness. I surely appreciate it."

When he left, Audrey returned to the casket, gazing at the peaceful face. This wasn't so hard. God had given her an opportunity to do one last thing for her fellow man, a good thing. Nellie had given her a different perspective about working here.

She rested her hand on top of her new friend's. "Thank you, Nellie."

It was then that she knew that she could handle anything Kirkland Burying sent her way.

Chapter 12

Sinking to the floor, Audrey pulled off her wet shoes the moment she got home. Two days after the wagon train arrived, the epidemic had turned macabre. New bodies were arriving at the funeral home daily. The work had become routine now, which disturbed her. The victims, and their grieving loved ones, deserved better than someone rushing through preparation in order to hurry on to the next victim. Willow came down the stairs as Audrey lay back in a chair and closed her eyes.

"Oh, poor thing. You're exhausted, but Tucker has called a town meeting about this dreadful epidemic. Something has to be done, not only about the bodies, but about the ones who are not yet affected. Do you feel like going?"

Audrey wanted so badly to refuse, to go upstairs and stretch out on her bed and sleep for days. But she knew Willow was right. Something has to be done. The only good light on this time was the fact that she saw Eli several times a day as he delivered the dead. The situation was quickly nearing a breaking point. The parlor couldn't keep up with its clients. "Let me change my dress, and I'll be ready to go."

She smiled. "You have time to eat a bite. Perhaps that will restore you."

"Well, we can always hope." Audrey climbed the stairs to the third landing, feeling as if the steps grew steeper with each passing day. A pox on Claudine for coming up with this poorly designed house. It was bad enough when she was fresh and energetic, but almost impossible when long work hours with inadequate rest and food sapped her strength. She took time to wash and tidy her hair before slipping into a clean dress and going downstairs.

Over supper she listened to Willow and Copper prattle. Too tired to join in, she smiled at appropriate places, nodded occasionally, allowing their conversation to flow past her like a peaceful stream.

Willow fell silent and reached over to take Audrey's hand. "You don't have to go tonight. Tucker will understand."

Audrey stifled a yawn. "No, I'm all right."

Copper pushed her plate aside and leaned back in her chair. "What are they doing with all those bodies?"

"There are fifteen now," Audrey murmured, "and still counting. Men, women, and children." Copper had been so busy trying to cook for the ill, watch Tate, and look after Wallace that she hadn't been brought up-to-date on the situation. Willow had her hands full with the sick. "The caskets are stacked in the icehouse until the rain lets up and the ground dries enough to . . ."

Copper winced. "Please. You don't need to elaborate. How horrible for the families. Where's the ice coming from?"

"I have no idea, and I haven't thought to ask."

"The millpond," Willow supplied. "During winter they cut huge blocks of ice and store them in the icehouse. They keep until winter comes again. This time of year, the ice must be very low." Willow covered the bread and stored it in the cabinet. "We need to be on our way. The meeting is about to start."

As they were about to leave, Audrey reached out to touch Willow's arm. "I'm so sorry that this illness has taken the luster away from you and Tucker. We'll still have plenty of time to alter Claudine's dress for your vows."

Her friend smiled, the lines around her eyes testimony to the long hours she'd spent nursing the sick of late. "That is so kind of you, but our time will come."

Wrapped in layers of warm clothing, the women waded through running streams toward the church house. Dim lantern light seeped from the windows, almost blotted out by the rain. September was drawing to an end and October was near.

Deet Jackson held the door open for them. "Come on in here, ladies. It's not a fit night for man or beast out there. How's Wallace?"

"He's sleeping, so we felt it would be all right to slip out for an hour or so," Willow explained.

Deet patted her shoulder. "Hard to watch, isn't it? But Wallace knows the Lord, and he's in safe hands. He's not been happy since Claudine passed."

"I know, and it's selfish of me to want to keep him here, but it's hard to give him up too." Willow touched the corners of her eyes with a folded handkerchief.

Audrey marveled at the care shown by this grizzled old

man. Deet Jackson, in spite of his appearance, had a soul filled with compassion.

Townsfolk milled about the stuffy room. A few strangers sat among the regular members, and Audrey suspected they came from the wagon train. Most had suffered the loss of at least one family member. Her heart ached for them. Her eyes searched the crowd and found Nellie's husband. How was the now-single father managing without his mate?

Her gaze sought and found Eli. He was alone tonight. Apparently Tate was home in bed. For a brief moment their gazes touched, then moved on.

Tucker rose and faced the crowd. Audrey had been so overwhelmed with work she had failed to notice how lined his features had grown. She glanced at Willow, whose eyes fastened on the man she loved. She must be worried sick about the additional load he carried.

"Glad you could all come. You know the reason we're here. We've got a major problem on our hands. As you know, a lot of people with the illness have died. Too many. We have a serious need to separate the well from the sick."

Doctor Smith nodded his agreement. "That's right, folks. What looked to be a simple sickness has turned into an epidemic. What do you have in mind, Tucker?"

"I was hoping maybe some of you would be willing to take the ones who are well into your homes. Get them in out of the rain, and keep them away from others who are infected with whatever this disease is. Give us a chance to get the disease under control or let it run its course."

Audrey studied the faces of the people gathered there. Murmured discussion rose and fell around the room. Finally Sully James rose. "Sounds like a good idea to me. Me and my missus can take five, if they don't mind sleeping on the floor. We'll put quilts down so they'll be comfortable."

"Thanks, Sully." Tucker's gaze moved around the sanctuary. "Anyone else? I know it's asking a lot, but a lot is at stake right now."

One by one the townspeople offered shelter and food to the people from the train. Then Cordelia Padget got to her feet and strode to the front of the church. As she faced the parishioners her features turned mottled. "Have you all lost your minds? These people are *sick* and dying. Why would you bring them into your homes? Let them stay with the train. In fact, pull those wagons out of Thunder Ridge, away from our homes and businesses. Let them fend for themselves."

Reverend Cordell rose. "Cordelia, think. The Bible says we are to give a cup of cold water in Jesus' name. Would you turn people in need away from your door?"

"In this case, yes. We have to look after ourselves. God doesn't expect us to kill ourselves in order to help another."

"Cordelia," the reverend protested.

The woman's eyes fixed on the pastor. "Is it your intent to bring death and destruction upon your flock?"

"Of course not, but to turn someone away because they might become infected—that's hardly a reason to forsake our duty. Who knows who might fall victim next. Why, it could be you, Cordelia. Would you have us turn you away?"

"I won't fall victim because I have the good sense to take precaution when danger is present. I don't intend to expose myself or my family to harm. The rest of you can do what you please, but I warn all of you against being part of this irresponsible plan."

Sully lumbered to his feet again. "Seems like we have an

obligation to help these folk. They came to us, and I don't see how we can turn them away. God's given us an opportunity to serve. How do we know he's not testing us in some way?"

Cordelia frowned. "God doesn't test his people by sending an epidemic. That's the Devil's hand. The rest of you can do as you please, but we have a child to consider. An innocent, trusting child. His welfare must come first."

"Others have children too," Copper protested. "They're helping."

Audrey whirled to stare at her friend. She'd never heard her be so vocal in front of strangers. The rain did have her on edge.

Cordelia lifted an impervious brow. "That's their business. We refuse, don't we, Horace?"

The banker's face turned brick-red, but he nodded. "As you say, love. Perhaps we could help in a monetary way?"

Cordelia's lips tightened.

Horace cleared his throat and rose. "I believe we've said our piece. Come, dear. Let's go home and see about Junior."

With a commanding glance around the room, Cordelia swept toward the door, her husband following in her wake.

Willow rose to speak. "I believe we can handle at least six. The only thing I ask is that they realize my uncle is very ill and I don't want him disturbed. No one will be allowed access to the second floor in order to shield him as much as possible from the illness."

Audrey recognized that Willow's sacrifice was great. If Wallace contracted the mysterious illness, he would be dead within hours.

Tucker smiled at her. "My thanks to all of you for your

help. We'll be assigning people to their new quarters straight away."

Reverend Cordell sprang to his feet. "Excuse me, Tucker, but we need to make provisions for the sick, too. Would anyone object to sheltering them in the church? They would be out of the rain, which could help. We may need to help with food."

"Good idea, Reverend." Caleb stood up. "Eli will help me transfer the ailing here."

"What about Sunday services?" someone asked.

Reverend Cordell turned sober. "Until the worst of this illness passes, I say we suspend services and each household conduct their own. The more this disease spreads, the harder it will be to stamp out."

A tall man with dark reddish hair and tea-colored eyes stood and spoke from the back of the room. "The name is Redlin. Josh Redlin. I'm the train's wagon master. I want to thank you all for what you're doing. I'll be happy to work with you transporting the sick, because we do need to get these folks in where it's warm and dry. Fall's closing in, and the chill is brisk in the morning."

Others voiced their agreement, and the meeting broke up. Some gathered in small groups to rehash the subject. Audrey rather hoped that Eli would offer to walk her home, but when she looked at his seat it was empty.

During the walk home, Copper said. "Audrey, Willow and I can help out at the mortuary. All you need do is ask."

Audrey looked at her askance. "You're offering to help? If I remember, you thought it would be too gruesome to work there."

Copper shrugged. "I didn't say I'd like it, but you seem to be surviving, and after all, what's a friend for if she isn't there to help? We help each other. It's always been that way, always going to be."

"She's right," Willow said. "We should have offered before. As soon as we settle our new guests, we'll help."

The offer was a huge load off Audrey's shoulders. "I'll admit I'm too tired and too overwhelmed to argue. You offered, and I'm accepting. Thank you."

"You should have asked earlier," Willow said as they entered the judge's house. "Now off to bed with you. Copper and I can decide where to put everyone."

Audrey was too weary to argue. "Maybe that good-looking wagon master will be with them. Did you notice him, Copper?" If she hadn't, the woman had been struck blind. Tall and handsome, even though that beard was in the need of a good trim.

Copper raised her eyebrows. "You think that man is good-looking?"

Audrey turned to eye her. "Don't you?"

Her friend shrugged. "Mediocre—at best."

Willow laughed. "You have a strange idea of average. He's a striking man. Not as handsome as Tucker, of course, but definitely more than passable, and how many times do I have to remind you. It isn't about a man's looks—it's what he is on the inside that counts."

As Audrey headed upstairs, a knock sounded at the door. She turned and opened it to find Eli and Tate. She was so stunned she just stood there staring at them. Eli's features were graver than usual.

"Sorry to bother you so late."

"It's not that late." Heat colored her cheeks and she stepped out of the way. Father and son walked past her and headed for the kitchen. She followed, pausing in the doorway.

Eli cleared his throat. "It seems that Tate has disobeyed again and sneaked off to the wagon train while we were meeting. I fear he's exposed to the disease."

"Oh, Tate." Audrey's heart sank. She reached out to touch the boy's shoulder. "Why did you do that when you knew it was so dangerous?"

The boy shrugged. "I can't figure me out. Grandma fell asleep and I thought I'd just catch a few frogs. Junior can't come to the cellar anymore, and I ain't got no one to play with so I took a walk and whadda you know. There's the wagon train and some folks were puking out the back of their wagons. Before I knew it, I was right in the middle of 'em."

"Don't have anyone," Audrey corrected.

"Huh?" Tate stared at her.

"I don't have anyone to play with," Audrey repeated.

"You ain't got nobody either? We could play together if you want."

Audrey gave up on the English lesson.

"Even if I wasn't worried about my boy, Ma's had another spell."

"We understand completely," Audrey interrupted. "He can stay as long as needed."

"I know you have your hands full at the parlor."

"Not so full that I can't look after Tate's interests."

"I've got his things outside on the porch." Eli nodded. "If it's all right, I'll bring them in now."

"Yes, of course. And we'll put Tate in that small room off mine," Willow said. "I'll go prepare the bed for him."

Eli brought in a small bag and climbed the stairs with his son.

Following, Audrey waited at the end of the hall and eaves-dropped. She shouldn't. But she couldn't help herself.

Tate's youthful timbre floated to her. "I ain't never slept in a house this big. Will I be scared?"

"You won't be scared," Eli said. "I promise you there's nothing to be scared of, and Miss Audrey will be right down the hall."

Audrey straightened. *Miss Audrey.* He was willing to turn his son's care over to her? She grinned.

"Does she sleep up here too? If I get scared I'll talk to her."

"You leave Miss Pride alone, Tate. Don't be bothering her, now."

"I won't bother her, but I wish she could come live with us. Do you think she would, Eli?"

"No, son. She can't live with us."

"Why not? She's nice, and she smells good."

"She just can't."

"But if she smells nice and talks nice, and she's smart too, why can't we have her? Nobody else wants her."

Audrey frowned.

"It's just not possible. We just can't. Now hush up and get ready for bed."

Audrey's heart constricted. It was impossible only because Eli Gray hadn't the slightest notion of consulting her about the matter. How did he know what she'd say? Who'd he think he was, the Almighty?

Tate, I'd be mighty tempted to take you up on your most gener-ous offer. A second smile escaped her. She'd love to see how Eli'd squirm out of that one.

Chapter 13

Within the hour, the exodus from the stricken wagon train started to arrive. Most were so exhausted they were still sleeping when Audrey came downstairs the next morning. Tate sat at the table eating mush and washing it down with great gulps of milk. "Morning, Miss Pride. Did you sleep good?"

She checked the near empty milk supply. "I slept very well, thank you. And you?" His answer didn't matter. She knew the sleep of an innocent child was an enviable one.

"I slept good."

"Well."

"Yep. I ain't a bit sick yet." He stuck out his tongue. "See?"

Audrey grinned.

Without interrupting his meal, the boy asked. "You reckon Eli will come for breakfast?"

"I don't know, and I seem to recall a discussion about you calling him by his first name?"

Tate ducked his head. "I forgot."

"It would be thoughtful if you could remember. I'll help you."

"I don't think he likes for me to call him Pa, Miss Pride. He gets this funny look on his face like he has a bellyache when I call him that." He spooned mush into his mouth.

"Oh, I think he likes it. I have a feeling your father is a very caring man, and he would be proud to hear his son call him by his rightful name." Audrey paused. Tate had been exposed to the sickness. It would break her heart if anything happened to this precious child. She'd prepare the cure her grandmother had recommended for almost everything. It might be difficult to find the herbs in this rain, but if she remembered right Jolie had a supply. She'd stop by the woman's house on her way to work and see if she could have some echinacea, garlic, and mint. She meant to do all she could to keep this child safe.

Willow entered the room, and Audrey turned to her. "Do you happen to have any echinacea in the house? I'd like to make some tea for Tate. It might ward off any exposure he encountered at the wagon train."

"You know, Betsy Pike used to dry herbs when she worked for the judge. Let me see what I can find." She smiled at Tate. "Good morning, young man."

"Morning, ma'am." Tate's gaze never left his meal. "You look mighty fetchin' this morning."

"You, sir, are spending too much time with Caleb. Entirely too much."

Willow rummaged around in the pantry and returned with several glass jars and tin boxes in her arms. "See if you recognize any of these."

Audrey opened the jars, sniffing to see if they still had fragrance. "Oh yes. These are exactly what I need. Is the kettle boiling?"

"Yes. I was planning to fix Wallace some hot tea, hoping it would restore him a bit. He knows about the guests in the house and agrees we needed to invite them here. You know, Audrey, he's such a compassionate man. Eccentric, perhaps, but so giving."

"From the snippets I've overheard, he's helped the whole town at one time or another." Audrey poured boiling water over the herbs and let the mixture steep while she filled a bowl with mush, and placed it on the table. As soon as the tea was nicely colored, she poured a cup for Tate. "Here you are. Drink up."

He sniffed the contents. "What is it?"

"It's a special drink that will keep you from getting sick."

"It stinks."

"That's just the way the herbs smell. Go on, take a sip. I think you'll like it."

He pushed the cup aside. "No thank you."

Obstinate. Like his father. "Now Tate. Please drink it for me. You don't want to get sick and be unable to splash in mud puddles, do you? This rain won't last forever." At least she didn't think it would. Even Noah eventually came out of the ark. "When it quits you can go outside and play if you're not sick."

"No thank you."

Willow pulled up a chair and sat down. "I've been meaning to ask you, Tate, would you do me and Tucker the honor of carrying at our wedding?"

His spoon paused. "Carry what?"

"Our wedding rings. I was thinking it would be rather nice to have you bear our rings, and when the reverend asks, you can hand him the token of our affection. Tucker can put mine on my finger, and I'll put his on his finger, and then after the pastor announces that we're man and wife, you can walk us back down the aisle."

Tate appeared to study the offer. "Will I be married?"

"No. Just Tucker and I, but you'll be a very important part of the ceremony. If you were to fall ill and couldn't attend I would be so distressed."

He eyed the half-eaten bowl of mush. "Distressed, huh. Is that the same as mad?"

"No. I would be disappointed, and sad, but not angry. Just very sad." She gently eased the cup of tea toward his bowl. "Now if you were to just sip on this tea every now and then, and manage to get the whole cup down, then I could rest assured that I would have a very handsome ring bearer for the wedding. Audrey made it just the right temperature. You don't have to blow it to cool it."

He sighed and reached for the cup, downing half the liquid in one gulp. Audrey held her breath, hoping he wouldn't choke. He made a face. "That's not good."

Audrey reached for a napkin. "Sometimes we have to do things that aren't good, but are good for us. Drink the rest of it, please."

"What is it?" a gruff voice asked.

She swerved to face Eli. When had he come in? His expression leaned toward hostile.

"Herbal tea. If he's been exposed to the sickness we need to take precautionary measures." As his frown deepened, she defined her stance. "I'm only trying to help."

"Don't fix him any more." He set a bucket of milk on the counter. Rain ran from his soaked slicker. "Aren't you needed at the parlor? Brought in two more victims a couple of hours ago."

Two more? Her heart sank. "I was just about to leave." Her heart went out at his appearance. Haggard, exhausted. He must have been up all night. "Can I get you a cup of coffee? Or there's eggs and biscuits?" Why did she have this insane urge to sit him down, strip away his sodden hat, wipe those unruly curls with a dry towel, and humanize him?

Ease that silent hurt.

Kiss away the pain.

He spared her a glance. "Women have been bringing food all night." He focused on Tate. "Eat your breakfast, son."

"I am, Eli. And I'm drinking black stuff so Miss Willow and Tucker can wear rings."

Eli centered on Willow. "Silas Sterling has taken ill."

Willow's hand flew to her throat.

"Not the illness," he clarified. "He developed a chill a couple of days ago, and he's taken to his bed. Thought you might want to know."

She nodded. "Thank you. It must be all this damp weather. I'll stop by sometime today and check on him."

"Best take care, Willow. You can't be coming down with a cold now." Nodding, Eli exited through the back door.

If the envy Audrey felt over his concern for another woman was any indication of the depth of her Christianity, she had fallen way short this morning.

Willow shook her head. "Eli can get crossways of his britches at times. Don't be discouraged."

Crossways of his britches? That certainly was an apt description of the man. She paused. And how did Willow know how she felt about Eli Gray?

Copper entered the kitchen, glancing at the swinging back door curtain. "Was that Eli I just saw leaving?"

"Yes, he brought fresh milk." At least he'd physically been there. Audrey was never sure where he emotionally spent his time.

Copper took a plate from the cupboard and helped herself to a biscuit. "I'll tell you what. It's going to take a lot of food to feed this bunch. I think we have extra guests this morning."

Tate licked his spoon. "Besides me."

Audrey reached to ruffle his hair. "Yes, young man, besides you. But you're a special guest."

Copper sat down at the table and heaved a sigh that seemed to come from her toes. "I do declare I'm at my wit's end."

Her friend's tendency for dramatics never ceased to amaze Audrey. If a real problem ever developed, she didn't know how Copper would handle it. "Now what's wrong?"

"Caleb stopped by earlier. Do you know the doctor quarantined Thunder Ridge this morning? I can't leave for Beeder's Cove. If I'd had any sense I'd have stayed there once I broke free from this swamp. No telling how long it will be before I can leave, and with my luck the school board will get tired of waiting and hire someone else."

"Oh, they won't," Audrey exclaimed. "That would be so unfair."

"Life is unfair, or hadn't you noticed?"

Tate pushed his bowl aside. "I'm done. Can I go play?"

Audrey absently nodded. Copper was in one of her moods. No reasoning with her when she was like this. The only thing to do was leave her alone. She loved her friend dearly, but there were times when it paid to walk a wide circle around her.

Someone knocked at the front door, and Copper rose to answer. She returned, followed by Josh Redlin, the wagon master. His commanding presence filled the kitchen in the same manner as the Gray cousins. He nodded to Audrey and helped himself to a cup, filling it from the stove before he sat down at the table. Copper watched his every move, lips tight. Audrey figured it wouldn't take much to set her off.

He took a sip of black coffee. "Everything settled here?"

Willow set a hot biscuit and the honey jar in front of him. "Most are still sleeping. They arrived so late in the night. As far as I know, none of them is showing signs of sickness."

Copper's voice turned sharp enough to slice bacon. "Mr. Redlin. Don't you think it's a little reckless on your part to stall out here so close to town? You could infect everyone here. Have you not considered the prospect?"

He turned cool eyes on her. "Sorry—I didn't catch your name."

"I didn't throw it."

"Copper Wilson," Willow supplied, and then cleared her throat. "Josh Redlin."

He didn't acknowledge the introduction. "I have considered the possibilities."

Audrey had a feeling he bowed to no man . . . or woman. He'd sized up Copper the moment he'd walked through the doorway.

He turned back to Willow. "The sick could use some nourishing broth. Would you care to make a pot?"

Copper slapped her hand on the table, rattling eating

utensils. "And just what are we supposed to make broth out of, and what are we supposed to use for wood?"

Josh remained focused on Willow. "I'll try to scout up some dry wood. Just broth of any kind will do."

Willow nodded. "We have plenty of chicken. And we have herbal tea."

"That would be real fine."

"Mr. Redlin."

Josh slowly turned to focus on Copper.

"Are you ignoring me?"

"I'm trying, but you keep interrupting."

Copper smacked her cup down on the table. "It's your fault that I can't go to Beeder's Cove."

His gaze didn't waver. "How's that?"

"You brought that wagon train into town. You could have stopped somewhere else."

"I could have."

"You have endangered all of our lives—the whole town."

"I have no control over illness."

"Maybe not, but you could have moved farther up the road."

"I also cannot walk on water, ma'am. The road was a swamp. Folks were dying. I thought it best to stop."

Audrey hesitated to intervene in this sterling exchange. She hated to get involved, but someone had to arbitrate before the two came to blows. "I agree this is a frustrating experience, but finger-pointing doesn't help, and really the situation is no one's fault. Who can predict when or where illness will strike? I would have acted as Mr. Redlin did. Stop, and try to gain control of the situation. I've only been working at the parlor a few days and suddenly I'm inundated with bodies, a position I assure you that I didn't expect. There are bodies to prepare, and it's so wet no one can open a grave, so the victims are mounting up in the icehouse." She knew she was blathering. Even Tate focused on her. "I thought I couldn't deal with even one, and now look at me. A person has to do what they have to do, and sometimes we don't want to do it, but we have to. Do it." She shut up. She was babbling like an idiot, and Josh Redlin's expression confirmed it.

Copper puckered. "That's such a pious, simpering thing to say. We're not pointing fingers. I could make some broth if I had the meat."

"I'll see you have wood for the fire," Redlin said, but not to Copper.

"I'll dress a couple of hens," Willow offered. "And if worse comes to worst, Cordelia has a smokehouse full of meat."

"Cordelia is holed up like a rat," Audrey confirmed. "She's determined that she and her family will be spared the illness."

"Cordelia is a rat." This came from Copper.

"You know your rats, do you, miss?" Redlin spared her a tolerant glance.

Audrey excused herself to get ready to go to work. Copper and Josh were like two hissing cats in a burlap bag, and she didn't intend to get caught in the fracas.

When she returned to the kitchen Josh was gone, and two women, Sadie and Adele, from the train were sitting at the table with Willow and Copper. Adele was an older woman, Sadie maybe ten years younger. "There you are," Willow said. "Guess what? Copper and I are going to help out at the parlor this morning."

Copper's features tensed. "This is Willow's idea. I say

we're needed more this morning to cook and feed the sick at the church."

Sadie, the heavy-set blond, grinned. "Me and Adele can cook and look after Tate. We'll get others to help. Willow's been kind enough to offer us shelter, and we mean to earn our keep. You go on and do whatever you need to do. We'll look after the judge and keep the ovens busy."

"But if you're infected . . ." Willow began.

The woman shook her head. "I'm not, and I'll take care of the judge myself. And I'll tie a handkerchief across my mouth when I enter his room. You don't need to worry. I never come down with so much as a sniffle. My grandma says I have a bull's constitution. She lived to be in her late nineties, and I'm just like her."

Adele nodded. "Don't you worry one bit. We'll take care of things here."

Copper squirmed. "That condescending wagon master is bringing dry wood."

"Copper!" Willow exclaimed.

"Well, he is arrogant."

Sadie laughed. "Don't you bother yourself about Josh Redlin. We know how to handle that good-looking man."

Copper's lips tightened. "Isn't he married? Pity the poor woman."

"No, ma'am, no woman's got her hooks in Redlin, and there's nothing wrong with me having my eyes set on the fellow," Sadie said. "I lost my man two years ago, and I don't mind to tell you I'm looking to replace him and Redlin's the prime candidate. You run along now and help Audrey."

Audrey drew on her slicker. Copper had managed to alienate two people this morning, Redlin and Sadie, and it was barely seven-thirty. And she was working at the parlor today.

Willow got to her feet. "I don't know how much help I'll be, but I'm willing to try."

Copper hesitated, and Audrey waited. She suspected when it came right down to working at the parlor, Copper would have second thoughts. Now Audrey hid a grin as the redhead considered her options before reluctantly giving in. "All right, I suppose we have to help if Audrey needs us."

"I need you, and I know Kirkland will be happy to see you. I'll make sure he pays you."

"You mean he might not want to?" Copper asked with raised brows.

"Well, he is rather tight-fisted when it comes to money," Audrey admitted, "but I'm sure he'll be fair." She hid a grin. Maybe she would set Copper up with Kirkland. Nah. Even she wasn't that mean.

Accompanied by rumbling thunder overhead, the women trudged through deep mud to the funeral parlor. "I declare, I never thought I'd live to see the day." Willow stepped around a sinkhole. "It's like living in a marsh."

"There's something wrong with this town," Copper grumbled. "First it can't rain, and then it can't stop. It's not normal."

Audrey opened the parlor's foyer door and ushered them inside, watching as their gazes roamed the dim interior. Neither of them had been in the funeral home before, and she was amused at their facial reaction. Whatever they had expected, this spanking clean room, with the stained glass lamps, the neat, orderly rows of chairs, wasn't it. The viewing room was bearable. She kept it clean, mopping out the mud people tracked in, and making sure the lamp wicks were trimmed so they wouldn't smoke. She'd given up on candles.

"The room where we'll be working is through here."

Three bodies were already laid out on the tables. How nice. One apiece. Recalling her first experience, Audrey wasn't sure how well Willow and Copper would cope, but she was grateful to have the help. She assigned each a corpse, and directed Claude to bring in extra water and washcloths.

"First you undress the body, and wash it."

Copper turned a fine shade of green. "Do what?"

"You have to undress the client."

"And give it a bath?"

"Yes."

"Surely you're joking."

"I'm not. I know how you feel. I felt same way, but it's not that hard once you get started. Actually, you'll find the work rewarding. These people were living, breathing souls only a few hours ago. They were mothers, fathers, brothers, and sisters. They felt they had their whole life ahead of them. I pray over each one of them, asking strength for the families. I hope you'll feel led to do the same."

Copper frowned as if she would like to argue, but after a moment of silence, she took the scissors Audrey held out to her and began cutting away the muddy, stained garments. Willow did the same, and Audrey relaxed. One hurdle down, but she had no doubt there would be others.

She turned her attention to her own task, moving methodically. "We need to hurry. The families will be coming for the viewing."

Copper ignored her, but Willow nodded without comment. Audrey started dressing her client. She was heartsick praying over so many deceased, but she couldn't voice her feelings to the others. They might quit. She noticed Copper's jaws were clenched, but she kept busy.

Audrey helped pull the garments into place. "Now, we fix the hair and apply face paint. It's not hard—we all know how to fix hair."

Reaching for a brush, Copper started. Audrey wished she had time to supervise more closely—after all, it was a difficult task the first time, but she had her own work to do. She added the finishing touches and stepped back to check for details. She turned to see how the others' work was coming along. One look and she stopped, aghast, not sure what to say.

Willow placed the brush on the table. "There. I'm through."

"What do you mean, you're through?" Copper demanded. "What have you done to the poor woman's hair?"

Willow bristled. "Well, at least she doesn't look like she fell into a tub of paint."

Color flooded Copper's cheeks. "What are you talking about? This woman looks lovely. Elegant, actually."

"It's the face. She looks like she fell out of a dance hall."

"Well, your woman looks like she threw her hair up and jumped beneath it."

Copper stepped over to view Audrey's client. She glanced back at her own. Then back. "Well, perhaps I did overdo the rouge a bit."

"A bit?" Willow said. "Scrape it off, Copper."

Audrey frowned. "Ladies. Remember our decorum. We don't have to act disrespectful."

When Willow turned to look at the woman she had prepared, she groaned. "Oh my stars. We can't let anyone see her like this. What can we do?"

Audrey swung into action. "Copper, you guard the door and don't let anyone in, especially Kirkland. Willow, you wash this one's face, and I'll work on the other's hair. We need to hurry because I can hear people gathering in the viewing room."

She knew she should have never taken this job.

Kirkland's voice boomed through the paneled wood. "Miss Pride? We have guests!"

"In a minute," Audrey chirped. "We're just finishing up!"

"Very well, but hasten." She heard the little clap.

Copper whirled to face Willow, her body theatrically pressed against the closed door to fend off intruders. "Hurry. I can't hold him off forever."

"I can assure you, he isn't going to burst down the door and trample you aside. He'll give us a few minutes." Hasten indeed. Audrey brushed on face paint, combed hair, and took a deep breath. "Not perfect, but better. Call Claude to come get them."

Minutes later Claude and Jim carried in the caskets. As soon as the three victims were safely in the viewing room, Caleb and Eli entered through the back way, bringing two more.

Copper took one look and burst into tears. Willow and Audrey joined in. Fatigue overcame Audrey, and she knew that her friends were feeling the same. The past week had been the most challenging in her life. So much death; so much loss and so much sadness in trying to prepare these women for their final resting place.

Clinging tightly, the women sobbed.

Eli and Caleb stepped in, and Audrey collapsed against Eli. His arms drifted around her, pulling her close. She leaned against his strength, totally spent.

She stood locked in his arms for a long moment before reality set in and he gently eased her aside. Stepping back, she wiped tears, grateful, but aware of Eli's rejection.

The moments in his arms had been fleeting and all too brief, but it was a place she'd thought she'd never be. She couldn't fuss overly much.

"Can I talk to you a minute outside?"

They stepped out of the room and stood in the narrow hallway. His gaze locked with hers. "This is going to be a rough day. You go home, and I'll help Kirkland."

When she protested, he laid a finger across her lips. "This is hard on you. Go home, take Willow and Copper with you."

His kindness proved to be the last straw. She broke down, sobbing into her handkerchief.

It was easier when he ignored her; this gentleness, this . . . intimacy that she longed for only intensified her hunger to capture his heart. Were they inching closer to each other? Or was this only Eli's way of releasing strain? She feared the latter, but for the time being she took comfort that his shell could be broken, if only for a short time.

Chapter 14

Claudine Madison's irregular home with all its redundant rooms finally found a purpose for the well. It quickly became a staging area for the town efforts to aid the sick. Townspeople brought quilts and made pallets on the wood floors, while the ailing were taken to the church and bedded down. Ten people were currently ill, some sicker than others. Women cooked and carried food and helped dish up nourishing broth and force-feed hot sweet tea. Sadie and Adele, deemed saints now, kept Tate away from the ill and worked long into the night.

Audrey wiped her forehead with the hem of her apron. It seemed unbearably hot in the church sanctuary this morning. Between trying to keep up with the parlor work and the ailing, she felt like a puppet. A very tired puppet. Lack of sleep and overwork sapped her strength.

Josh Redlin came through the front door this morning and threaded his way through the room, speaking to the ill. This had to be hard on him too. Responsibility for the well-being of every family on the train must weigh heavily on him. Now he approached the table where the women washed dishes. Willow and Audrey greeted him, but Copper turned her head and ignored his entrance. Audrey sighed. Copper and Josh had flared at each other more than once over the past week, and yesterday she'd declared she wasn't speaking to the man. If only. The moment one or the other crossed the drawn line, the temporary ceasefire would shatter.

"Good morning, ladies." Josh leaned against a corner of the table. "Too bad the church doesn't have large enough cooking facilities. The wood stove won't hold all the pots and it's hard to carry food back and forth from the Madisons'. Anything I can do to help?"

"Yes, you can carry these pots out to the wagon." Willow indicated the stack of clean kettles. "I think we're through in here."

"Be glad to. Appreciate what you're doing to help out." With one hand, Josh picked up three of the cast-iron kettles that formerly held broth. "Anything else?"

"Yes." Copper swung to face him and Audrey clamped her teeth. "You can get that quarantine lifted so I can leave for Beeder's Cove. It's thoughtless to keep us tied to Thunder Ridge with no way in or out."

He leveled a straight look at her. "I didn't impose the quarantine. If you don't like it, talk to Dr. Smith—or better yet, Horace Padget. It was his idea."

"You could persuade the doctor to lift the quarantine."

His jaw set. "No, ma'am, I couldn't. Horace Padget seems to be running the show, and I can't talk to the man because of his wife's fear that her family will be affected.

I'm not about to go up against Padget just so you can leave."

Copper faced him, hands on her hips. "It's not about me. Other wagon trains have to detour around Thunder Ridge, which is what you should have done. Then we wouldn't be in this fix."

"And a lot more people would be dead. Is that what you want?"

"Of course not. What a crass thing to suggest."

Josh smirked. "Crass? I'm being nice, Miss Whatever-Your-Name-Is."

"You can't see past the end of your nose, Mr. Rude. I've never met a more ill-tempered man."

He politely swept off his hat with his free hand. "And you have the disposition of a rattler with the hives. Now if you'll excuse me, I'll carry these pots back to Judge Madison's." He clamped his hat back on his head and marched toward the door with Copper right behind him, berating him with every step she took.

Willow shook her head. "Why do you suppose she's so hateful to that man? It isn't his fault people got sick. I truly believe he did the only thing he could."

"I don't know what's gotten into her, but they took an instant dislike to each other." Audrey wiped the table with a damp cloth, and then dried her hands. "I've never known Copper to be so short-tempered with anyone."

"Particularly with a man with Redlin's appeal," Willow mused. "He's handsome, has strong moral values. There's nothing about him offensive."

"Nothing that I've found," Audrey agreed.

On the way home they passed the banker's house sitting

on top of the hill. Cordelia was on the porch with a broom, and from the volume of her voice she was upset about something. "And don't you come back again."

"Stop!" Audrey ordered. "That's Tate. He must have slipped away from Adele and Sadie's eye." She cupped her hands to her mouth. "Tate Gray, you come down here!"

The boy moseyed down the hill, eyes downcast as he approached. "Cordelia's bun's too tight this morning."

This child was spending entirely too much time around mill workers. Audrey glanced past him to see the woman discard the broom and charge down the hill like an ill-tempered bull.

Pulling Tate behind her skirt, Audrey braced. "Is there a problem, Cordelia?"

"That . . . that hooligan won't stay away from here. Shows up three or four times a day . . . trying to infect my Junior."

"I am sorry. Adele and Sadie are supposed to be watching him but they have their hands full with the well guests at the Judge's house . . ."

Cordelia went on as though she hadn't heard a word. "I swear I sweep him off this porch and he's back before I can get inside. Then I go to the root cellar, and there he is with Junior playing with the canned goods—stacking the glass jars to the ceiling. It's enough to put a body under."

"I just want to play," Tate explained. "I like Junior. Why can't he play with me?"

"I'm not about to let every ragtag and bobtail that comes along infect my son. Not with that terrible epidemic striking down people left and right," Cordelia spluttered, eyes fixed on Tate. "The very idea of that child coming here, when he's been told to stay home."

"If she doesn't want Junior to play in the cellar, I could go inside and play," Tate bargained. He turned to meet Audrey's eyes. "Her face is pretty red, ain't it?"

Cordelia drew herself up, looking down her nose. "It's disgraceful. Have you ever heard the like? That child needs to be taught manners." She turned and marched back up the hill, slamming the front door behind her.

Tate huddled against Audrey's skirt. He gazed up at her with hurt eyes. "Why doesn't Junior's mother like me?"

"Oh, I'm sure she does," Audrey began, but he interrupted her.

"No, she don't. She makes me leave."

Willow spoke up. "Oh, Tate, Cordelia doesn't mean to be so rude. Sometimes you have to overlook her words."

"Which," Copper said, "is hard even for adults."

Drawing him closer, Audrey said, "Tate, perhaps you should stay away from the Padgets' house until the sickness is over. Cordelia is afraid Junior will get sick. She's just trying to protect him. And if she doesn't want you around here, then you should stay away."

"I've been bad again."

"No, not bad, but sometimes we need to ask God for guidance. When you know there's something you shouldn't do but you do it anyway, it's wrong."

Tate sighed. "'Pears like I just can't win. No matter how hard I try to be good, I can't do it. But I'll try, Miss Pride. I'll start praying right now, and I'll pray for Pa too. He needs it more than me, because he's older and bigger."

Audrey noticed that at least Tate had called Eli Pa. She was making some headway. Her thoughts skipped back to Eli's considerate gesture the day he sent her home from the mortuary. Perhaps she was making progress with both father and son.

The women delivered Tate into Adele and Sadie's hands, and then climbed the stairway. "Why doesn't anyone check on Mrs. Gray?" Audrey inquired. It seemed rather odd they'd leave the ailing woman to herself.

"She's a quiet sort," Willow mused. "She's asked that we send a note before we come. Her illness makes her sleep a lot."

"What is her illness?"

"I'm not certain. Some sort of growth in her side. She seems to be losing ground steadily."

Audrey shook her head. How would Eli manage to care for Tate when his mother passed?

Late afternoon, Kirkland was ready to lock up for the night. Audrey already had her cape on preparing to leave when the door burst open and Copper dashed inside. "Oh, Audrey. Willow's been hurt."

"Willow? What happened?"

"She went with Tucker this afternoon, and while she was moving some of the stock to a drier location, she slipped and fell. One of the horses spooked and kicked her in the head."

Audrey stared at her, stunned. "Is she . . ."

"She's alive, but unconscious. Tucker carried her home. Oh, Audrey. He's sent for the doctor." Copper grasped Audrey's arm, urging her out the door. "Hurry. They need us at the house."

The women ducked their heads against the rain, running through puddles. Audrey fought back panic. Willow, hurt?

She couldn't lose Willow. The thought was too ghastly to entertain.

They reached the house, and she raced upstairs to Willow's room. Tucker sat beside the bed, shoulders hunched, his forehead etched with worry. Audrey moved to touch his arm. "How is she?"

He shook his head. "She hasn't come to. Why did I let her go with me? She didn't have any business helping with the stock. I should have known better. This is my fault."

Audrey patted his shoulder. "Now, don't borrow trouble. She'll surely wake up anytime now. She's just worn out from all the work and the blow to her head. She'll be fine." Audrey tried to convince herself she spoke the truth, but Willow lay so still, looking so pale and lifeless. What if she didn't wake up? But she had to. Audrey bit back tears.

Knowing it wouldn't do to have Tucker see her upset, she went to the kitchen to make a cup of tea. A knock sounded at the door, and Audrey answered to find Eli. One look was all she needed to see he was in a flaming fury. "Did you tell my son to pray for me?"

Good lands. Tate had mentioned their earlier conversation on the way home from the Padgets'.

Audrey stared at him, trying to focus. She was too worried about Willow to care what he was upset about. "I might have, why?"

"You know what he just told me? Said that when he asked the blessing that he asked God to not let me get crossways in my britches so often. Did you put that notion in his head?"

"It's possible." She was too weary to argue. "Are you aware Willow was hurt this afternoon?"

Apparently her question failed to register. "I want you to

explain what—and why you said such a thing to Tate." He paused. "What did you say?"

"A horse kicked Willow. She's unconscious. Tucker's upstairs with her. We're all sick with worry."

Eli paled. "I didn't know—I was working upriver today and just got back half an hour ago. Tate caught up with me at the mill, but he didn't mention an accident."

"Tate is supposed to be in the house, but with all the confusion Adele and Sadie can't keep up with him. He slips off, and in spite of everyone trying to keep an eye on him, he's quick."

"What's this about Willow?"

"She's unconscious." Audrey blinked back tears and stepped back. "Do you want to come in?"

He entered the kitchen. "Is it okay if I go up?"

"Of course."

He started toward the stairs then turned and looked back. "Sorry I was so uptight. Tate's remark—it's a minor thing. Just struck me wrong."

Audrey nodded, and he turned and slowly climbed the stairs.

During the night, Audrey and Copper took turns sitting with Willow. It was Audrey's turn, and Willow lay deathly still. Audrey bathed her with cool water. If only she would open her eyes. Show some sign of life. She knelt by the bedside, gripping Willow's hand in hers. "Oh, Willow. Don't die. Please don't. I can't bear the thought of losing you, and Tucker would be a broken man. He loves you so dearly. We all do."

She knelt there for what seemed like hours, then the hand she held twitched slightly. Audrey lifted her head. Willow's eyes were open. "You're awake! Oh, thank God. I'll go get Tucker . . ."

"Audrey?" Willow's voice wavered. "Wait."

"You've been hurt," Audrey said gently. "But you're going to be all right now. Just lie still . . ."

Willow shook her head. "Promise me."

"Anything." Audrey vowed, kneeling now beside the bed. "Anything, love. Just name it, and I'll do it."

"If something happens to me, don't let Tucker marry Meredith Johnson."

Audrey stared back at her, mouth open. "Meredith Johnson. Willow! How can you think of such a thing? You've been gravely injured and . . ."

Willow's grip tightened. "Listen to me. I mean it. I want him to have a good wife, and if anything happens to me, Meredith will have him in a flash. She's too young and too irresponsible for him, and I can't bear the thought of him marrying anyone else but you."

"Me!"

"Yes, you. I want you to marry Tucker if anything happens to me." Her voice turned so weak Audrey had to bend closer to catch her words. "Promise me."

"Nothing is going to happen to you. Don't talk like that. Besides, Tucker won't want me. He loves you."

"But I could die, Audrey. The pain . . . Promise me."

Audrey swallowed. How could she deny her request, but what Willow was asking was impossible. "You don't understand. I love another man."

Willow weakly shook her head. "You promised."

"I know, but . . ."

She opened her eyes. "You love . . . someone? Who?"

Audrey wiped her eyes. "Eli. I love that blasted Eli." Until that moment she hadn't realized how much she loved him, but her feelings only grew stronger with every passing day. She could never marry another man unless Eli forever kept himself locked in an emotional vault. She covered her mouth, ashamed of her previous oath.

Willow sighed. "You could grow to love Tucker, just like I would have grown to love Silas."

"I love Eli." Saying the words out loud made the impasse even more hurtful. *Why, God? Why did I fall in love with a man who is so unavailable?* Willow's hand relaxed, going limp. Audrey gasped. "Willow? Don't go back to sleep—talk to me!"

The still form on the bed now slumbered. "No." Audrey murmured. "Willow?" She rose to her feet, one hand clasped to her heart, but she detected the slight rise and fall of Willow's chest. She was alive. Unconscious, but alive. *Oh, thank you, God. Thank you.*

Audrey sank back into the chair, hands clasped in her lap. Whatever tomorrow brought, at least for now, Willow was alive—and had finally woken up.

She glanced at the clock. Three A.M. Tucker should be back to check on Willow. She went downstairs to see if he'd arrived when she heard a knock at the door. She slid the lock and opened the door to see a young woman drenched to the bone, shivering. "Yes? May I help you?"

"I need help. My husband . . ." The woman struggled to gain control.

"Your husband?" Audrey had never seen this woman. She wasn't part of the wagon train.

"He's dead. Back there, in our wagon." She pointed down

the road. "He was so sick—I did everything I could . . ." She crumpled, dropping to her knees.

Audrey reached out to help her to her feet and into the house.

"He's dead," the woman repeated. "I need help moving his body . . . he's too heavy. I can't move him."

"First let's get you warm and then we'll see about your husband." Audrey led the woman to the table and hefted the teakettle, which still had hot water. "I'll fix you a cup of tea, while you give me directions to your wagon."

"I saw your light from the road. It's so dark and raining so hard. I thought I'd never find anyone to help me. The road is washed out." Her breath caught on a sob.

Audrey put her arms around the thin, heaving shoulders. "There, now. You're safe and among friends. As soon as I get you into dry clothing I'll find someone to help with your husband. What's your name, dear?"

The woman wiped her eyes. "Yvonne. We've been on the road for a month or so, and we were doing fine until the rain hit and the roads became impassable. Then Frank took sick. I tried to care for him, but he died."

Helping the young woman up, Audrey moved Yvonne up the stairs. One pallet remained empty.

The stricken woman dressed in dry clothing and then fell asleep as soon as her head touched the pillow. Audrey quietly went downstairs, slipped on her cape, and grabbed her slicker. Copper appeared in the doorway. "What's happening?"

"I have to find someone to move a body. Can you watch Willow and the others?"

She nodded. "What time is it?"

"Very late."

* * *

A dim light shone in the mill office as she made her way there, praying that someone was working late. Treacherous muddy ground made solid footing impossible and she slipped, almost going down twice.

Wiping grit off her hands, she reached the mill and shoved the front door open. Eli sat at a desk working on a sheaf of papers. He looked up when she entered, then leaped to his feet. "Willow?"

Audrey allayed his initial fear. "There's been no change." Leastways none he needed to hear. She repeated Yvonne's story, and Eli shook his head. "I'll find her husband. Go back to the house, out of the weather."

"I'm coming with you." She thought he would protest, but evidently he knew when to pick his fights.

"Come on then. The sooner we get started, the sooner we get back."

The rain slacked to a heavy drizzle when they left the mill. Eli saddled a couple of horses and Audrey rode beside him, praying to find the body quickly and move it back to the icehouse before it started pouring again.

A half mile out of town they spotted the wagon mired at the side of the road. The horses stood slumped, heads hanging. They found the man's body covered with a tarp to protect it from the rain. Indeed, Yvonne had done the best she could for him. Audrey faded briefly into Eli's arms, and he held her gently.

"Just so much death," she whispered as his hold tightened.

He gently released her and tied their horses to the back of the wagon, helping Audrey climb on board. He clucked to the team, and after a half hour of rocking the wagon back and forth, Eli freed the wheels and started the slow journey back. Audrey glanced over her shoulder at the covered corpse. "It seems such a waste."

"Death usually does. It's hard to keep faith when nothing makes sense."

She touched his arm. "You would know about that. I realize you've been through so much, Eli, and I know I can't even begin to understand how much."

He was silent for so long that she feared that she had offended him. But he finally answered, and she could hear the pain in his voice. "I came home from the war a few months ago, expecting to find Genevieve waiting for me. Didn't know about the boy. Didn't know she'd died giving birth to my son. I wasn't there to bury her."

"You can't continue to blame yourself."

"I know that, but I figured she would have to bury me, if she was lucky enough to get my body back. Other men came home to their wives. I came home to a grave. It does something to a man."

Audrey sat silently, fighting back the urge to hold him, comfort him. Eli was eaten up with grief and regret. She couldn't intrude on his past. Not tonight when he had finally started to open up to her.

But it was a beginning, and that was what she'd prayed for. An opening, and if she let him talk, maybe the healing would begin.

Chapter 15

Dawn broke. Audrey stood in front of the kitchen window, drained. The parlor work was reduced. Willow lay upstairs unconscious, and another grieving widow tossed on the last available pallet. Audrey had about reached the end of endurance. And to top it off, Sadie thought Tate's exposure to the illness had passed, and with all the upheaval the boy would be better off at home. Audrey would miss the child dreadfully, but she agreed. There was too much sadness in the house. Way too much for a young, impressionable boy.

Eli had talked on the way home last night, spilling his grief. Once the words started to form he couldn't seem to stop, and Audrey had witnessed a man putting aside his dreams, facing reality. Maybe late in coming, but nonetheless she felt he saw the world as it was this morning, not as he wanted it to be. Perhaps seeing the struggles of the wagon train had allowed him to realize just how much this kind of senseless loss was the way of life.

Mid-morning, Deet brought worrisome news that Silas's cold had worsened and gone into his chest. He wasn't doing well. It seemed as if Thunder Ridge was being struck from every direction.

Company brought Audrey out of her reverie. She answered a knock on the door to find Dr. Smith standing in the drizzle. "This is the first moment I've been able to come. Caleb said Willow's been hurt?"

"She's upstairs. I'll take you to her." Audrey heard the doctor puffing as he climbed the stairs behind her. He had to dread coming to this big old house. On the third landing, she motioned toward the door to Willow's bedchamber and then stepped aside to allow him entry. He acknowledged Tucker, who was sitting on one side of the mattress. The doctor pulled up a chair on the other side and sat down, pensive. Audrey watched as he felt for Willow's pulse, then raised one of her eyelids and let it close again after a moment's observation.

Tucker spoke. "She's been like this since the accident."

He hesitated and then said. "Only time will tell if she recovers. She's taken a bad blow to the brain. I'd hoped she would have regained consciousness before now."

Audrey remembered her brief, awkward conversation with the injured woman. "She did, but only for a moment. Then she dropped off again."

He pursed his lips. "Encouraging. I suggest you keep on with what you're doing. Don't try to feed her. In her unconscious state she would be inclined to choke. Keep someone with her at all times, and if . . . when she wakes, summon me immediately."

Audrey trailed him downstairs. She had caught the doctor's stumble over "when she wakes." His tone didn't exude confidence.

"Hear we have another victim."

"Yes, a man. His wife showed up on our doorstep. Eli has taken him to the icehouse."

"More tragedy. I thought we'd turned the corner on this illness."

"The wife's health seems to be all right. She's still asleep."

The only thing Audrey could do was pray, and she intended to do so at every moment: on her knees, while standing at the stove, while working at the parlor—her hands might be busy, but her mind was constantly in touch with God.

Late afternoon, she tiptoed toward Wallace's bed. He opened his eyes, looking directly at her, and she smiled. Thank heavens. It was the most alert he had been in days.

"Just checking to see if you need anything. Would you like some broth, or a bit of egg custard? Copper made a fresh batch this morning."

"No, thank you." At least that's what she thought he said. His voice was little more than a muddled whisper.

"Some fresh water?" She lifted the pitcher, casting a practiced eye over the contents. "The rain barrel is full." When he didn't respond, she said, "I'll be right back."

She returned with fresh water to find the judge asleep. She tiptoed out without disturbing him. Sadie met her on the stairs. "And how is the poor man today?"

"About the same."

Sadie shook her head. "Ah, and it's a pity. Adele and I have been talking. We need to be doing more, but the folks staying here need attention. There's extra wash and cooking, and the other four women have all they can do to keep up with their folk. Adele and I are the only ones without families to look after. You and Copper have your hands full taking care of the judge and Willow. Anything you need, you just tell us and we'll get it done. We'll take over all the household chores, and there'll be no argument from you."

Audrey smiled. "You don't have to do that, Sadie."

"I know I don't have to, but I want to. I appreciate Willow opening her home to us. We didn't have nary a place to go, and with that banker's wife showing what she's made of, it's a wonder anyone would take us in."

"Cordelia's all right." And when had she *ever* expected to defend Cordelia Padget? "She's just frightened. Perfectly understandable in view of the situation."

"I suppose a lot of people in town are scared of us. Can't say I blame them. I'd be scared too, but you took us in, just like it says in the Good Book. 'I was a stranger and you took me in.' When you're the one being taken in and cared for, it makes you humble, let me tell you."

"I'm sure it does." Even though Cordelia had brought criticism on herself, Audrey felt uncomfortable taking part. She understood the banker's wife. Her position in town had shielded her from life's harsher blows. Now she was faced with a situation money couldn't ease. It had to be difficult for her.

Sadie nodded sagely. "Yes, ma'am. It makes a difference. I'm going to be a lot quicker to help someone else from now on, I promise you."

"We all need to do better," Audrey assured her, moving down the stairs to the kitchen. "I suppose we'd best start on the evening meal. How many will we have at the table tonight?"

A long plank sat in the parlor for the wagon train refugees to eat their meals. Crowding so many into the kitchen was a huge task.

Sadie rolled her eyes heavenward, her face a study of concentration. Finally she nodded. "Ten."

"Ten? Have we added someone?"

"There's a couple of men who have taken to dropping by and eating with us. They're staying at that Pansy woman's house. Seems she's a close friend to the banker's wife, and apparently not much of a cook."

"Pansy Henderson," Audrey supplied. "And we have added another. Yvonne, the young widow who arrived during the night."

"Oh yes. Sorry to hear about her husband." Sadie trailed Audrey into the kitchen, still talking. "I'll get a pan of spuds and start peeling. You want fried or boiled tonight?"

"Fried, I suppose." Not that she cared. She wanted Willow in the kitchen, going about her daily chores, not lying upstairs on that bed in the same position, still as the wind before a big storm.

Oh God, if anything happens to her it will break my heart. I can't give her up. I just can't. Never mind what I promised I'd do if she . . . She didn't let her mind go any further.

Audrey filled a pan with warm water from the teakettle and searched in the cabinet drawer for a clean cloth. If it didn't stop raining long enough to get some laundry done, she didn't know what they were going to do.

Around six the next morning, Audrey carried up a cup of tea and a bowl of mush to the judge. She eased open the door with her foot and entered, placing the tray on his bedside table. Wallace lay on his back with his head tilted and his mouth open. His eyes were closed, but something about the position of his body caused her to look closer. She edged near the bed, hoping to see the rise and fall of his chest.

"Wallace?"

No response.

Audrey reached to touch his shoulder, finding it cold and lifeless. The judge had died in his sleep. Alone, while she slept a floor above him.

Backing slowly away from the bed, she felt for the doorknob. Copper. She'd have to tell her and alert Tucker. Sometime during the night he had left to catch a few hours of sleep. Sadie had volunteered to sit with Willow until he returned. She eased onto the landing and closed the door behind her.

Copper stood at the stove stirring oatmeal when Audrey entered the kitchen. She turned as Audrey entered, eyes widening. "Now what's wrong?"

Audrey slumped down in a chair and rested her arms on the table. "It's the judge."

"He's worse?"

"He's dead. I just found him."

"Oh. Oh, I'm so sorry! Are you all right?"

"Thank the good Lord that he's finally reunited with Claudine."

Copper stepped away and sank to a chair. "He's been ill for so long. Actually, his passing is a blessing. Poor Willow . . ."

"Will miss him something terrible," Audrey supplied, not daring to consider that the judge's beloved niece could meet the same fate. It was entirely possible they could bump into each other at the Pearly Gates. Audrey got to her feet. "I'll ask one of the men to go fetch Tucker."

When she returned to the kitchen Adele had commandeered the stove.

"We'll get breakfast out of the way first," the woman said. "Then you and Copper have a wake to plan."

Audrey nodded. How could she have forgotten that? "We can't send him to the parlor. Willow would want him here."

Copper passed by, reaching out to touch her shoulder. "You and I can prepare him just fine."

"Are you sure? You know how you feel about . . ."

She nodded. "I can do it. Willow wouldn't want strangers taking care of him, and we're family."

"Of course we can do this for her. I'll go up to Wallace's bedroom and lay out the clothes."

Audrey climbed the stairs, thinking how fickle life could be. The move to Thunder Ridge hadn't turned out the way she had anticipated. Every day took a new turn, but then she supposed that life was intended to be a surprise. If you woke up every morning knowing what the day would bring, you most likely wouldn't get out of bed. One good thing had come from all these problems . . . she had been drawn closer to faith. In the light of death, life took on a new perspective.

This morning, she felt surrounded by God's presence, and it was a comforting feeling.

Tucker arrived shortly. When told the news, he sat down with Audrey and Copper to plan the wake. They decided to have it in the parlor, and the men from the wagon train would move out the plank table and set up chairs. Audrey and Copper agreed to prepare the body, and Tucker promised he'd see that the pine box was delivered. He'd ask Eli to drop by the funeral parlor and fetch the needed supplies for

Audrey. He left to set the plans in motion, and Audrey and Copper brought water and set to work.

Audrey cut away the rumpled nightclothes, and together they bathed and dressed the sunken body. Copper picked up a hairbrush. "I'll do his hair. You check and see if Eli has brought the face paint yet."

Eli sat at the kitchen table, a small bundle lying at his elbow. "You brought it?"

"I brought it." And wonders of wonders, he smiled. Directly at her. "Kirkland wasn't happy about not getting the business, but I told him we'd take care of our own. Hope you don't mind."

Take care of our own. The words were like an elixir. "Not in the least. Thank you." Audrey picked up the small bag. "As soon as we finish we'll need the box."

Eli nodded. "It's here. Claude and Jim helped me bring it over. It's on the porch, ready to bring in when you say."

"You've thought of everything." Audrey gave him a special look and left the room. Willow should be there. It wasn't right she should be lying in an upstairs bedroom fighting for her life while they buried her beloved uncle.

Copper raised her eyebrows when she entered the judge's chamber. "You have the paint and the box? I was afraid Kirkland might refuse to give it."

Audrey smiled. "Eli can be very persuasive."

"Speaking from experience?"

Audrey refused to answer. She gently but sparingly brushed on the paint, bringing a healthy glow to the sunken cheeks. Then she nodded to Copper. "Tell them to bring it up."

The men carried in the casket, and lowered the body into it. As they started downstairs with the pine box, Audrey hurried to the attic. She quickly thumbed through the photo album looking for the wedding picture. When she found it, she made her way back downstairs, the picture clutched in her hand.

Copper arranged lamps at the head and foot of the casket. The men were setting up chairs for the expected mourners. Audrey approached the box, fighting back tears. In her hands she held a symbol of Wallace and Claudine's undying devotion. She placed the wedding photo in the pine box, propping it so that it would be easily seen, and then slid her arm around Copper's waist.

"Do you think Willow would do the same?"

"I think she would be enormously pleased." Copper brushed away tears.

Yes, Willow would be pleased. A lightness settled around her shoulders. At least she could do this much for her best friend.

The first of the mourners arrived early in the afternoon. Tucker ushered them into the parlor. Friends and neighbors approached the casket, whispering among themselves. Within moments, the parlor filled to capacity. Everyone in Thunder Ridge had come to show his respects for Wallace Madison. Everyone but the Padgets. Evidently the banker and his wife were sticking to their self-imposed quarantine.

Audrey leaned against the sofa arm, suddenly very tired. Eli materialized at her side, sliding an arm protectively around her shoulders. "Come sit. You've done all you can do."

She let him lead her to the kitchen, sitting her down at the table. He seated himself across from her and bent forward. "I have something that I need to get off my conscience."

She braced herself, not sure what wrong she'd committed this time.

"May I speak?"

"You may."

Clearing his throat, he studied the tablecloth pattern. "I need to tell you I'm real proud of the work you've done with the wagon train families. Not just with the food and caring for the sick, but for what you've done at the funeral parlor. I've seen the difference your compassion has made. For the folks who lost family members . . . to be able to view their loved ones looking so presentable, that's a good thing. I was wrong about you, Audrey Pride, and I apologize."

She listened, her heart going out to him. It took a strong man to confess his weaknesses.

He nodded. "Wrong of me, to warn Tate away from you. I thought by the way you came into town that afternoon that you didn't have a brain in your head. The boy loves you. You've made a difference in my son's life." His features softened. "I . . ."

Suddenly she could sense that he was so close—so very close to acknowledging a mutual attraction.

"You want to say . . ."

"I—"

Drats! Caleb and Yvonne entered the room and sat down at the table. She wanted to nicely ask them to leave, but she couldn't. Nor could she control her hammering pulse. Eli thought her worthy of Tate's love. She couldn't be offered a nicer gift. Was it possible that he felt that same love? Perhaps not as intense, but growing. If not love, then a willingness to change? She'd never know. The moment was lost forever. If he had feelings, they would have to be expressed another time.

Chapter 16

Audrey had been to the parlor and returned home when Caleb delivered the wood late the next morning. She invited him in, but he hesitated in the doorway. "No, guess I'd better get along to the mill. I just dropped by to see if . . . everyone was all right." His gaze traveled around Audrey's shoulder into the kitchen where Yvonne was working at the sink.

The young widow had admitted after the judge's services that her husband had been ill a good part of their journey. They were looking for better climate when the final fever took Frank. It was good to know that the malady that had stricken the wagon train wasn't the cause of Yvonne's loss. Seemed Frank had been sick a good long spell and Yvonne had been expecting widowhood for some time.

"We're fine," Audrey assured him. "And thank you again for moving the judge to the icehouse. Everyone was so helpful; Copper and I really appreciate it."

Caleb brushed off her thanks. "Looked like the whole town turned out, except for Cordelia and Horace."

"Well, I understand their fears."

"Rumor has it Cordelia's lost her mind. She won't let anyone in the house, and Horace can't leave the place. Guess his two employees run the bank."

"She is aware that the illness is abating?"

"She knows, but she refuses to believe it."

Audrey shook her head, thinking about the poor woman and her pathetic attempts to isolate herself and her family from trouble. Hard times had a way of coming even when uninvited. "I'll fix something, maybe bake a cake, and go see about her." The visit was long overdue, but chances were Cordelia wouldn't let her into the home. If not, she'd leave the offering on the doorstep and hope the banker's wife didn't feed it to the dogs.

Yvonne turned from the sink, dressed in a light blue calico that Copper had loaned her. She made a fetching sight with her blond hair drawn back into a smooth chignon. She looked nothing like the terror-stricken, half-drowned waif who'd appeared on the judge's doorstep earlier. She sent a shy smile at Caleb as she passed the open doorway, and the red stain of a blush crept into his cheeks. Caleb didn't want a spitfire like Copper, and Yvonne wasn't a spitfire in any sense of the word. She was quiet, gentle, unassuming, and pleasant to be around. In spite of her loss, she was quick to help in the kitchen or with feeding the refugees from the wagon train.

When it seemed apparent that Caleb had caught the scent of fresh-baked bread, Audrey opened the door wider. "I just took a pan of cinnamon buns out of the oven. Surely you can stay for a few moments."

The hat came off swiftly. "I could spare a minute or two."

Audrey ushered him into the room, and he took a seat at the table. Minutes later Audrey slid a plate of warm cinnamon rolls in front of him. For a man who artfully wooed women, the big mill worker was suddenly tongue-tied, so she decided to help him by asking the questions she knew he was fair to bursting to ask. "Where are you from, Yvonne?"

"South Carolina."

"Oh yes. You have a lovely Southern accent." She motioned to the table. "Sit down and keep Caleb company. You've been working all morning."

Her features turned a colorful shade of pink, but the woman sat down. "Y'all talk nice too." She lifted a hankie to her eyes. "Can you tell me about Frank? I don't know where they've taken him."

Too late, Audrey realized the fast pace of events had left the poor woman in the dark, and she'd been too polite to ask. She explained where Frank had been taken.

Caleb reached over to lay his large hand on top of hers. "It's not a proper place for women, but I'll be happy to take you there, ma'am. The icehouse is just down the road a piece."

Audrey smiled, thinking of the times he'd glibly let her wander around on her own. Who would have thought fun-loving Caleb could be so gentle?

Or Eli be so attentive. Her heart thrummed when she thought of how tenderly he'd held her the night they'd found Frank. And then the unexpected admission that he'd changed his mind about her being . . . what had he said? Something about her not having a brain in her head? Silence stretched until Audrey decided Caleb was truly in over his head. She picked up the conversation.

"Had you and Frank been married long?"

Now why had she asked that? It was too soon for the young widow to discuss personal information with her loss so fresh in her mind.

"Five years. Frank was our neighbor. Pa got sick, then Ma. We lost our crops—and in a few months I lost Ma and Pa. The next year, I lost the farm. I didn't have anywhere to go, so Frank suggested we get married so he could look after me. He was a lot older than me, but I owe him so much." She dabbed her eyes with the linen napkin. "I tried to take care of him when he took sick, but he just kept getting worse. Then he decided we'd best look for better climate, but during the long journey he got even sicker. Then the rains came and it was wet and cold and . . . he died. And I didn't know what to do."

Caleb's expression was as sober as Audrey had ever noticed. "You don't have to worry now. The citizens of Thunder Ridge will see that you're taken care of. Your wagon is in a shed at the mill, and we're taking care of your horses and personal effects. It's going to be all right, ma'am. You're not alone now."

Yvonne clung to his hand, eyes brimming with unshed tears. Audrey sensed life had been hard for her. Perhaps it would be better now.

Patting the widow's hand, Caleb turned back to Audrey. "Any change in Willow?"

"None."

Audrey closed the door when Caleb left and set to work. A quick trip to the chopping block, a dose of scalding water, a little time spent plucking the wet feathers, and an hour later the fragrance of frying chicken and chocolate cake filled the kitchen. Copper entered the room and wrinkled her nose. "Isn't it a little early to be fixing dinner?"

"I'm fixing the Padgets' supper."

Copper eyed her as if she had lost her mind. "Whatever for? The old crow won't let you come within a hundred feet of her, and she's perfectly capable of cooking her meals."

"Caleb says she's barricaded herself inside that house, refusing to see anyone. I'm going to check on her."

Sadie, who had entered behind Copper, stored the cleaning supplies, clearly eavesdropping on the conversation.

Copper frowned at Audrey. "You're wasting your time taking food to Cordelia and Horace. They won't appreciate it."

"Probably not, but I'm going to take it anyway." God knew, even if Cordelia might not, that her intentions were honorable.

Copper banged a pot down on the stove. "I suppose I ought to take that ill-tempered Redlin something for his supper. He insists on staying with the wagons and stock, and he can't have a campfire with all this rain."

Sadie laughed. Not a ladylike chuckle but a full-throated belly laugh.

Copper turned to look at her. "What?"

"Gets under your skin, does he?"

Copper twitched. "I'm merely trying to show him some Christian charity, and believe me, it isn't easy."

"A man like that ought to be treated like a king. Now if I was to marry the man, I'd put him on a throne."

"I'd crown him, all right," Copper muttered. "With an iron skillet."

Adele walked into the kitchen in time to hear the exchange and laughed. "He's lucky she hasn't crowned him with the whole stove, as riled as she gets."

Copper firmed her lips. "He deserves a swift kick in the behind. Josh Redlin is the most aggravating, arrogant, self-centered man I've ever had the misfortune to meet."

Sadie grinned. "I could overlook a few flaws for a man that good-looking."

Copper heaved a sigh. "You're welcome to him. And as for taking food to Cordelia, Audrey, I never suspected you were such a saint. Why do you want to risk a tongue-lashing?"

Audrey, who had listened to the women's sparring, felt a spurt of irritation. "Actually, I never thought you could be so judgmental."

Copper whirled. "Judgmental? Because I speak the truth about Cordelia?"

"I know the truth about Cordelia, but I wholeheartedly agree with Sadie about the way you treat Josh Redlin. It's downright maddening the way you treat him. If I were him . . ."

The young lady's porcelain complexion flushed bright red. "You're taking his side?"

"I surely am. He'd be more agreeable if you were kinder."

Copper threw a dishcloth on the counter and flounced out of the room.

Sadie nodded wisely. "That woman's got it bad."

"Her behavior toward the man is peculiar." Audrey packed food in a basket, covering it to keep out the rain. "I'm going to carry this over to the Padgets'. Keep an eye on things here, will you?"

"Does that include keeping an eye on Copper and Josh?" Sadie joked.

Audrey chuckled. "That's up to you. How much do you value your life?"

She pulled on her cape and started out for the banker's house.

Climbing the steps to the front door, she turned to look back at the town. From here Cordelia could keep an eye on the comings and goings of just about anyone who ventured in or out. Small wonder the woman knew everything that went on.

The redbrick home with its white-pillared porch was a fine establishment. An appropriate show for Cordelia's exaggerated opinion of her appointed place in life.

A latch clicked, and Audrey turned around to face the door. The heavy wood swung open, and there stood a Cordelia she'd never seen before: hair hanging in untidy coils around her face, hollow-eyed, clothes wrinkled and stained. She had a dishcloth held protectively across her mouth, and her expression was downright haunted. The two women stared at each other for a minute before the banker's wife barked:

"What do you want?"

Audrey held out the basket. "I brought your supper."

Cordelia's gaze clouded with suspicion. "Why would you do that?"

"Because I—we, the town, are worried about you. I came to see if there is anything we can do to help you."

"We're fine. Have more died?" Her inflection rose. "More deaths? More!" She was screeching now.

"No more," Audrey hurried to say. "There's been none in the past few days. I hadn't seen you lately, and I wondered if you might need help of any kind." She didn't know how she could make it clearer. The people in town cared . . . or at least she did. Even with the Padgets' peccadilloes, concern for the banker and his family was evident. Was that so hard to conceive?

"Willow is ill—"

"It's her fault. I warned her to stay from those sick people."

"No, she—"

"She brought it on herself!"

Audrey indicated the basket. "May I bring this inside?"

"No!" Cordelia recoiled as if Audrey had handed her a rattlesnake. "I have no intention of allowing anyone inside this home until this dreadful epidemic has run its course. Now go away and don't come back until you're invited." She tried to slam the door but Audrey's boot stopped its movement.

For a moment the two women's eyes locked in silent combat.

"Cordelia," Audrey pleaded softly. "The epidemic seems to have run its course. Please, come out of this house and join the townspeople in helping these homeless wagon train families. They'll move on soon. There's no reason for alarm now, and no longer a reason to imprison yourself and your family. Is Horace Junior all right?"

"He's fine, no thanks to you or the others." The battle-worn woman swiped a hand across her forehead. "Will this madness never end? What if it sweeps the town, wiping out the entire population? What will you have to say then?"

Closing her eyes, Audrey silently prayed for a way to comfort the distraught mother. "No one can know what tomorrow will bring; we can only trust that God is in control of the circumstances."

"He wasn't watching over that wagon train."

"Now that's not true. Not everyone died, and he tells us that every man is appointed his amount of time. He provided a good-hearted town for the wagon families to recover in. What more could you ask?"

Cordelia stared at her, then snatched up the basket and stepped back inside, shutting the door. The lock slid into place.

Audrey waited a moment, wondering if anything she'd said had reached the woman. The last thing Cordelia needed was a pious sermon on faith. Her qualms were logical. What mother would allow her child to be subject to a fatal illness if she could prevent it?

Turning away, Audrey descended the long stairway back to the path, wishing that she could be as rational about her wants and fears regarding Eli as she pretended to be about Cordelia's misgivings.

It would sure make life a whole lot simpler.

Chapter 17

A djusting her cape, Audrey glanced at the sky as she walked home. Dark clouds raced across the horizon. Not a single break in the overcast sky.

No one could believe how long this had lasted. Three long weeks of gloom, doom, and wet feet.

She hesitated at the judge's front door, strangely reluctant to go inside. Perhaps Cordelia's panic had influenced her more than she realized. She wasn't afraid of the illness. She was determined to do all she could to help the well, the sick, or the dead, but a sense of doom filled her, like a rudderless ship on an unknown course. Nothing in her life made sense, and she wanted to sit down and cry.

Instead, she squared her shoulders and turned the latch.

Copper ran down the stairs to meet her. "I'm glad you're back. I think Willow's worse. She's tossing around, murmuring incoherently. I think we need to send for the doctor."

Audrey paused in removing her cape. "I'll go fetch him."

"Hey, are you all right?"

No, she wasn't all right. She wanted to yell at God and ask him why he hadn't heard her prayers. He couldn't take Willow. He just couldn't. She turned to face Copper, seeing her own fears reflected in her friend's eyes. Setting her hat aside, she held out her arms, and Copper leaned into the embrace. Tears mingled as she drew strength from her friend. Finally, Audrey straightened. "Everything will be all right. It has to be."

"Of course it will. It's foolish to worry about something that we have no control over." Copper wiped her eyes. "The doctor will assure us that nothing's changed. Willow's just restless. Hurry. Go fetch him . . . and keep the faith."

Audrey closed the door behind her and stared bleakly at the rain-washed street. She believed, of course she did, but it was difficult to let go and surrender to God's will. *Help me to trust, and to accept whatever happens.*

Wasn't that the meaning of true faith? Sometimes her courage was less than she cared to admit.

She made her way to the doctor's office aware she'd left without her hat. She would catch her death for sure. She arrived to find the doctor's office locked. The old mill worker who sat outside the building, keeping dry under the overhang, said he'd send the doc to the judge's as soon as he returned.

Copper waited at the foot of the stairs when she entered the house. Audrey shook her head in response to her friend's inquiring glance.

"He's not there. The old whittler promised to send him the moment he returns."

"I guess that's the best we can hope for. Your hair is dripping wet. I'll get a towel."

Audrey pulled off her cape and followed Copper into the kitchen. "The doctor knows the urgency. He'll come as soon as he can." To her surprise, she found Deet and Sadie at the kitchen table. The remains of a piece of chocolate pie sat on the old-timer's plate.

Shoving the dish aside, he got to his feet. "Got to get back to my stock." He gave Sadie a courtly bow. "Thank you for the pie. I deeply appreciate it, and I'll be back for more, I can assure you, ma'am."

"I think I'll bake Tate cookies." Audrey hung her cape on the peg when the door closed behind the mill worker. "The child's waited long enough for a fresh batch." Anything to keep her hands busy and her mind still.

"Better not. Eli doesn't want you coddling the boy."

"Oh, I don't think he'll think that a batch of fresh cookies is coddling the boy." Audrey reached for a bowl, savoring the knowledge of Eli's barriers slowly starting to crumble.

The cookies came out of the oven about the time the doctor arrived. Copper opened the door and let him in. Both she and Audrey climbed the stairs behind him to Willow's room. He hesitated in the doorway. Audrey glanced past him to see Tucker, haggard and worn, leaning forward in his chair, elbows on his knees, gaze riveted on Willow's thrashing form. From the set of his shoulders, she had a feeling he was braced for the worst. He looked up at the doctor, his expression pleading for good news.

Dr. Smith pulled a chair to the bedside and reached for Willow's wrist, checking her pulse. Then he placed his hand against her neck, apparently testing the strength of her circulation. Audrey wished she knew more about medicine, so she would understand what he was doing. After a few moments, he looked at Tucker, his expression grave.

"What's happening to her?" Tucker's voice was hoarse with concern.

"I can't be certain. There's a possibility that blood has pooled on the brain."

"A clot?" Tucker's expression crumbled. "Can you do any-thing?"

Dr. Smith hesitated, obviously reluctant to answer. Then he slowly shook his head. "I don't have the knowledge to op-erate. She's been unconscious for a long time. You need to understand she may not regain consciousness. A blow like that . . ." He laid his hand on the mill owner's shoulder. "I'm sorry, son."

Tucker focused on Willow, and then pushed out of his chair and plunged toward the door. Audrey could hear his boots thundering down the stairs. Leaving Copper to sit with Willow, she followed the doctor to the floor landing. He paused with his hand on the doorknob. "Is someone always with her?"

"Yes. She's never alone."

"That's good." His gaze fixed on the rain-swept landscape. "Look after Tucker just as carefully. It looked like he'd never find the woman who'd capture his heart, and now that he has Willow, he may lose her. It's times like this that I wish I'd never become a doctor."

Audrey watched the older man move slowly to his buggy before she reached for her canvas cape and slipped outside, warm cookies and Eli momentarily forgotten.

Where would Tucker have gone? He'd want to be alone, someplace where he could think. Pray for acceptance. Rail at God.

Not the mill. He'd be sure to run into Caleb and Eli there. The livery or the mercantile? Not likely, not in his mood. He wouldn't go to the church; right now he was angry with God. That left the river.

She turned her steps toward the destination, hearing the roar of turbulent waters long before she reached it. At first she thought she had guessed wrong, but then she saw him, standing perilously close to the bank, sheltered by overhanging branches. She approached cautiously, not wanting to startle him. He turned in her direction, his expression blank, as if he didn't see her.

"Tucker?"

"Is she worse?"

"No change. I was worried about you."

"Concentrate your prayers on Willow."

"I'm praying for Willow, but God is big enough to cover two people at once." She moved closer, wanting to reach out and comfort him. At the moment, Willow's irrational request for her to marry this man didn't seem nearly as implausible. If Willow had been willing to marry and dedicate her life to Silas Sterling without love, then Audrey could do the same for her best friend. Yet her heart cried out for Eli. They were getting so near an understanding.

Tucker turned and looked out at the raging body of water. "I came down here, not sure if I wanted to go on living. I've been searching for Willow all of my life, and now she's going to be snatched away from me and there's not a thing I can do about it." He rammed his fist into the tree trunk. Audrey averted her eyes. "I should have never let her go with me that day. Never let her help with the horses. I knew it was dangerous, no place for a woman. It's my fault."

"No it isn't. You know Willow. She felt the need to help."

His face contorted with agony. "My life won't be worth living if I lose her. I faulted Eli for not getting over Genevieve and remarrying, but I didn't understand what he was going through. Now I know. Death is threatening to claim the one person I love above all others, and I don't think I'm man enough to take it." He turned pleading eyes on her. "God help me . . . I can't go on without her."

"You will go on if that becomes necessary. Life won't be pleasant, but you'll be given sufficient strength. If God sees fit to take her you will survive, just as Eli has survived."

"For what? An empty life like Eli has chosen?"

"Yes, chosen. Eli has chosen to live alone," she reminded.

He massaged his bruised hand. "No one could ever take Willow's place." He gave her a searching glance. "You're in love with Eli, aren't you?"

"Dreadfully so, I'm afraid." It was her turn to seek solace in the roiling river. She was aware of Tucker's eyes on her. Wishing she had kept quiet, she drew a deep breath. "I've never told anyone but Willow, but I think I've loved him from the moment I met him. And I adore Tate."

"Does Eli know?"

"Just you and Willow, and if you ever say anything, I'll deny I said it."

"Why deny it? He feels the same about you."

Tucker's words barely penetrated. When they did, she turned to face him. "How can you say that? He was very kind at Wallace's wake, and there have been occasions when I think he might care somewhat, but I don't dare let myself hope."

Tucker fell silent long enough to make Audrey regret her frankness. Finally, he said, "Eli's got an odd nature. Once he sets his mind to something, it's hard for him to turn loose. He's like a jackass without a cause. Just bucks and jumps without any particular place to go with his feelings. He thinks since he wasn't here when his wife died, he owes her his loyalty, like it would be unfaithful to her if he took up with someone else."

She nodded. Eli had said as much. He was like Cordelia—running from trouble before it headed in their direction. He'd loved and lost once; he couldn't lower those barriers overnight.

They stood in silence until Tucker turned to face her. "Love's the only thing that makes sense in this upside-down world. I wouldn't take anything for my time with Willow. Even if I lose her now, I'm richer for having loved her. Don't give up on Eli. He needs you, the way I need Willow. He just doesn't know it yet."

She nodded again, unable to speak around the lump forming in her throat.

Perhaps God would be merciful, and Willow would recover. Or perhaps her allotted time on earth was over.

But the last thing Audrey was prepared to admit was that death would be the victor.

Later she stopped by the mill with fresh cookies and coffee. She needed Eli. His presence in her life was the only sunshine she knew. The business was dark. A lone worker remained, closing up. He eyed the tray of cookies and coffee. "Eli's working the river."

Her face fell. "Is he expected back shortly?"

"No ma'am. They'll be working most of the night to keep the river clear." He nodded toward the tray. "What you got there?"

She extended the offering. "Cookies and coffee. Help yourself."

"Much obliged, ma'am."

Yes . . . much obliged.

She turned and carried the empty tray back up the hill.

Chapter 18

The judge's house was silent when she came home. The wagon train guests had been considerate, staying near their pallets or working outside the house. With the sickness waning, the train would soon move once the rain stopped.

Audrey closed her eyes, holding tight to Willow's hand as she sat beside the bed. Tired, so tired. Waiting was the hardest, the long days of uncertainty; at times she thought she'd scream. Other times she prayed for one more hour . . . sixty more minutes for Willow to return from wherever she lay in this deep slumber.

She sat up straight, listening, cocking her head toward the door, senses strained, trying to find the source of her concern. Her eyes drew to the window. Nothing. No raindrops hitting the pane to slide like tumbling children. No thunder crashing, no lightning flares. Stillness.

Surging from the chair, she ran to the foggy glass and

wiped the pane clean. A glimmer of light flickered over the rain-washed landscape. The sun? It had been so long since she'd seen it. The clarity was startling. Had the storm finally broken? The incessant downpour over? She leaned against the pane, seeking confirmation of the miracle. The sun poured golden rays over Thunder Ridge.

She returned to the bed and took Willow's hand. "I know you can't see the sun, but it's shining brightly all over the fields. I believe it's God's assurance that you're going to open your eyes and smile at me. We're going to laugh, and hug, and I'm going to fix you some broth. Tucker will come, and . . . oh, he loves you so much, Willow. So very much! We're praying for you. Everyone in town is praying. Sunday services have been canceled because of the rain, but the reverend reminds everyone he meets of the prayer chain." She pressed closer. "Wherever you are, I pray you can hear me. Come back to us, Willow. We need you. I need you."

The door opened and Sadie entered the bedroom. "There now, love, you run on downstairs and I'll sit a spell. You're worrying yourself sick. The sun is shining. God's in his heaven, on his throne. You can't change a thing by sitting here until you grow to the chair."

Audrey drank in the older woman's wisdom. "She's going to be all right, isn't she, Sadie?"

"It's in God's hands, lovey. Our way is not always his way."

"Waiting is so hard."

"Nothing worth having comes easy." Sadie sat down in a chair and rested her work-roughened hands on the arms. Her sun-streaked hair was swept up in a bun, and the calico dress she wore had seen better days, but to Audrey she looked like an angel, sent to comfort her. Sadie never hesitated to share her faith.

She smiled. "You're good for me, Sadie. I'm glad God saw fit to send you this way."

"We've both been blessed. Now you go rest. Or maybe go outside and enjoy the sunshine. I'll let you know if there's any change.

Sadie and Adele had cooked and cleaned, right along with Audrey and Copper, with nary a word of complaint. Because she was a widow, Sadie had been traveling with Adele, another widow. Colorado was to be a new start for the women, a chance to make a new life on their own. Audrey couldn't imagine the past few trying days without these wise women's help.

She descended the stairs, thinking how quiet it was without the rain beating against the windows. Later she'd go to the attic and empty the buckets and pans again. With God's grace, the flood might be over. Right now, she just wanted to stand and soak up the warm rays bathing the soggy fields.

She stopped by the kitchen window and took another peek. Tate was in the field back of the house, running and jumping like a newborn colt. She watched, smiling. How wonderful to see the boy relishing the sun's warmth. That was what childhood should be, happy and carefree. The boy clapped his hands together, and then opened them. A grasshopper flew from his hand. He lifted his face to the sky, laughing. Water stood in streams, but that only enhanced the child's joy.

Tate chased after another hopper, and Audrey yielded to temptation. She wanted to join him. As foolish as it might be for a woman her age, she needed to run and laugh and enjoy being alive.

Casting a look at the pot of boiling potatoes, she rushed to the door, giddy with the bright sunshine. Did anything feel as good, or look as exhilarating as sunlight! Stripping shoes and socks off, she wiggled her toes.

She bounded down the steps and raced around the house to where Tate was playing. A grasshopper flew past, and her feet automatically gave chase. A light breeze ruffled her hair and tugged at her skirt. She laughed at Tate's surprised expression.

"Miss Pride! You're barefoot!"

"I am, and I can chase grasshoppers too. Why, I'll bet I can catch more hoppers than you."

His face lit with expectancy. "No, you can't. I'm the best grasshopper catcher in the world."

"It's a contest. Ready, set, go!" Audrey's bare feet flew over the ground, chasing the elusive insects. She didn't care if her hem was already soaking wet. She needed to feel like a child again, to giggle senselessly, to rid herself of the stench of illness. The earlier weariness melted like snow in a spring thaw. She sucked in fresh air and raced through the fields, laughing in triumph, her hair tumbling loose from its ribbon. The rain had ended, and life suddenly made sense!

"What in the world are you doing?"

Audrey skidded to a halt and turned to locate the voice. Copper stood at the edge of the field wearing a bewildered countenance. "Have you lost your mind?"

"No, for the first time since coming here, I'm in my right mind! The sun is shining, the rain has stopped, and the grasshoppers are here for the chasing. Take off your shoes and join us!"

Her friend's eyes skimmed the soggy ground. "You're chasing grasshoppers—barefoot, in this mud and dirty water. May I ask why?"

Audrey laughed. "Because they're here to chase!"

"Because they're here to chase. You have clearly lost your mind. I warned you about working in that parlor."

Audrey lunged for her hand. "Come on . . . you know you want to play."

Copper's strained features suddenly lightened. "Why, certainly. I can't think of any better way to spend a sunshiny afternoon than to chase grasshoppers, barefoot."

"You're really going to play with us, Miss Copper?" Tate yelled as he flew past.

"I really am." Copper toed off her shoes, removed her stockings, and then lifted her skirts and jigged across the muddy field. "Since I don't see any jars, I assume this is a catch-and-release game?"

"Of course," Audrey said. "Who'd want a jar full of grasshoppers?"

"I would," Tate said. "Can I have one?"

Audrey paused to kneel beside him. "If you were a grasshopper, where would you like to live? Would you like to fly out here in the open field and all this sunshine, or be stuffed in a canning jar?"

Tate considered the options. "How big is the jar?"

Audrey burst into laughter. "Not nearly big enough."

"Don't believe I've ever seen a jar big enough to hold me," Tate said. "You got one in the house?"

"A jar big enough to hold you?"

He nodded.

"No, but that's not the point. Would you like to be shut up in a jar?"

Tate shook his head no, and she elaborated. "Neither would the grasshoppers. They belong out here in the sunshine. God didn't create them to be canned. So, while it's all right to catch them, they should be turned loose to enjoy all of nature."

Tate studiously rolled his eyes. "Let's just catch them. We won't put them in a jar."

"Good boy. Now, let's see who can catch the most and turn them loose."

Tate's sturdy boots flew across the field. Copper ran beside him, dipping and swaying with each catch and release. Audrey headed into a patch of the winged insects, lunging. She ended up with one fat grasshopper, its wings harsh and brittle, and the body soft and plump.

She sprinted across the field on feet that had suddenly sprouted wings. The three ran and shouted, joy overflowing with freedom after being limited by rain and sorrow for days on end.

The mill door opened, and Audrey spotted Eli and Caleb looking up the hill for the source of merriment. She waved, and then turned to chase after Copper.

The two men watched for a moment, then walked up the path to the field.

"What's going on?" Caleb called.

"We're celebrating the sun!" Copper slapped his arm. "Take off your boots and join us."

She turned and bolted across the field with Caleb close on her heels. Tate bent double, laughing. "Run, Caleb, run! Catch her!"

Audrey saw Eli standing at the edge of the fun. Would he join the game? "We're having fun," she called as she passed.

"So I see." He removed his hat and studied the clear sky. "Well, it's a fine day for it."

"Hey, Pa," Tate yelled. "Catch me!"

Eli grinned. "Let's see how fast you can run." His boots and socks landed beside him, and Eli took out after his son.

Tate dashed across the field with his pa on his heels. The uncharacteristic sight sent Audrey skidding to a halt. She stood watching father and son romp across the sun-drenched field, splashing water, Tate's youthful screams filling the sweet, rain-washed air.

Caleb swatted her on the shoulder as he dashed past. "Tag. Miss Audrey's it."

She tore after him as Copper cheered from the sidelines. Tate resumed his grasshopper quest. Audrey, feeling brave, tagged Eli. "You're it."

A grin suddenly broke across his handsome features, and she watched years melt away from his face. He lunged, pursuing her across the uneven ground. She could hear him gaining as she raced away from the group, zigzagging from left to right, trying to escape. His breath increased to harsh, uneven gasps coming close on her heels. Grasping her shoulder, he spun her around. She whirled, laughing. Her hair had come loose and hung around her shoulders. She must look a sight, but she didn't care. For the first time in a very long time, she felt young again.

Eli's gaze focused on her disheveled state, and it seemed to Audrey that he was seeing her for the first time. As he held her at arm's length, his air of detachment disappeared. This was Eli as she'd longed to see him. Laughing, eyes alight with fun. He rested his hand on her shoulder. "I've caught you, Miss Pride. Now what shall I do with you?"

She bit her lower lip, trying to still the sudden quiver. "I have no idea, Mr. Gray. I'm completely at your mercy."

Heat penetrated her rosy cheeks. Was this she? Audrey Pride being so utterly bold and . . . flirtatious?

The twinkle in his eyes suggested that he shared her sudden enlightenment. "Ah, yes? Well, then I'll have to think of a suitable penalty."

She searched for a proper response, but for once came up speechless. Her eyes locked with his, and what she saw there almost took her breath away. The warmth of his smile, the way his gaze absorbed her as he examined his prize. His eyes moved gently and reverently over her features.

Whatever barriers had once stood between them had vanished. She silently thanked God for the sunshine. For the utterly perfect day and for the special bond she hoped had begun between them. Because at the moment, nothing was clearer. She adored this reticent man who had turned away from her at every corner. She felt the same unquenchable passion that Willow had for Tucker.

Oh, God, make it possible for him to return my affection. I'll never ask for anything again . . .

A burst of laughter caught her attention. Yvonne had joined the others, and along with Caleb and Copper was now chasing grasshoppers with abandon. Audrey caught her breath, thinking that they were all mad with delight, saturated with the golden rays of the sun after so many days of gloomy skies and hard rain.

Eli reached for her hand, and together they waded barefoot across the field with a hidden bond knitting them together. They joined the others at play, their hands separating. He didn't directly approach her again, but Audrey felt his presence, caught an occasional glance, a curious smile.

"Hey, is this a private party, or can anyone join?"

Audrey turned to see Josh Redlin approaching the merriment. The wagon master looked particularly fine today. The sun touched his auburn hair, turning the freshly washed mass a shiny red. Now that the illness had run its course, the deep worry lines previously rimming his eyes had vanished.

Copper's features closed. "Mr. Redlin."

"Miss. I heard the fun, and knew you'd want me to join in." He smiled.

She sniffed. "You flatter yourself, sir."

He sighed, gripping his right side. "Ah, another glancing blow." The man loved to annoy her, Audrey noted.

He straightened, flashing another white grin. "For a moment I thought the sun had thawed your disposition, but I see I was mistaken."

Copper nailed him with a frosty glare. "And I, sir, am saddened by your faulty observation. It seems you are plagued by the shortcoming."

"Ah, yes. I am a rogue. It takes a woman of great insight to recognize my failings. May I congratulate you, Miss . . . ?"

She crossed her arms. "You know my last name, and no, you may not congratulate me."

"Ah. Pity." The sound of Tate's squeals filled the field. "Shall we join in?"

Copper heaved a sigh and turned on her heel. "I'll leave you children to your play. I have work to do." Turning, she flounced across the field toward the house.

Josh glanced ruefully at Audrey and stated the obvious. "She doesn't like me."

Shrugging, Audrey couldn't argue. "She's usually sweet-natured." Not always . . . but more so than she was with Josh Redlin. The man clearly got under Copper's skin.

"She's a spitfire." Caleb paused to join the conversation.

Josh's eyes fixed on Copper's retreating figure. "That she is. She'll throw a party when I leave town."

Audrey looped her arm through the wagon master's. "And I promise not to attend. We've grown accustomed to having you around."

He grinned. "Your hospitality is much appreciated, but we'll be leaving soon as the roads are passable."

"I'll be sorry to see you go."

His eyes turned toward the sound of the judge's slamming back door. "To tell the truth, I like it here in Thunder Ridge. A man could do worse if he intended to put down roots."

As much as Audrey delighted in the thought, she was happy Copper hadn't heard it. The observation would inflame her.

There wasn't enough room for Redlin and Copper in the same small vicinity. Beeder's Cove might be several miles away, but the distance wouldn't be nearly enough to temper that explosion.

Chapter 19

⌒

Audrey woke to the sound of rain drumming the window. The sunny, welcome respite hadn't lasted long. She sighed. Never had the saying "Into each life some rain must fall" been so appropriate. Thunder Ridge was getting a lifetime supply all at once.

Throwing back the quilt, she padded to the window. The sky was dark as sin. Rain slanted in a driving curtain between Wallace's house and the sawmill. The pond was now a lake creeping toward the town's businesses. She dressed and went downstairs to find Copper awake and starting breakfast. "Kirkland sent young Todd Everett to say you're not needed at the parlor this morning."

Audrey filched a piece of ham. "I'll enjoy my respite, I've made a good deal of money, money I shudder to think about, but I can survive on my savings for a good while."

Copper forked a piece of meat onto a hot skillet. "Why don't you come to Beeder's Cove with me? If the Widow

Potts doesn't have room for the both of us, we can surely find a place for you to board, and the job opportunities may be better there."

"Thanks, but Willow will need me here to help with the wedding."

"Perhaps—but if the worst happens . . . and you know it could . . . please come to Beeder's Cove with me."

"Nothing's going to happen. It just can't. And besides, I'd only be in your way. You're starting a new life, new pupils. I'd be a nuisance you don't need."

"Audrey Pride, I can't believe you said that. We're like sisters, and you'll never be in my way. Don't you ever say a thing like that again."

Audrey bit into the pilfered meat. "I'm sorry. I know you mean well and I always want you in my life too. If we should lose Willow, it will just be the two of us."

Copper sat the plate on the table and put her arms around Audrey, hugging tight. "Nothing but death will separate us. We have no control over that, but nothing in life must come between us."

"Which reminds me." Audrey broke the embrace and reached for a letter lying on the table. "This came for you late yesterday afternoon."

"It's from Aunt Nancy. She's insistent about me coming for a visit."

"Your aunt in Ellsworth, Kansas?"

She nodded. "Mother's sister. I visited her once when I was a child and Uncle Wilt was still alive. She's invited me to visit but I've never found the time."

"Ellsworth? Isn't that where Ester moved when she left Timber Creek?"

"Yes, she had a brother and sister near there." Copper sighed. "Esther was such a fighter. Without her, I doubt that we'd have lasted very long in defending Timber Creek against the rebs. If I decide to visit my aunt I'll make sure and look up Esther. I think she moved somewhere near Fort Dodge, but not in the town itself."

A knock sounded and Audrey turned to answer. She was greeted by Caleb's smiling face. "Can you spare a cup of coffee?"

"I believe I can. What brings you out so early?"

"Just came over to check with Tucker about moving what lumber we have over to Miller's barn loft. Town's going to be flooded by nightfall. We can't hold back the river any longer."

"Flooded." Audrey sank to a chair. "What then?"

"Then we all leave for higher ground."

"But the roads aren't passable."

"We don't have a choice. Some of the men are rounding up enough boats to move everyone to safety."

Audrey's thoughts turned to the icehouse and all those victims waiting for burial. She couldn't bear to think of the judge's body being somehow desecrated by a flood. And Willow. How would they move her in her precarious state?

"We can't just leave."

"We can't sit here and be washed away." Caleb reached for the cream. "Where's Tucker?"

"With Willow. The poor man hasn't slept in days other than what little he snatches by her bedside. If something doesn't break soon . . ."

Caleb sobered. "He won't listen to me. He won't leave her side."

Copper brought a hot biscuit and some ham and set it in front of him. "I'll bet you haven't had breakfast."

"Not yet. I wanted to speak to Tucker and then I'll go home and fix something. I've been at the mill all night fighting water."

"Was Eli with you?" Audrey asked. "Perhaps he'd like something to eat. I'd be glad to take something to him."

"No, he went home about an hour ago. He'll be around later and let me grab some sleep. Men are holding the water at bay but it's about got us beat."

Copper turned from the stove where she was scrambling eggs. He eyed the skillet. "How do you get those eggs so fluffy? Mine are always flat and dry."

She broke into a grin. "I suppose I could spare a few bites."

He winked at Audrey. "Why, hadn't thought about it, but eggs would taste real good."

Copper set a plate of ham, fluffy clouds of scrambled eggs, and two more steaming biscuits in front of him. "Here. There's more where these came from."

"Ma'am, there's not another woman in this town who can scramble like you." He bit into the eggs, and then reached for the salt shaker. "What're you having for supper?"

Copper laughed. "Think you can charm me into cooking for you? Think again. I've got enough to do around here."

Audrey listened to the friendly exchange, harboring a grin. Now why couldn't Copper get along with Josh Redlin as well? Caleb and Josh had good personalities and neither was lacking in the looks department.

Yvonne walked in the kitchen. "Good morning."

Caleb's chair scraped back and he sprang to his feet. "Morning."

Yvonne nodded demurely.

"It's not all that good," Copper said. "It's raining again."

"I see that. May I help?"

"No, I've got it. Sit down with Caleb and I'll get your breakfast."

Yvonne smiled, erasing the tight lines around her eyes. "Yesterday's sun was nice."

"It was at that," Caleb said, fumbling behind his back for the chair. "We could stand a few more days like that." He smiled and pushed the cream pitcher closer.

After breakfast Audrey stopped by the parlor. The viewing room was empty, though it needed sweeping. The last family had left muddy tracks. She found her employer in the downstairs sitting room, deep into a book. He glanced up when she entered the room. "Miss Pride. I sent word that you weren't needed today."

"Yes, I got the message, but I thought I'd stop by and clean a little."

"Ah. Well, business has slowed considerably."

No work meant her wage would be cut. "There isn't anything else I can do? Cook? Perhaps clean your private quarters?" In the past his living area had been off limits, but fifty cents couldn't be overlooked because of personal preference.

He seemed to consider the offer. "Not really. Why don't you take a week off, without pay, of course, unless work picks up unexpectedly? You look as if you could use a good rest."

She looked like she needed a rest? Pausing, she considered the past hectic days and let the remark pass. "Very well. You will send word when I'm needed?"

"Of course." He absently shooed her away. "Have a restful period."

That evening Audrey helped Copper bathe Willow and dress her in a fresh nightgown of white muslin, with tucks and lace. "She looks almost bridelike, doesn't she?" Copper mused, as she brushed Willow's hair.

"She does. She's beautiful, even like this."

"Just as beautiful on the inside too." Copper laid the brush aside. "I wonder what goes through Tucker's mind, sitting up here, hour after hour."

"I don't know. Sorrow. Helplessness." Audrey gathered up soap and towels, and the women left the room so Tucker could once again take his place in the bedside chair.

Outside the parlor window, rain lashed the panes. Lightning flared, illuminating the yard for an instant, faded, and then flashed again. A cannon blast of thunder rocked the house.

Audrey glanced up from her handwork. "Does a body ever get used to this?"

"Never." Copper drew a needle through her needlepoint. "I don't intend to get used to it. The moment the roads are passable, I'm leaving for Beeder's Cove."

"Won't you miss the people here?"

Copper shook her head. "I'll miss you. And Willow and Tucker, but nobody else. If the three of you weren't here, I'd never want to step foot in Thunder Ridge again."

"You'd miss Caleb."

Copper's jaw dropped. "I wouldn't miss him. Why would you say such a thing? Just because I took pity on the man and fixed him a plate of decent scrambled eggs doesn't mean I have affections for the man."

Drawing thread through her tatting mat, Audrey smiled. "I think you two make a perfect pair. Caleb with his nonsensical teasing and you so quick to rise to the bait."

Copper made a face. "Granted, the man has a pleasant personality, but we're mismatched. He needs a sweet, delicate flower that will look up to him. Yvonne is exactly the kind of woman he needs. Someone he can protect. Beneath all that teasing, Caleb is a gentleman."

"Ah, you have noticed."

"Of course I've noticed. I'm very perceptive when it comes to men." Sighing, she rested fiery tresses against the chair baluster, eyes dreamy. "I want a man with fire in his soul—someone who isn't afraid to take a chance, to live. Adventurous—but a godly man." She glanced over. "Mind you, I'm not looking. Perhaps it's my role in life to remain single. A woman dedicated to nurturing youthful, innocent minds. Yes, I wouldn't be surprised if that's what God intends for me."

Balderdash! Audrey feared for a moment she might actually have voiced the contradiction. Copper a spinster? As pretty and vivacious as she was? That would be a waste. She hadn't met her mate, but, given time, she would. She was born to marry, and all this nonsense about spinsterhood was just that, nonsense.

Copper grinned. "Besides, the sooner I leave Thunder Ridge, the sooner I'm rid of Josh Redlin."

"You won't be leaving before he does. The roads are impassable. If the town is forced to evacuate, he and his party will go with us."

"You know what I mean. He'll have to leave one of these days, and I say good riddance."

Audrey bit off a thread. "Uh-huh."

"It can't be too soon for me. He's like a skunk lurking around, looking to shoot off a foul scent when the occasion presents itself."

Copper's eyes glowed with an inner fire, and Audrey wondered if she was speaking out of frustration, or if she really felt this adamant about a man who would be most women's dream come true. She'd never known Copper to be so dead set against anyone.

Yvonne entered the parlor. "Don't let me disturb you. I'm just looking for something to read."

"You're not disturbing us." Copper motioned for her to sit. "We're just visiting. Why don't you join us?"

"If you're sure I'm not bothering you."

"Not in the least. Please. Sit."

The young widow sat down, reaching for a nearby book of poems. The women sewed or read until Audrey finally broke the easy silence. "Do you plan to join the wagon train when it leaves?"

The widow turned pensive. "I've considered the possibility, but I'm not sure Mr. Redlin will allow me. It's not easy for a woman alone to travel with the train."

"Why would he care?" Copper asked.

"Oh, I can handle a team, but if a wheel came off or anything breaks, I'd be helpless. I'm not knowledgeable about equipment like Frank."

Copper focused on her needlepoint.

"Besides, Frank didn't like traveling with a group. He was very much a loner. That's why we were traveling by ourselves. It got lonely for me, sometimes, but that's the way he wanted it."

"Did you always do everything he asked?" Copper's dark expression suggested she wouldn't dream of being so malleable.

"Always. I owed my husband my life. He took me in when I had nowhere to go. I don't know where I'd be today if it wasn't for Frank and his goodness."

The soft rise and fall of the young widow's voice lent a sense of calm to the room. It wasn't hard to recognize the young lady's genteel nature, the deep compassion for a man who had saved her from who knew what.

Copper was right: Yvonne was a perfect match for Caleb, and perhaps since her marriage had been born of necessity and not love, Yvonne's grieving period would be shortened.

Yvonne and Caleb. Audrey smiled. The two went together like a pair of silver slippers.

Chapter 20

Jolted awake, Audrey sat up in bed and tried to orient her senses. A shadowed form loomed nearby, and she heard a muffled sob. "Come quickly. Willow is worse."

"Copper? Is that you?"

"Yes. You're needed in Willow's room."

Audrey threw back the sheet and swung to her feet. *She can't die, Lord. Please . . . not when she's fought so hard to stay alive.*

"She's burning up with fever, tossing and turning, muttering those senseless words. It's frightening."

Audrey pulled on a robe as they left her bedroom. "Have you sent for the doctor?"

"Yes . . . and Jolie."

How did you bring down a raging fever? Copper had bathed Willow in cold baking soda water—was there something more that could be done? She trailed Copper down the hall to the door of Willow's room, which stood open. Tucker bent over the bed, talking to Willow, his tone urging calm.

"Don't, love. You'll hurt yourself."

She rolled away from him, and he caught her and eased her back to the mattress. Audrey moved to the opposite side of the bed. "How long has she been like this?"

"Half an hour or so. She's been getting steadily worse for the past couple of hours." He glanced up. "Stay with her . . . I'm going for the doctor."

"I thought he'd been sent for."

"Adele went, but that's been twenty minutes ago."

"Of course. Go."

Nodding, he left in a run.

"Tucker?" Audrey called after him. "Take the kitchen lantern. It's filled with oil and the wick trimmed."

Copper pushed past him. "I'll get it for him."

Willow muttered a string of indecipherable sentences. Audrey laid her hand on her friend's forehead. Burning up. This afternoon she'd been almost cool. Copper's footsteps sounded on the stairway. Seconds later, she stood in the doorway. Audrey turned to meet her eyes and saw the same fear she felt raging through her mind.

A breathless Adele returned with a small pail. "There's hardly any ice left. It's all melting."

Audrey took the bucket. "Thank you, Adele. Now go have a cup of tea and send the doctor up the moment he arrives."

Copper approached the bed. "Is it possible Willow has the same mysterious sickness . . . ?"

Audrey pressed a hand to her throat. "Oh . . . I'd never considered that possibility . . . but no. This is the first time her fever has soared so high."

"Look at her," Copper urged. "She has the same hue, the same grayness."

Audrey refused to accept the thought. Willow suffered from a blow, not the grave sickness that had claimed so many lives.

Footsteps pounded on the stairs, and a few moments later Tucker arrived with Dr. Smith in tow. The doctor shrugged out of his rain cape and snapped open his medical bag. He tucked the ends of his stethoscope in his ears and motioned for them to hold her still while he held it against her chest. Removing the instrument from his ears, he placed his hand on her forehead and then on her throat.

"We have to get that temperature down."

Audrey nodded. "Tell me what to do."

"Ice. You and Copper go to the icehouse and bring back all you can carry. I need Tucker here to hold her down. If she keeps flailing around like this, she'll do even more harm."

Audrey glanced at Copper and read her thoughts. *The icehouse? Where all those bodies are stacked like sacrificial cordwood?*

Could they do this? She glanced at the bed and back to Copper and saw quiet resolve. She was so proud of her friend at that moment she wanted to cry. They could do this.

Copper nodded and Audrey confirmed, "We'll get the ice."

"There won't be much," Tucker warned. "The supply is nearly depleted."

"Pray there'll be enough." The doctor bent to Willow, countenance grave.

The women took the stairs without speaking. Copper took a couple of buckets from the kitchen while Audrey relit the lantern. They took time to join hands in a silent prayer. *Father, we're helpless without your mercy. Let there be enough ice to help.* Hunched before the driving rain, they set off.

The lantern threw out a dim radiance, barely illuminating the path. The icehouse sat at the edge of town, dark and scary in the best of times, petrifying on a windy, stormy night.

Copper broke the silence. "Hurry up. I want to get this over with."

"I'll hurry, but I can assure you nobody is going to leap out of their box and get you."

"So say you."

When they reached the structure, Audrey handed the lantern to Copper and reached for the door hasp. Easing the heavy wood open, she peered inside the pitch-back depths. The stench of death overpowered her.

Copper pressed close, lifting the lantern higher. Rows of pine caskets lined the brick building. In the center were a couple of melting ice blocks, and an ax.

Taking a deep breath, Audrey braced her resolve. This would be no different than having a client lying neatly on a table awaiting her service, only she wouldn't have to touch or even see the body. Pure meanness set in, and she reached back and pinched Copper's ribs.

Squealing, her friend bolted out of the door, nearly tearing the wood off its hinge.

Audrey stepped out and took her firmly by the hand. "I'm sorry. I couldn't resist."

"You're wretched!" Copper accused.

"True, but if you could see your face right now you'd know why." Probably as comical as Audrey's had been her first day of work at the parlor. "Come on, I'll protect you."

"You go." Copper hung back, clearly peeved. "I wouldn't be a stitch of help."

"You have to hold the light."

"I don't have to do anything but die."

"In which case, you will, and very soon if you don't help me."

"I *can't* go in there."

"Yes you can." Audrey grasped her arm and pulled her into the black abyss. Copper's breath came in ragged pants. "Hurry up."

Audrey reached for the ax. "This will only take a minute."

Swinging the pick, she chunked off a sizable hunk of ice. Even she was made a little uneasy by the grotesque shadow the lantern light threw against the walls: a cloaked figure swinging an ax with all its might.

Copper's tinny whimpers filled the stillness. "This is wretched."

Audrey lifted the ax over her head and brought it down with a resounding whack. A second lump of ice cracked, and she hit it again, breaking off enough small and medium-sized pieces to fill the buckets. Setting the ax aside, she picked up a pail and gave it to Copper. Grabbing her own pail, she stepped outside and closed the door.

Rain lashed exposed skin, hindering their speed. The lantern barely shed enough glow to show the path. Rough, mud-slick ground proved treacherous underfoot. Audrey slipped, almost spilling her bucket. Still they trudged ahead, putting one foot in front of the other. Upon reaching the Madison house, they removed their rain-soaked capes and toted the buckets upstairs, where the doctor dumped the ice in a bedsheet, instructing Tucker to twist it into a pack to fit against Willow's feverish side.

Dr. Smith turned to Audrey, his voice rough with impatience. "What are you standing there for? We need more ice."

Audrey glanced at Copper, and they silently turned and left the room.

The stormy night closed around them as they slogged through the mud and running water on their way back to the icehouse. Lightning flared overhead, and thunder roared. Imagined terrors waited outside the tiny circle of light. The wind picked up, howling like a banshee.

Inside the icehouse, Audrey held the lantern while this time Copper chopped enough ice to fill the buckets a second time. A sound suddenly caught Audrey's attention.

Something moved in the darkness behind the stacked caskets.

Inside the block walls, it was quiet enough that she could hear a scratching sound. She caught her breath, glancing at Copper, who was blissfully unaware of the swish as she diligently whacked the large block.

The sound wasn't coming from the boxes. Audrey ought to know. She'd prepared at least half of them. She knew Mrs. Helman had on a flowered dress, and Mr. Hutchison wasn't wearing his store-bought teeth because he'd lost them somewhere on the trail.

"Is anyone there?" she called, ashamed of the way her voice fractured.

Cooper immediately dropped the ax and whirled to face her. "What?"

Aware the noise could well be her imagination, Audrey modified her response. "I . . . I asked, 'Anybody there!' You know . . . teasing—because we both know there's . . . nobody there."

"Well, stop it." Copper lifted the ax and whacked off another hunk.

Green round globes glowed behind a box.

Audrey's blood curdled. That was not her imagination. She carefully set the lantern on a box and eased closer to the source.

Copper chopped away.

The eyes moved closer. She whirled, ready to abandon Copper and save herself when she spotted a fat opossum wander into the light, moseying toward her.

To Audrey's dismay, Copper spotted it about the time it spotted her. She squealed, and the lantern wavered.

Audrey whirled to steady it. "Do you want me to die of heart failure? I cannot bear the thought of walking back to that house in the dark."

Sinking to her knees, Copper closed her eyes. "This is absolutely appalling!"

"Just hurry."

Minutes later, Audrey closed the opossum inside the icehouse and secured the hasp. If it'd gotten in there on its own, it could surely get out on its own.

The women set off with the load. A rising stream of water blocked their pathway. Too tired to go around, they waded through. They reached the edge of the yard, and Copper suddenly went down, dropping her bucket. Ice flew in all directions. Audrey set down the lantern and helped her up.

"Is anything broken?"

Copper moaned. "I think I've turned my ankle."

Audrey scrambled to retrieve the precious ice, and then

turned back. "Lean on me." She slid her arm around the girl's waist and helped her to stand. "Don't get upset. I'll hold you steady. Can you hop to the steps?"

"I'll try."

The women forged across the rain-soaked yard, Audrey assisting Copper, who now carried both ice buckets. When they reached the house, Copper dropped to sit on the bottom step. "Let me scoot up. It would be easier than trying to climb them."

Audrey didn't argue. Copper might be little, but she and the ice were a bundle to support. She took both buckets and set them aside.

Easing herself up, one step at a time, Copper made her way to the top. From there, Audrey helped her inside. Not confident enough to tackle the stairs, she opted for the kitchen. Copper sank into a chair. "I'll be all right. You take the ice upstairs before it melts."

"I'll be right back and we'll get some ice on that ankle." Audrey hurried outside and gathered the ice and carried both buckets inside before returning for the lantern.

Again Dr. Smith used the ice to fashion a pack and then gave her a commiserating glance. "We need more."

Audrey nodded and plodded downstairs. She could not make the trip back to that icehouse by herself, but she had to, for Willow's sake. She stood at the top of the steps, staring uncertainly into the darkness. She had to have help. But whom could she turn to?

Eli? Caleb?

Eli it was.

Holding the lantern low enough to illuminate her steps, she hurried down the road.

The Gray house was dark when she reached it. She tapped on the door, not wanting to wake Tate or Mrs. Gray. When she didn't receive an answer, she rapped louder. The door swung open, and Eli appeared, snapping suspenders into place.

"Willow's worse. We need ice to bring down her fever."

She had wakened him from a sound sleep. His tousled hair whipped in the rainy gale. "What?"

"I need help! Copper and I made two trips, and then Copper hurt her ankle, and I can't go back there by myself. I just can't." To her mortification, she broke into tears.

He drew her close, her slicker drenching his bare chest and trousers. "Calm down. I'll help you. Just let me get some clothes on."

"Thank you." She openly bawled. "Thank you ever so much."

She waited on the porch, gaining control of her emotions until he returned. Taking her by the arm, he helped her off the porch. "I'll get the buggy."

A buggy. Of course. They could carry more ice that way. Why hadn't she and Copper thought of that earlier? Audrey relaxed, so thankful to have someone else in control. Willow would be fine now.

Eli stopped the horse in front of the house and helped her up onto the seat. She huddled against him, for protection, but mainly because she wanted to. He didn't object. She drank in his presence, his strength, and closed her eyes, powerless to explain why it took a crisis to bring them together. Why couldn't they have one sane moment of togetherness without pending doom?

"There's an opossum in the icehouse."

He glanced down at her. "How do you know that?"

"I've been there twice already tonight. I don't know what it's doing there, but it gave me quite a start."

She could feel his grin. "I'd think so."

He put his arm around her and drew her closer. "So the icehouse bogeymen got you?"

"Of course not." She snuggled nearer, drinking in the exquisite moment. "But it was rather startling when the little dickens walked out and stared right at me. It was so very spooky in there, and all those clients gave the icehouse quiet a macabre air."

Eli laughed—a strong, manly timbre. "A fine undertaker's assistant you are. I'd think you'd be used to the deceased by now."

One thing she wasn't used to: this intimacy. But she didn't question it. She relished it, and longed for more.

They reached the icehouse, and Eli made short work of the opossum, turning him out in the rain. Then instructing Audrey to remain in the buggy, he swung a few swift blows with the ax, and loaded the chunks of ice. Thunder blasted overhead, and she covered her ears as Eli picked up the reins, and in a few minutes they drew up in front of the Madison house.

"I'll carry the ice upstairs."

Audrey swiftly swung out unassisted. "I'll do my share. Time is short."

He filled a bucket for her before picking up his own load. When they reached the upstairs bedroom, he paused in the doorway, his face draining of color. Willow twitched and jerked uncontrollably, her sweat-soaked hair hanging in strings. She moaned, as though in anguish.

"Dear God . . ." He set down the buckets.

Audrey's gaze sought Tucker, who sat hunched over, grief shadowing his tight features, praying.

"Bring it in," the doctor ordered. "It's melting almost as fast as we get it in place."

Eli empted the buckets while Audrey went to check on Copper. She found her sitting at the kitchen table, her foot propped on a chair. "What's happening? I'm about to go out of my mind sitting here. Willow . . . ?"

"No change. Eli and I brought the last of the ice. If she needs more there is none. Can you make it upstairs if I help you?"

"I can try."

"I'll get Eli to lend us a hand." Audrey caught him as he was starting upstairs with the last bucket of ice and explained the situation.

"Let me deliver this and I'll be right back."

Ten minutes later he entered the kitchen. Gathering Copper around the waist, he helped her to stand and take a cautionary step. Noting the limp, he swept her up in his arms and carried her up the stairs. Audrey trailed, actually envious of her friend's injury. To be carried in his arms . . . Protected. Loved to the very depths of her soul by this man . . .

She shook desire aside. She'd just been given a rare moment of privacy with Eli Gray. God was good.

If only he would be good enough to spare Willow, she would never ask another thing of him.

Chapter 21

The hall clock chimed three, and Willow lay encased in ice packs. Audrey had been bathing her forehead with cool water, a priceless commodity until recently. Suddenly she straightened, unable to endure another moment of waiting. "I'm going downstairs. Does anyone need anything?"

The doctor, Tucker, then Eli refused the offer. Copper dozed in a nearby chair, her injured foot propped high.

Sadie met her at the bottom of the stairway wearing her sleep bonnet. "Is the poor girl worse?"

"It would seem that way. The doctor is with her. I need a breath of fresh air."

"Why don't I fix you a nice cup of hot tea?"

"No, thank you, Sadie. I just need a little air."

"Then I'll sit with you."

"But it's raining."

"I won't melt. Done proved that days ago." The woman

drew a shawl around her nightgown. "Shall we sit on the stoop?"

Audrey followed Sadie into the damp night air.

"Heard a ruckus earlier and feared that Willow might have worsened." Sadie sank to the damp step. "How bad is it?"

"Bad."

Sadie shook her head. "Such a pity."

"Sorry if we bothered you. We've been going back and forth to the icehouse. Willow's fever is dangerously high."

"Poor little one."

"I have this need to do something, but there's nothing I can do." Audrey slumped against the concrete step.

"Wait on the Lord. That's all a body can do."

"Oh, Sadie. How do you stay so firm in your faith? You never waver."

The woman pulled her wrap closer. "I've had my share of doubting, but I've walked with the Lord for quite a few years now, and if he's taught me anything, he's taught me his way ain't my way, but his is the best way, whether I can see that or not."

The distance in the older woman's voice convinced Audrey that she was now lost in personal thought. Finally Sadie sighed. "I know what you're going through. Losing someone you love is hard. I had a husband once. Lost him in a mining accident; lost my daughter to the influenza, and my son to snakebite. There were many a time I felt like folding up. There weren't no reason to go on living, but God's kept me here on this earth, and I've found out some days aren't so bad anymore. Don't know why he cared to keep me around—he knows there were times I've begged him to take me. Land, girl, I've been to the end of my rope so many times I prayed for someone to saw off the limb, but the good Lord's held tight. You might think he's forsaken you but he hasn't. You have to bury that assurance deep in your heart and hold on during the storms because there's one thing I do know for certain, there's going to be storms." She suddenly stood up. "And you're right. It is raining too hard to sit out here. I'm drenched to the bone, and the last thing this household needs is another patient. Come inside, dear. We'll make coffee and take it to the men whether they want it or not."

It was nearing four A.M. when the two women climbed the stairs to Willow's room bearing a tray of coffee and cups. Audrey opened the bedroom door, and Sadie carried the tray inside and deposited it on a table. She filled cups with the dark, fragrant brew, and Audrey deposited them into hands that automatically wrapped around the cups' warmth.

Straightening, Sadie whispered. "I'm going back to the kitchen and do the only thing I can do: pray. If you need anything, just let me know."

Her words brought comfort. It seemed to Audrey that the woman's prayers might reach higher than hers. God heard all of his children's pleas, but it did seem as if Sadie, with all her life's sadness, might have the Lord's ear.

Eli set his cup aside and abruptly left the room. Audrey heard his heavy boots descending the stairway. Despair engulfed her. When he was near she could cope. When he wasn't she was adrift.

Willow moaned, drawing all attention to the bed. She appeared to have calmed somewhat. At least she wasn't so restless, and the agitated twisting and turning had eased. Dr.

Smith stood beside her, alert to her state. Tucker held her hand. She seemed to respond to his voice and his touch in a way she didn't for the others.

The doctor had dressed Copper's ankle, and told her to keep off it. She sat in a chair, keeping vigil.

Footsteps sounded on the stairs, and Eli returned, followed by Caleb. Tucker lifted his head, acknowledging their presence. Caleb rested his hand on his cousin's shoulder for a moment before going to stand by the window. Audrey's heartbeat quickened. Why had Eli gone for Caleb? Did he sense the end was very near?

Caleb spoke quietly. "Eli says she's quieter than she was."

Nodding, Tucker shifted in the chair. "The fever's still high." His eyes indicated the sheet of ice encasing Willow's body.

"It could be the sickness, or it could be her body fighting off the blow. We just don't know," the doctor said.

She moaned, and the heartbreaking whimper sucked the air from Audrey's lungs. Excusing herself, she stepped outside the room and sank to the floor, tucking her skirts around her legs.

A shadow fell over her, and she looked up to find Eli standing above her. After a moment's hesitation, he slid down to sit beside her, their shoulders touching. They sat in companionable silence. Audrey supposed he didn't feel like talking any more than she did.

Why would God take Willow when she was needed by so many people who loved her? Sadie and her losses rose to her mind. *All right, God. I'm through fighting and questioning. I surrender Willow to you. She belongs to you, not me. Your will be done.*

A sweet peace crept through her. The sting of loss lin-gered, but she could let go now. She leaned forward, resting her head on her up-drawn knees. In the end, she didn't have a choice.

She sat deep in thought, unaware that Eli had moved. She glanced up to see him carrying a rocking chair. He put it beside her. "Here, it's softer than the floor."

Audrey shook her head. "I'm fine."

He bent and scooped her into his arms, ignoring her pro-tests. For a moment she lay cradled against his chest, her cheek brushing the rough shirt fabric before he deposited her onto the cushion. She leaned back, eyes closed, afraid to look at him for fear he'd see the love and longing in her eyes. Love that could only add to his burden. How she hoped and prayed that he wouldn't permit life to pass him by before he emotionally buried his wife. Tate needed a mother: Eli needed a wife and helpmate.

He needed her.

She needed him.

They'd made strides in their relationship, but not enough to please her. Would there ever come a time when she could walk into his arms and be welcomed there?

Why torture yourself? If Willow died, she would fulfill Willow's wish and marry Tucker, if Tucker would have her. It would be years before he was ready to love again.

Years.

She might very well be an old woman by that time, and the promise would go unfulfilled. No one would have her, and yet there was only one she would open her heart to.

Outside, the storm howled and raged like a restless predator. Audrey had come to despise the sound. It was as though the storm was the enemy, come to snatch Willow and sweep her away.

No sound drifted from the sickroom except for the heavy wind banging a loose shutter.

She slipped her hand into Eli's, feeling his fingers close around hers. They sat, waiting. She couldn't bear this lonely vigil alone. *If you must take her, God, please do so swiftly. Tucker can't bear any more.*

Eli got to his feet, favoring his right leg as if he had a cramp from sitting too long on the hard floor. Darkness lifted outside. She sat staring at the early gray daylight that gradually shone through the hall pane, but her mind and heart were on the struggle going on inside the bedroom. Willow's illness had opened her eyes. Life was short, and filled with purpose.

What was her purpose? She didn't seem to have one. No matter what she attempted, she failed. And Eli . . . what was his purpose? To raise Tate alone? To exist in an empty life when Tate grew into a man and took a wife of his own? What would Eli do when his mother passed, and there was no one to look after Tate? Hire some stranger to see to the boy's needs?

Caleb stepped into the hallway. "Doc Smith says you'd better come."

Audrey's gaze shot to Eli, fear blocking her throat. He reached out a hand to pull her erect. Then with his arm around her waist, he turned her toward the doorway. She closed her eyes. She couldn't go into that room—could not witness her best friend's death. From Caleb's grave expression, she knew the summons could mean nothing less.

Her hand tightened in Eli's. "You can't put her in the icehouse. Not with all those others . . . It's cold and damp and animals can get in there. Promise me that you won't put her in the icehouse."

"Shhh," he soothed, and drew her closer to his side.

Willow lay quietly, no longer twitching or moaning. Shadows thrown by the kerosene lamp danced across the ceiling. Copper quietly sobbed.

Tucker stood by the bedside, haggard, tears rolling down his cheeks. Caleb leaned against the wall, arms folded. Eli gently eased Audrey closer to the bed, holding tightly to her shoulders. His warm breath fell on her ear. "She'll be at peace. I try to think that someone she loves will be with her to take her hand and walk her to the other side."

Audrey nodded wordlessly, her heart melting. Hot tears slid down her cheeks. Willow looked like an angel resting among the white sheets. Beautiful. Serene . . . so utterly peaceful, and if she knew her friend, at peace with God.

Hours or maybe only minutes passed. No one said a word; all eyes fixed on the still form lying on the bed. The faint rise and fall of her chest confirmed that life's flame still flickered.

An explosive blast of thunder jarred the house. Windows rattled. Copper muffled a moan. Audrey caught her breath, feeling faint. The sound never ceased to startle her.

Willow's body jerked. Her eyes opened, and she blinked. "*Blast* that thunder!"

Tucker gave a hoarse cry and dropped to his knees beside the bed. Dr. Smith poured a glass of water. "Lift her to a sitting position."

The room exploded with relief. Everyone spoke at once.

Tucker slid his arm behind Willow, gently lifting. The

doctor held the glass to her lips, and she drank greedily. When she lifted a hand to feebly push the glass away, Tucker lowered her head back to the pillow. Dr. Smith rested his hand on her forehead. "Your prayers have been answered. The fever has broken."

Audrey sagged against Eli. Copper slid off the chair and limped over to join the group at the bedside. "She's going to live. Really?"

"Surely she will," Audrey whispered. God wouldn't take her now after giving them renewed hope, would he?

The doctor began removing the ice packs. "Let's get these wet sheets off the bed and get her into dry clothes. She's soaking wet."

Tucker lifted Willow, while Caleb and Eli stripped the bed. Audrey brought fresh sheets, and they spread them over the mattress, tucking in the ends and sides. Then the men stepped outside while Audrey changed Willow into a dry nightgown. As soon as she allowed the men back inside, Tucker sat down in the bedside chair, reaching for Willow's hand. She gave him a drowsy smile before dropping into a normal sleep.

Dr. Smith shrugged into his coat and rested a hand on Tucker's shoulder. "She should be all right now. I'll stop by later in the day."

Tucker reached to grip the doctor's hand. "Thank you. I'll never forget what you've done."

The doctor shook his head. "I didn't do anything. I've never felt so helpless in my life. All the credit belongs to the Lord."

Once the doctor left, Caleb helped Copper to her room. Tucker sat watching Willow, his features haggard with relief and lingering concern. Audrey tiptoed away to allow him privacy. He didn't need her or anyone else now. Willow would live, and Tucker would be just fine. More than fine. He'd be a happily married man soon.

And Audrey was no longer obligated to marry a man she loved, but not the romantic way.

She followed Eli and Caleb downstairs, thanking them for their help. When they left, she went to the kitchen. Sadie sat in a chair drawn up to the table, head down on her folded arms, sound asleep. Audrey touched the older woman's shoulder. "Sadie?"

She lifted her head, features white with strain. "Yes?"

"The fever broke. The doctor thinks Willow's going to be all right."

The older woman's face lit with joy. "That's wonderful, love! I knew he'd bring her through. God is good."

Audrey nodded, smiling. "That he is, Sadie. He is extremely good."

Chapter 22

Sunshine streamed through the windowpane—brilliant, warm, life-giving sunshine. Audrey parted the bedroom panels to see a drenched landscape. Rivulets of running water meandered over sodden fields and through trenches that had been cut through roads and yards. An eagle soared overhead, white head dazzling against a cobalt sky. No thunder, no lightning, not a single raindrop to mar a brand-new day.

She hurriedly splashed water on her face, and then pulled a clean dress from the closet. The sun was out and Willow was alive! Sadie and her favorite saying cut through her mind. "God's in his heaven, all's right with the world."

Running a brush through her hair, she then pinned it in a tidy knot on the back of her head. Sadie and Adele did well, but the house still needed a thorough cleaning, and there was a mountain of wash awaiting her. Everything they owned was damp and muddy, and the bedding needed to be washed and aired.

She snuck a peek in Willow's room and found her awake and smiling. "There you are. I wondered if everyone had gone off and left me."

Audrey laughed. "Surely you're teasing. This room has become a second home to most of us. We've spent more time here than anywhere else."

Willow sobered. "I don't remember anything about it. Wouldn't you think I'd remember something?"

Audrey wanted to ask if she remembered the promise she had wrung from her. *I want you to marry Tucker if anything happens to me. Promise me.*

Tucker would have had something to say about the matter. He wasn't a man to marry casually. He adored Willow. No one on this earth could have taken her place. Love was a funny thing. What mysterious spell caused a man or woman to fall so hard for someone that no one else would do? She loved Eli, and she dared let herself hope that in time he'd return the same affections, but he'd yet to say the words. But his actions last night had been those of a man—

Willow's voice broke through her meanderings. "Exactly how did the accident happen?"

"You really don't remember any of it?"

"Nothing. I know Tucker's explained it more than once but I can't seem to grasp the circumstances."

"Don't worry. Your memory will clear soon. You were helping move some of the horses from the wagon train when you slipped and fell. It's rained for nearly a month here— footing is treacherous. The horse got excited, and before Tucker could gain control the animal kicked you in the head. You've been unconscious for days. We didn't know if you would live or not. Then you developed a very high fever and your condition worsened. Oh, Willow, we were so afraid we were going to lose you."

Willow closed her eyes. "How did Tucker handle the situation?"

"That man practically lived in this room. We had to force him to go home and get some rest. He was here day and night—refused to leave your bedside except for necessity."

Willow smiled. "He really did that?"

"He really did. He loves you. I don't know what he would have done if you hadn't recovered."

"He's a special man."

"A very dedicated man, and you're worth every moment of his adoration. You make a good pair. I'm so glad he came into your life."

"So am I." Willow glanced at the window, blinking back tears. "And now? Am I going to fully recover?"

"You're on the mend, and the doctor thinks you'll be up and around soon—though he warns it will take time to regain your strength." Audrey straightened the bedsheets. "There's no hurry. We'll look after everything until you're back to your old self. The folks from the wagon train are still here, but they'll be moving on as soon as the roads are passable. The sickness has run its course, and we're well on our way to returning to normal, whatever that might be."

Copper hobbled into the room. "And you're never to have anything to do with horses ever again. And that's an order."

A faint grin hovered on Willow's lips. "What happened to your ankle?"

"I slipped and fell. Audrey and I were carrying buckets of ice to pack you in, and I went down. My fault—I should have been more careful."

Audrey wanted to relate the hectic trips to the icehouse, but she decided the tale could wait. Willow's shadowed eyes could barely stay open.

"Ice? You went to the icehouse? Where all those bodies are . . . ?"

Copper shuddered. "It was horrifying."

Willow shook her head. "I see nothing's changed since I've been sleeping."

Oh, much had changed. Audrey knew the moment would come when they would have to tell her about the judge's death. "You've been very ill but you're getting better." She turned to Copper. "We're running low on supplies. I thought I'd stop by the general store and pick up a few needed items. Do you need anything?"

"I'll make a list. Willow, will you be all right up here by yourself? We'll check on you often, and of course Tucker will be in and out."

"I'll be fine, Copper. I'm so very tired."

"You must sleep. The rest will be good for you." Copper rearranged the pillows. "I'll make broth for lunch."

Willow wordlessly nodded.

"Good. You rest now. We'll be back later." She bent to place a kiss on her friend's cool forehead. "Welcome back."

Audrey followed Copper out of the room. "How's your ankle?"

"Better. I can manage the stairs if you go ahead of me and let me take my time." Copper sat down on the top step and scooted down to the next one.

Audrey eyed the snaillike progress. "You're going to go down all two flights that way?"

"Do you have a better idea? I'm afraid to hop for fear I might lose my balance and tumble to the bottom."

"All right, if you need me I'll be downstairs."

Copper eventually hobbled into the kitchen and started a list. Audrey went to Wallace's room and found a cane, which she brought to the ailing friend. "Here. Maybe this will help."

Copper accepted it and took a cautious step. "Yes. It helps enormously. Thank you. Now find me a man's hat and a wad of chaw and I'll be ready for the old folks' home."

Audrey giggled. "When I get back from the store I want to strip the beds and wash all the linen. We need to take advantage of the sunshine. No guarantee it will be here tomorrow."

"That's a pessimistic thought. I prefer to look on the bright side."

"Fine, but remember this is Thunder Ridge."

"Where it never rains," they parroted in unison.

Audrey laughed. With the list tucked in her pocket, she set off for town shortly afterward. People were out and going about their business. She hadn't seen this many folks stirring since arriving in Thunder Ridge. Apparently everyone was taking advantage of the break in the weather.

She located the items Copper wanted and set them on the counter. Tom Curtis peered at her over his spectacles. "Sure am glad to hear your friend is doing better."

"Thank you. We indeed thank the good Lord for her progress."

He totaled up the purchases. "Will that be all, Miss Pride?"

"For the time being. Looks like business is brisk."

"Guess the sun brought them out. Now if I could just get a supply wagon through it would be nice. We ain't had one coming into or going out of Thunder Ridge since it started raining."

"Yes, it's been a real nuisance but I understand it's been a blessing too."

"That's a fact, Miss Pride. We'd been as dry as cornmeal for so long it was beginning to look like we'd have to abandon the town and go elsewhere. 'Course that illness was bad, but I suspect that Redlin fellow has the grit to do whatever he sets out to do. He was might near desperate when he stopped here, with his people sick and dying."

"It would seem that was the sole reason he chose to stop here." She had a feeling Josh Redlin would be mighty hard to restrain once he set his mind to a task. And she wouldn't be a bit surprised if the wagon master could, as Copper implied, be rather stubborn at times.

"I hear tell the roads are all right a few miles out of town, but it's pure trouble getting from here to there. But then, I guess someone real set on coming might be able to swing it, though I can't see why they'd want to. Ain't nothing here a body would be that interested in seeing."

"Oh, I don't know, it's a lovely little town."

"It is at that, but the weather is something fierce. Either too wet or too dry."

"Or noisy," she added.

He agreed. "That thunder sure did jar a person's senses."

She paid for her things and left. On her way home she passed the funeral parlor, but it didn't appear much was going on. Perhaps Tom could use help at the store. She must remember to ask him.

Copper was waiting for her, and Audrey helped put away the groceries and went upstairs to strip the beds and gather up laundry. From the looks of the pile of unwashed clothes, they would be hard put to get it done today. Copper had managed to fill the iron wash kettle and build a fire under it. The water, while not scalding hot, was warm enough to start the wash. Audrey carried cool water from the rain barrel and filled one tin tub for rinsing. The second tub held a blend of hot and cold water, with a cup of shaved lye soap Copper had prepared. The first load was put to soak while Audrey sorted lights from darks, putting them in separate piles. Most of the garments were stained with red clay. She scrubbed them on the washboard, rinsed, and then wrung them out and hung them on the line to dry. A brisk breeze soon sent sheets and clothing flapping on the line.

After the wash was finished, and the first load of dried laundry brought inside, Audrey climbed the stairs, with Copper bumping up the steps behind her. Willow was asleep but woke when they entered the room. "What are you going to do now?"

"Give you a bath and wash your hair. How does that sound?" Copper asked.

"Like pure heaven. I can't wait."

Audrey had carried a bucket of warm water upstairs. Now she and Copper removed Willow's gown and gently bathed her. She had lost weight, her body heartbreakingly frail. Copper washed her hair and toweled it dry, and then spread the clean tresses across the pillow. Audrey expected Willow to ask about Wallace, and it was a relief when she didn't. Tucker had requested that he be with Willow when they told her of her uncle's passing.

Willow sank back against the pillow, her eyes closed.

Copper motioned for Audrey, and they slipped out and made their way downstairs.

Audrey was gathering wash off the line when Tate appeared. "Afternoon, Miss Pride. You doin' mighty fine?"

"Mighty fine, Tate. And you?"

"Tolerable, I suppose."

She smothered a chuckle. "What brings you visiting?"

"I was wondering if you had any cookies you didn't need. Seems I've got a powerful hankering for sweets this afternoon."

"I imagine we could find a few. Why don't you open the door for me so I can carry in this clothes basket and I'll see what we have?"

"Be glad to oblige." He skipped ahead and held the screen open while she carried the large basket inside. "I miss staying with you, but I have obligations. You understand."

"Yes, obligations are important. How is your grandmother today?" She set out a plate of spice drops baked that morning.

"Just weary." Tate bit into one and sighed with gratification. "Did you make this?"

"Made them fresh earlier today. Do you like them?"

"Uh-huh. I reckon you're about perfect, aren't you?"

Audrey laughed. "Perfect? Not me. I make a lot of mistakes."

Tate shrugged. "You suit me just fine. I bet you'd suit Eli too, if I asked him."

Audrey's jaw dropped. "Don't you dare ask him any such thing, Tate Gray. That would be most embarrassing."

"I don't see why. If he likes you and you like him, then you could come live with us and bake cookies every day."

"You listen to me, young man. Little boys do not ask adults questions like that. It's not polite."

He bit into a second cookie. "If you say so. Can I take some these to my grandma? Might make her feel better."

"Of course, I'll wrap a few for you and your grandmother. I'm glad you dropped by today."

"I'll be back. Will you have more cookies?"

She smiled. "I'll make certain that I do."

Tate filled his pockets with cookies while she wrapped a few more for Mrs. Gray. Minutes later the back screen slammed shut.

In a short time a second visitor arrived. Caleb trailed Audrey back to the kitchen, but refused a cup of coffee. "I just dropped by to see if you needed anything."

"No, I went to the store this morning. Willow's doing fine, and Copper and I are catching up on the wash and the housework. Seems Adele and Sadie fell a little behind in their chores." The older women had hearts of gold, but their bodies weren't as cooperative as their spirits.

"That's good. Town's starting to stir except for Horace and Cordelia. They're still barricaded in that house. Claim they're not coming out until the wagon train leaves, and that may be a while yet. They want to bury their dead before they move on."

Tucker stuck his head around the doorway. "I knocked, but nobody answered. Figured it was all right to let myself in." He focused on Audrey. "Are you available?"

"Of course." She untied her apron, knowing it was time to do the chore they had been dreading. They must tell Willow about the judge's passing before she heard it from others. "I'll be right there."

"Want me to come, Tuck?"

"No, I'd appreciate it, Caleb, if you'd go and check on the crew. Work's backing up on them. Someone needs to help."

"Sure thing. I'll go right now."

Audrey climbed the stairs behind Tucker, not looking forward to the task ahead. Willow was awake when they entered the room. Her pleasant smile faded when Tucker took her hand and sat down on the side of the mattress. She frowned. "You have bad news, don't you?" She bit her lower lip. "It's Uncle Wallace. No one's said a word, and I've been afraid to ask."

His eyes gentled. "While you were unconscious, Wallace passed on."

She met his eyes. At first she did not comprehend, and then her eyes slowly filled with tears. She turned her head away as they began to slide down her cheeks.

Tucker handed her a kerchief that was lying on the bedside table. "He was old and tired and sick. God took him home."

She nodded. After a moment she said, "I know I shouldn't grieve. He's finally with Claudine."

Audrey stepped closer. "Yes, and with God. He hasn't been truly happy in a long time."

"I know. He's much better off now."

Tucker eased her to a sitting position, his arms cradling her as he rested his cheek against the top of her head. "They had a strong love, and the judge lived a good long life. No one can ask for more."

Willow buried her face in his chest, and Audrey quietly excused herself and then tiptoed from the room.

There were just times when a man and woman needed to be alone.

Chapter 23

⁓

Two weeks later, Audrey was still scraping mud off the front stoop. The clean, fresh-smelling air stirred her senses. The sun was shining, and the ground had dried enough to hold funerals.

Wallace had been buried in a quiet family service. The Gray cousins, Copper, and Audrey had attended. Willow wasn't strong enough to go outside, but she was resigned to the fact that she wouldn't be going anywhere until she regained strength.

After week's delay, the wagon train was preparing to leave. The ground was firming up and the creeks had gone down. The men from the train, plus men from town, were working together to mend the roads.

Dr. Smith drove up in his buggy and climbed down. "Morning, Audrey. Thought I'd drop by and check on Willow on my way out of town. How's she doing this fine morning?"

"Still very weak, but gaining ground every day."

"Good, good. You want to come up with me?"

"Of course. She'll be happy to see you." The long climb no longer daunted her. Most days she could make it all the way to the top of the stairs without stopping to find her breath.

Willow sat in a chair, drinking in the sunlight. Her features brightened when Audrey issued the doctor into the room. "Good morning, Doctor. What brings you out this early?"

"I just stopped by to check on you before I left town. Figure it will be a few days before I get back."

"I'm doing well. I expect to be back to normal in another few days."

He shook his head. "No, my dear, you won't. You've been gravely ill, and you have months of recuperation ahead of you."

Willow's lips drew into a fine line, and Audrey knew that she wasn't pleased. "I can't accept that. I'll bounce back. I'll be getting married soon."

"No one would be more pleased than me to see the bloom back in those cheeks, but as far as the job goes, you are not going to be able to teach the fall session, or for that matter, perhaps all year. And a wedding? Well, we'll talk about that in due time. I know you don't want to prolong love, but you must take care and not overdo. The sort of blow you suffered could still bring about serious ramifications."

He fished around in his bag and brought out a bottle of tonic. "I want you to take this according to the directions, and send for me if your headache worsens."

"I barely notice the headache now. I don't have time to sit up here and be pampered. I have a wedding to plan."

"In that case, you need to take very good care of yourself. It would be a shame to miss your own celebration." He patted her shoulder. "I must be on my way. You take that tonic, now, and I'll check on you when I get back."

Audrey escorted him downstairs and out to the carriage. Poor man. He'd been busy day and night, caring for the sick. It would be good if he'd follow his own advice and take care of himself before he collapsed from the strain.

"Thank you for stopping by."

"That's my job, but you ladies make my job a pleasure. But"—he smiled—"a loaf of your fine pumpkin bread would surely hit the spot."

"You'll have two loaves the moment you get back."

Smiling, he picked up the reins, and the buggy rolled off.

She returned upstairs to find Willow in tears. "Here now . . . what's wrong? The doctor said you were going to be fine."

"Oh, Audrey, he's only pacifying me. I'm not getting my strength back. I'm weak as a newborn colt. It's going to take me a long time to recover. I've tried to pretend otherwise, but I have to face the truth."

"But you will get better eventually." Audrey sat on the side of the bed and wiped her friend's tears with a clean handkerchief. "You'll fully recover in time."

"I won't be able to teach this year. I wouldn't have the strength, and there've been no preparations made for the term. School should be in session now." Willow met her eyes. "Would you consider taking the position for me?"

Remain in Thunder Ridge? Near Eli and Tate? Of course she would love nothing more, but she must be realistic. "The school board might not want me."

"Of course they'll want you. Why wouldn't they? Blackberry Hill plans to ask you to teach when they reopen their school."

"I have no objections, but it would be Thunder Ridge's decision, and I'd have to discuss it with Blackberry Hill's school board." She could hardly teach in two places at one time, yet her heart was certainly here with Eli and Tate.

Willow took the hankie and wiped her eyes. "I'll talk to Tucker. He'll know what to do."

Willow's request stayed with Audrey throughout the morning. She wanted to remain here so badly. It would be the answer to her prayers. And while she couldn't stay in the judge's home after the wedding, the school board would help arrange room and board.

She found Copper packing in her room. With roads becoming more passable each day, her friend was able to move to Beeder's Cove. Audrey stifled a pang of melancholy. It wasn't fair. After all they had gone through, they were going to be separated anyway. What a pity they couldn't all remain in Thunder Ridge. Couldn't all marry cousins. Handsome, aggravating cousins.

Copper folded a cotton work dress and laid it in her satchel. "I'm thrilled about the new job, but I hate to leave you and Willow."

"I hate to see you go, but we'll manage. We can't hope to stay together always." No matter how badly she felt about the separation, she couldn't stand in Copper's way or dim her excitement about her new position.

"I know you're right. After all, Willow moved away from Timber Creek and we all survived and remained close. I'm sure it will be fine, but it will be different. I suppose I just don't want anything to change." Copper slipped her Bible into the open case and swiped at moist eyes.

"Life is full of changes. We just have to adapt and go on."

She sighed. "Caleb will be here soon. Do you mind carrying these cases downstairs? I don't think I can handle them down the stairs just yet."

"Of course," Audrey replied.

After the luggage was placed downstairs beside the door they went to the stoop to await Caleb's arrival. Twenty minutes later, he and Tucker drove up in a buggy just as Josh Redlin arrived on a flashy black stallion. The morning sun glinted on the wagon master's auburn hair, and Audrey reflected that he certainly was a fine figure of a man. Too bad Copper couldn't see his virtues.

He tipped his hat. "Miss Audrey, Tucker, Caleb."

Audrey noticed he ignored Copper. A glance in her direction revealed she hadn't missed the oversight. Red tinged her cheeks, and her eyes flashed intolerance.

"Where's Eli this morning?" The question slipped before Audrey realized the implication. Heat colored her cheeks.

Redlin broke into a slow grin. Purely masculine. Purely ornery. "I believe he's working up by the river this morning, ma'am."

Audrey opened her mouth to deny that Eli's whereabouts were of concern, to say that she was merely making conversation. But then she closed it. Her intentions were as clear as the nose on her face.

Redlin addressed Tucker. "I was wondering if you could give me a hand? We've got a couple of broken wagon tongues. Thought you'd have some lumber thick enough to make new ones."

"I'm sure I have. Let's go take a look."

"Much obliged. We're getting ready to pull out as soon as the wagons are in shape to travel. Should be around week's end."

Josh dismounted and led his horse, walking beside the mill owner as they made their way to the work site. Copper turned affronted eyes on Audrey. "That's what I don't like about that man. He is always so testy. Did you notice he didn't even acknowledge my presence?"

Audrey grinned. Yes, "testiness" was certainly in the air, but it wasn't brought on entirely by the wagon master.

Caleb glanced at the sky. "Looks like it's clouding up again. Please Lord . . . no more rain."

Copper straightened her hat. "I'm ready if you are."

While he stowed her bags in the buggy, she turned to Audrey. "I've already said good-bye to Willow. Oh, Audrey, I'm going to miss you."

Audrey stepped into her waiting embrace. "Come back soon."

"Every weekend," she vowed.

Audrey hugged her, fighting back tears, and then Caleb helped Copper into the wagon and drove away, leaving Audrey standing alone, waving. Maybe things were actually going to work out.

That afternoon Audrey moseyed past the Padget fortress. Redlin had moved the wagon train closer to load needed supplies. The train sat nearly at the foot of the banker's house, a fact Cordelia would surely loathe.

Audrey stopped to say good-bye to so many she'd come to love. She worked her way through the crowd, greeting people, realizing when they left she'd likely never see them again.

Suddenly a scream rent the air, followed by an ear-piercing crack—breaking boards—nails being ripped free of lumber. A horrendous crash jarred the ground and then a low rumble. Audrey jerked around to locate the source. Bystanders fell silent. Then Frank Richardson, the assistant wagon master, pointed. "Look there! The house is gone."

Audrey followed his astounded gaze, gasping in disbelief. Where the Padget mansion had once stood, a raw gash of mud and rocks now scarred the face of the hill. A tangle of boards and glass piled at the foot of the steep slope showed where the house had ended up. Apparently it had just slid downhill, the result of heavy rains.

Frank's words released the onlookers, and the crowd sprang toward the site. Audrey ran with them, unable to believe her eyes. Cordelia? Junior? Horace? Were they all right? Surely they were in the house, true to their self-imposed exile, even though word had been sent that the crisis was over. When she reached the edge of the pile of rubble, men were already digging, pitching boards aside and searching for life.

The noise summoned the mill workers. Josh Redlin arrived and organized the men into groups, handing out orders. The women milled around, panic written on their faces. Audrey's heart skipped when Tucker and Eli raced past, joining the rescue process.

Shattered glass glistened in deadly shards. Audrey spotted Caleb standing by Josh, waving his arm toward the far side of the rubble.

A shout went up from the group working in front of where a crowd had gathered. "Someone's down here!"

"Alive?" Sadie asked. "Oh, I pray."

When Audrey felt someone next to her she looked down to find Tate. He stared at the pile of rubble, expressionless.

She reached to protect his eyes from the sight. All the weeks of exile to protect themselves from the illness, and the Padgets had come to ruin.

"Where's Junior?" the child asked.

Where was Junior? Audrey's eyes skimmed the ridge. Had the youngest Padget miraculously found an escape before the house collapsed?

"I'm not sure, Tate. They're searching . . ."

She placed her arm around the boy, trying to shore him up. The women stood to the side, holding collective breaths. Tucker held up his hand, and the men stopped working.

Eli dropped to his knees, bent to the ground to peer into the opening. "Over here!"

The men sprang into action, heaving boards aside, working quickly. After what seemed an eternity, Eli slid down into the hole, followed by Sully James.

Reverend Cordell hurriedly brought a strip of canvas and lowered it to the two men. The crowd waited. A red-haired man handed down ropes, and Audrey watched with bated breath as they slowly began to haul something to the surface. Gradually the makeshift sling came into view. Cordelia was yakking a mile a minute.

"Well I never . . . what happened? Someone will answer for this atrocity—get out of my face!" She held her hand over her nose when Sully pressed too close. "You could be sick!"

Reverend Cordell bent over her for a moment, and then straightened. "She's okay."

A mighty cheer went up. Audrey realized she had tears on her cheeks. Cordelia was a thoroughly disagreeable human, but no one—or not many—would have wished her ill.

Volunteers carried the woman to the closest house for shelter, and the search resumed for Horace and Junior.

An hour went by before they located Horace. Like Cordelia, he was vocal, but alive. Dr. Smith had arrived by now and was checking for injuries. They carried Horace to join his wife, and Eli approached Audrey. "We can't find Junior."

Audrey caught his hand. "He would have been home."

Eli turned to stare at the pile of rubble. "God help him."

"I know where he is."

Eyes pivoted to stare at Tate.

"Where?" his pa asked.

With a humph, the child pushed past the onlookers.

"Tate!" Eli warned. "Don't go near that house!"

"The house is gone, Eli," Audrey murmured.

"Don't go near that— Tate! You come back here!"

Tate marched on, his step determined. When he reached the incline, he began to climb.

Eli's hands shot to his hips. "Where is that boy going?"

The root cellar. Of course. Willow grinned. Those two boys played in that cellar more often than Cordelia could imagine. *Please God, let Junior have been, for once, in the wrong place at the right time.*

Thunder sounded, and eyes shot to the sky. A dark bank hung in the west.

By now Tate had scaled the incline. He stood, dusted off his knees and hands, and marched to the site where the house had formerly sat. Eli was halfway up the incline when the boy moved a couple of boards and jerked open the cellar door.

Junior Padget scrambled out, bawling. "*Ma! Ma! Where are you! I've been yellin' and yellin'!*"

Audrey hurried up the hill and took charge of the boy. She, along with Eli and Tate, led Junior down the incline, quietly calming him. The child's voice could be heard for a mile. "My house slid down the hill! I'm going to tell Ma!"

* * *

When Audrey returned home she found Willow downstairs in the parlor. "How did you get down here?"

"I decided to try Copper's trick. I scooted down the stairs. I couldn't bear that bedroom one more moment. Where is everyone?"

"Wait until I tell you." Audrey related the afternoon's happenings. "You would have to be there to believe it."

"The entire house slid downhill?"

"Just whooshed right on down. One minute it was sitting there, the next, whoosh."

"And the Padgets aren't seriously injured?"

"There doesn't appear to be anything serious though the doctor is with them now. Junior seems to be no worse for the wear, and Cordelia and Horace are alive and in good voice."

Footsteps sounded on the porch, and Audrey hurried to open the door. The three Gray cousins and Tate entered, followed by Dr. Smith. Audrey ushered them into the parlor, wondering about their grave expressions. Had the Padgets been more gravely injured than first thought?

"How badly are the Padgets hurt?" Willow asked.

Dr. Smith cleared his throat. "Cordelia has a broken arm and numerous bruises and scrapes. Horace has broken ribs and a mild concussion. Junior was playing in the cellar where it seems he spends most of his days playing with . . . er, Tate."

"Tate," Eli warned.

The boy scooted behind Audrey's skirt.

The doctor continued. "The child was frightened, but not hurt. Of course, it could have been worse. If Tate hadn't known about Junior's habit of playing in the cellar—rather strange, I'd say, but with Cordelia's propensity for fear, the poor child needed some outlet. Anyway"—the doctor reached to ruffle Tate's hair—"Tate saved the day."

Audrey shook her head. "Can't you see the irony? Cordelia and Horace refused to shelter others, so utterly convinced that they could keep harm away from their doorstep, and now they've lost their home and are at the mercy of the very people they refused to help."

Dr. Smith gave a weary smile. "It's true that we usually reap what we sow. I do have a piece of bad news though." He glanced at Tucker, and Audrey feared the main purpose of this visit was not to inform them of the Padgets' problems, but something more dire. Her suspicions proved true when the doctor said, "Before I could leave town one of Sterling's staff summoned me. Silas passed away a short time ago. Pneumonia fever. I did everything I could, but his age and the advanced state of the affliction were too much for him."

Audrey glanced at Willow when Tucker moved to take her into his arms. Sadness collapsed the young woman's features. "Silas? Gone? He was such a wonderful, generous man."

Tucker held her as she broke into tears.

The doctor got to his feet. "Sorry to be the bearer of sad news. You've certainly had your share lately. I must be going now. I still have to get to Twin Roads before darkness falls."

Eli walked him to the door, and Caleb said, "He's worked day and night to help the sick. It's a wonder he hasn't come down with the sickness."

Tucker put a handkerchief in Willow's hand. "Sterling was a mighty good man. You could have done worse than marrying him."

"But I love you."

He smiled, pulling her back to his chest. "I said you could have done worse, I didn't say you didn't choose wisely."

"Pretty sure of yourself, aren't you?"

"Only when it comes to you."

Willow sat up straighter and touched the hankie to her nose. "I could never repay Silas for his goodness. He paid off the mortgage on this house."

Tucker frowned. "I thought the judge owned the house. There shouldn't have been a mortgage."

"I thought the same, but not too long ago a man arrived to inform me the judge had taken out a large note using the home as security."

Eli shook his head. "Padget would never give a large loan to a man the judge's age."

"Horace didn't. Seems that Uncle Wallace arranged for the loan from a large Amarillo bank. I can only conclude that the bank officer knew and trusted the judge's integrity and therefore granted the unusual five-year conditions. When a representative arrived to collect, I had no means to pay. Had it not been for Silas's compassion, they would have foreclosed on the house."

Tucker shook his head. "This happened recently?"

"The day you proposed to me."

"Oh, is that the way it was? I thought you proposed to me," he teased. "The day it finally started raining."

She smiled. "Yes, the day Audrey and Copper came to town."

And destroyed the water tower. No one said it, but Audrey was sure the thought had passed through the minds of everyone sitting there, including hers.

"The day it started raining," Tucker said. "Where was I when this was going on?"

"At that particular hour? Ignoring me."

He grinned and tweaked her nose. "I knew you were around."

Audrey glanced at Eli. Did he have the same tendencies as Tucker? Pretend that she didn't exist but deep down be acutely aware that she was "around"? Tucker stood up. "Well, Sterling's generosity was well-known. Let's hope Silas carried through with the offer."

Willow glanced up. "Are you suggesting he didn't pay off the mortgage?"

"I'm saying there's a chance he didn't have a time for business matters. The rain started, then the sickness. Then Silas fell ill."

"Oh my goodness. I hadn't thought about that." Willow appeared to worry the idea over in her mind. Then she tilted her chin. "I refuse to consider the possibility. Silas was a man of his word. I'm certain he paid off that mortgage before the collector left town that morning. Everything is in order. I'm sure of it."

Sighing, Audrey reached for her hand. "Come now. You've been sitting up far too long. You need to rest."

Tucker bent and kissed his fiancée good-bye. "I'll stop by later this evening."

Moments later the door closed behind the men. Eli had not said good-bye.

"He did pay off that mortgage, didn't he?" Willow asked as Audrey helped her to the staircase.

"Of course he did. Now stop worrying."

Silas paid off the mortgage. To think otherwise would only be inviting more disaster, and the last thing they needed was more trouble.

Chapter 24

The moon was up when Audrey locked up, then climbed to the third story landing. She already missed Copper and her wry comments. The house was lonely without her, and Audrey could hardly wait to write and tell her about the day's unorthodox happening. The Padgets were blessed to escape the destruction with so little injury. They were now settled in the Widow Gleason's spare bedroom.

Before settling down for the night, Audrey stopped by Willow's room to see if she needed anything. She was awake, staring into space.

"Can't sleep?"

"I've slept enough to last me months." She shifted. "I'm fretting. Every little thing exhausts me."

"Just relax and let us take care of you. It won't be long until your strength returns, but you know Dr. Smith said you would have a long road to recovery."

"It's just so frustrating. Tucker has been patient, but I want to get married, Audrey. I love him so very much."

Smiling, Audrey sat down on the edge of the bed. "Well, if Tucker's agreeable, I don't see why you shouldn't have your wish as long as we don't tax you in any way. The man practically lives here anyway; he might as well marry you and move in."

A smiled touched the corner of Willow's mouth. "That was an uncharitable observation, Miss Pride. And the doctor said—"

"That you must rest, and we'll make sure that you do just that, but taking vows doesn't take a whole lot of energy, does it? And Tucker will be overjoyed."

"No . . . oh Audrey. Are you suggesting that I marry quickly and without any fuss?"

"That I am. And perhaps with a wedding soon, the wagon train will stay on a few more days. Your new friends wouldn't want to miss the occasion. Now, do you want to talk all night, or do you want to plan a wedding?"

Willow struggled to sit upright while Audrey reached over and removed the pins from Willow's hair. "Let me brush out the tangles while we visit." Her mind flashed back to Eli and the way he had touched her hair the night of Willow's miracle. Softly, almost reverently. Had he longed to loosen the pins and thread his fingers through her hair? Willow's acceptance of the offer drew her back to reality.

"That would be ever so nice."

It took a moment to locate the brush. Audrey sat down and proceeded to tame hair that was beginning to regain its glossy shine. "You have Claudine's wedding gown. What else do you want?"

"If I remember right, there were some very nice silk dresses in that trunk. Do you mind going up to the attic tomorrow and locating them?"

"I don't mind, but why do you need silk dresses?"

"They're for you and Copper . . . ouch! You're pulling."

"Sorry." Audrey worked the bristles free of a tangle. "What about flowers?"

Her friend sighed. "There hasn't been a flower around here in years."

True. The vegetable garden flowers had gone to seed. And with the flood following on the heels of the drought, a bloom didn't have a slacker's chance in this town.

"I could carry my mother's locket on a Bible."

"That would be nice."

Willow yawned. "I'm sorry. I tire so easily."

Laying the brush aside, Audrey helped lower Willow's head to the pillow. "We'll talk more in the morning. Do you want the window opened?"

"No. I know fresh air is good, but have you noticed an overpowering stench?"

"Rotting vegetation. Water standing in the ditches and fields has created an awful odor."

The patient closed her eyes. "I've missed so much. So much I'll never regain."

"Not being able to recall all that rain is a blessing, my dear. I've never been so wet for so long in my life."

"It can't rain on my wedding day. It just can't."

Audrey laughed. "Lucky the bride the sun shines on."

"And I am so fortunate."

"We are both most fortunate. And now, my love, you need to rest so you'll be fresh and bright-eyed when you see your true love in the morning."

Willow murmured. "In the morning."

Audrey blew out the light and stopped to rest her hand on

Willow's shoulder. "Sleep well, my friend. Come Saturday, we're going to have a wedding."

In her bedroom, Audrey pulled off her dress and slipped into her nightgown. She must find Redlin at first light and tell him about the wedding. He would be certain to delay the departure a few more days. The weather had held; a few days shouldn't make a great deal of difference, even though Old Man Winter was breathing down his neck.

Her mind turned to her own life. Tucker had spoken to the school board, and they were willing to let her take Willow's place. She would remain in Thunder Ridge.

She knew Willow and Tucker would welcome her here, but newlyweds needed privacy. With her income, she could find someplace to stay. But where? She knew almost everyone in town by now, and she couldn't think of a single person with extra space but the Widow Gleeson, and her house was tiny and already full with the Padgets. Yet someone in the area would surely welcome additional income and company. Yvonne would need living space; perhaps the two could share a room.

The turn of events was both a curse and a blessing. She would stay in Thunder Ridge, teach school, and pray that with time, she and Eli would grow closer. The possibility wasn't as farfetched as she'd once thought, but logic told her that she still had endless miles of bad road ahead of her.

Early the following morning, Audrey found the wagon master and relayed the wedding plans.

"Going to tie the knot, are they?"

"Yes. Willow doesn't want to wait any longer. I'm accepting the teaching position. I thought Saturday would be nice for a wedding."

"Don't blame her for not wanting to wait." He tightened a cinch. "Never know what tomorrow is going to bring. We can delay departure until Monday."

Later she climbed the steps to the attic carrying a lantern. The room wasn't as gloomy as she'd expected, but she still wished Copper was there to help with the task. She felt intrusive going through Claudine's personal effects. Would Wallace have minded? *Sorry, Judge. I'm only doing Willow's bidding.*

She set the lantern down on the planked floor, close to the trunk. Kneeling in accumulated dampness, heedless of the effect on her skirt, she timidly reached for the handle. When she folded the lid back, a scent of lavender wafted the air. Had Claudine packed these lovely garments away, knowing she would never wear them again?

When she lifted out the folded items of clothing, she found most of them unsuitable for what she needed. Finally she found a sky-blue silk that would do for her. The design of a pink silk would have been perfect for Copper, but it was the wrong color for her hair.

However, Audrey could wear it, and give Copper the blue.

On impulse, she dug deeper. Reaching the last layer, she found a dress of mint-green with deep flounces of cream-colored lace. She held it up to the light, searching for flaws and finding none. It was perfect, and she was sure it would fit Copper with very little alteration.

She carefully placed the discarded garments back in the trunk, and closed the lid. Folding the gowns over her arm, she made her way downstairs. The door to Willow's room stood open, and she spotted Tucker sitting in a chair beside the bed. Audrey carried the dresses in and spread them on the coverlet. Willow's eyes widened. "They're perfect."

"I thought so. Copper will look stunning in the green one."

Tucker lifted a brow. "Who's having a party?"

Willow grinned. "You are."

"I am?"

"Bridesmaids' dresses, silly."

He stared at her.

Willow sighed. "Our wedding. You do plan to marry me, don't you?"

"Of course I plan to marry you, and you're getting stronger every day, but—"

"Oh Tucker! It will be ages before I'm strong enough to walk down the aisle as part of a big wedding. I don't want to wait that long. I was thinking Saturday."

Tucker sprang to his feet. "A week from this Saturday?"

Audrey intervened. "No, this Saturday. Josh has agreed to delay the wagon train departure until Monday, and there's absolutely no reason to wait. You're getting married this Saturday, Tucker."

Willow nodded. "It has to be on the weekend because I can't get married if Copper's not here. Caleb can fetch her home. You don't mind, do you?"

The groom broke into a wide grin. "Mind? I could be ready in an hour."

"Saturday," the bride-to-be reiterated, grinning at Audrey. "If I can keep my eyes open long enough to recite my vows."

Tucker frowned. "You can't overdo . . . the doctor said—"

"That she had to stay quiet and we'll see that she does." Audrey lifted the dresses. "I'll hang them in Copper's room to air. Looks like we have a wedding on our hands."

Tucker reached for Willow's hand. "Just tell me what to

do, and what time to be there. I don't know much about weddings. This will be my first one."

"Mine too." Willow flashed him a mischievous grin. "And our last one."

He bent to kiss her, and Audrey slipped out of the room.

On Friday evening, Caleb brought Copper home from Beeder's Cove. Audrey waited at the door, enthusiasm brimming. "It's so good to see you!"

"It's been a long week. The children are wonderful but quite exhausting. How's Willow?" The two women shared an exuberant hug, blocking the doorway.

"Have you started classes yet?" Copper asked.

"Not yet. I'm working on lessons in my spare time. We should be able to start classes soon. We're really running behind."

Copper stretched out her arms and turned in a circle, "Oh, I'm so happy for Willow, I could just dance." She winced and paused. "My ankle hasn't fully healed. It still bothers me fiercely."

Caleb cleared his throat. "Where do you want your bag?"

She turned and blinked. "Well, I want it upstairs, but if it's too difficult for you, just leave it here and I'll carry it up."

He quirked an eyebrow. "I believe I can manage to take it upstairs. I thought you said your ankle was bothering you?"

"I didn't say I couldn't walk."

Yvonne entered the hallway. "Copper, you're back. How's the teaching job?"

Copper smiled. "Wonderful. Come, let's all have a cup of tea and I'll tell you all about it."

Yvonne laughed. "Beeder's Cove seems to have agreed with you. I declare you're prettier than ever."

"And that's outright flattery." Copper slipped her arm through the young widow's and walked her toward the kitchen. "What have you been doing while I've been gone?"

Yvonne's voice faded as they walked away. "I've been trying to find employment, and a place to live. I can't impose on Willow much longer, especially now that she's going to be married."

Shame filled Audrey. She hadn't given much thought to the young widow's plight. Her own future was uncertain enough, but Yvonne had no one to help her.

She paused in front of the door of Willow's room and softly rapped. "May I speak to you and Tucker?"

Willow's voice floated back. "Why so formal? We've never stood on formality before. Come in."

She entered and approached the bed. "Copper's back. She'll be up to see you soon."

"Good—I can hardly wait to talk to her."

Audrey sat down. "I just realized Yvonne is in a terrible spot. She has no way to support herself, she has no family in this area, and like me she doesn't want to impose on you any longer than she has to."

"You're not imposing, either of you," Willow said. "I want you here. Tucker wants you here."

"I do," Tucker said.

"Perhaps so, but we feel we are imposing, so please hear me out. With me taking Willow's teaching position, I was thinking I would talk to Kirkland about giving the funeral parlor job to her."

Tucker grinned. "What makes you think she'd want it?"

"Kirkland isn't so bad, and he clearly will need an assistant on occasions. It wouldn't be much, but it would help Yvonne. Should I ask without consulting her?"

"You could ask," Willow said. "But it would be up to her whether she wanted the job. She is more than welcome to remain here."

"Good." Audrey smiled. "I'll speak to Kirkland first before I raise her hopes. I feel much better. Thank you."

"Ladies, it's getting late." Tucker leaned to kiss his future bride. "I'll see you in the morning."

He left, and Willow smiled at Audrey. "I hope this works out for Yvonne. She's a wonderful, caring woman."

"She is. Now I must get some rest because I have a busy day tomorrow. We're going to have a wedding."

Willow frowned. "You'll have help, won't you?"

"More than I need since the wagon train is staying until Monday. Copper is going to make the cake. Now your job is to pray for sunshine."

Silas Sterling was buried Friday morning. Saturday morning the sun burst forth from a fresh-washed sky. At one o'clock the townspeople began to gather in Wallace's parlor. Eli and Caleb had brought benches from the church and borrowed every kitchen chair in town. Copper had taken silk roses from one of Claudine's hats to fashion a bridal bouquet. An arch for the bridal couple dominated the doorway—compliments of none other than Eli.

Audrey fingered the lovely white carving.

"Do you like it?"

She didn't have to look to know the love of her life was standing behind her. She could feel him. Drink in his unique scent.

"It's lovely."

"It was mine and Genevieve's. I made it."

"For her."

"For our wedding."

"She was a very fortunate woman."

She felt his arms on her shoulders, slowing turning her. For a moment he captured her gaze, and time stood still. "I know you feel that I am cold and uncaring."

"No . . ."

"Well, I am," he said. "Or I like to tell myself that I am." A grin broke across his face. "Tate says that I need a woman in my life."

"Really. Perhaps the Widow Gleeson?"

"Perhaps."

"Or Meredith Johnson?"

"Better. I do have the pick of the litter, don't I?" Still grinning, he lightly touched his lips to hers. For a moment she lost balance, so much so that he had to steady her. Gazing deep into her eyes, he said softly, "Wait for me."

The petition ricocheted through her mind. It wasn't necessary to clarify the plea; she knew what he was asking. Saw it in his eyes, heard it in his soft appeal.

It didn't take a moment for her answer. "I plan to. Forever, if that's what it takes."

"It won't." He lowered his mouth and kissed her fully, then eased her aside as the bride entered, leaning heavily on Tucker's arm. Her face was radiant with happiness. Caleb stood ready to follow behind with Copper.

Tate proudly led the procession, carrying the rings on a pillow.

Eli smiled down at Audrey and held out his arm. She placed her hand in the crook of his elbow, matching her steps to his. Her heart beat so loudly she was sure he could hear it. She'd waited a lifetime for this moment—this man. She could wait awhile longer.

The reverend read the vows. The ceremony was quick, but poignant. In a matter of minutes, Willow was Mrs. Tucker Gray.

The bride looked tired, but happy. She pleaded to remain downstairs at least long enough to share a piece of cake with her husband. Who could deny a bride?

Audrey slipped outside to absorb her happiness. Eli had asked her to wait for him. That she could do. However long it took for him to accept his past, she could wait.

A buggy rounded the corner and stopped in front of the house. Latecomers. They'd missed the nuptials, but cake and punch were being served. Two men got out and approached the stoop. They weren't dressed in finery. Just plain work clothes, and soiled work clothes at that.

"Is this the Madison place?"

"Yes . . . though the judge recently passed away."

"Are you a relative?"

"Acquaintance. May I help you?"

He held out a piece of paper. "Clifford Brown. I work for Amarillo National Bank, and I'm here to auction off the house." He held up a sheet of paper. "Here's the eviction notice."

Audrey's heart hit her stomach. Auction off? Eviction notice? She closed her eyes, willing the men away. This day was too perfect, too surreal to desecrate. When she reopened them, the two men were still there.

With a sinking sensation, she realized that not even a wedding or a promise from Eli could stop trouble.

Not in this disaster-prone little community.

Chapter 25

Audrey turned to look back at the closed door. *Oh, please don't let anyone come out now.* What should she do?

The younger man, burly, with a large black mustache, edged closer. She stepped in front of him, literally daring him to cross the threshold. "We've had a wedding today. Can't you at least wait until the guests leave?"

"We can't wait, ma'am. This rain has left my crew weeks behind. Now I ask you to step aside and please let us be about our business."

"Sir, I insist you wait outside until I find the present owner. She can talk to you here much better than in a room full of people. Please wait."

She fumbled behind her for the doorknob. The man looked as if he would follow her when she finally located the handle and turned it. She gave him the sort of look she reserved for wayward children. "You stay here. I'll be back in a moment."

Inside the house, she closed the door and went in search of Tucker. She found him in the kitchen talking to Eli and Caleb. He caught her eye, and immediately crossed to her. "What's wrong?"

"Men from the mortgage company are here. I made them wait on out front."

He shook his head. "Let me guess. Silas didn't have time to pay off the mortgage."

"And now they're here to repossess the house."

"They intend to take the house now?"

"I'm afraid so. Will you talk to them?"

He followed her to the front porch, closing the door behind them. "What's the problem, gentlemen?"

"You in charge?" the older man asked

"My wife is, but she's been ill. Can I help you?"

"We're here to auction off the house for moneys due," the black-mustached man said. "I understand this is a bad time, but we're only doing our job. Sorry."

Tucker nodded. "I understand. You realize this is a shock to us right now. We've just had a wedding. We understood the mortgage payment had been paid."

Stalling, Audrey thought. Could he persuade them to leave until the party broke up?

"Wallace Madison knew about the loan, and knew he wasn't making the payments. He had to know we'd show up."

"Mr. Madison suffered a stroke and recently passed away. His niece, my wife, lives here now, and she hasn't been well."

The man nodded. "Condolences regarding your recent loss. I regret having to bring you this news, but it can't be helped. Can your wife bring the loan up to date? Or perhaps I should ask, can you?"

Tucker shook his head, and Audrey wanted to cry. What would this do to Willow, who was still so fragile? How could they tell her the house didn't belong to her anymore?

Tucker remained calm. "We won't give you any trouble. Give us time to pack and dispose of the furnishings. We'll move as fast as we can in order not to hold you up."

The older man hesitated, and then motioned to the other. They retreated a few steps, talking animatedly before turning back. Audrey waited beside Tucker. The older man nodded. "We'll be back first light. You must have the payment or vacate the premises then. We'll post notices in the morning that the house will be auctioned off at noon."

Grim-faced, Tucker agreed.

The men left, and Audrey followed Tucker back inside. He located Willow in the front parlor and pulled her aside. Motioning for Eli to follow, he led the way into Wallace's library. Willow clung to Tucker's arm, her features drained. Audrey's heart ached at what must be done. Willow was just beginning to recover from the accident, and now this. Eli moved to stand beside her. "What's going on?"

Willow appeared unaware of their whispers. She glanced up at Tucker. "What is it?"

He took a deep breath and glanced at Audrey. She indicated a comfortable leather chair. "Sit down."

Willow gave Audrey a searching look, but obediently moved to sit down, folding her hands in her lap. "All right, I'm seated. Now what's all of this secrecy?"

Audrey met Tucker's gaze, and at his nod began. "The men from the mortgage company are here to foreclose on the house. Apparently Silas didn't have time to pay off the loan."

Willow's face drained of color, but she remained silent. Eli reached for Audrey's hand and held it. His warmth strengthened her. Why had it taken so long—so incredibly long for him to thaw? She still had a long road ahead to truly win his love, but they'd come half a journey in the past few hours.

Tucker knelt in front of his bride. "It isn't the end of the world. We've faced a lot of problems and come out on top; we'll do the same this time."

"I don't see how. We haven't a penny to spare, and Uncle Wallace's note is for five thousand dollars." She met his gaze. "Do you have a plan?"

"Honestly?" His eyes searched Willow's. "I don't know how I'll meet this week's payroll. They intend to auction the house off tomorrow noon. I gave my word that we'd be out by then."

"They'd do that on the Lord's Day?"

Tucker's eyes met Eli's. "Apparently so."

"So everyone will know." Willow brushed a stray lock of hair off her forehead. She looked so very tired. Audrey had to get her back to her bed.

"Oh Willow." Tucker lightly caressed the back of her hand. "I wish I could work a miracle for you, but I'm all out."

Willow reached out to touch his cheek. "I don't mind giving up the house. Wherever we live, as long as we're together, that's all I need."

Audrey's hand tightened in Eli's. He returned the grip. Their eyes met, and the silent exchange reiterated his earlier request. The contact was enough that Audrey knew love wasn't so impossible. Miracles still happened, even if Tucker was out of them. If the Lord gave her Eli and Tate, she'd be three times blessed. Love. Eli. And a child.

She had all the time God allotted her to experience the blessing.

Willow straightened. "These people are our guests. Friends, neighbors, the judge's trusted confidants, and it isn't fair to let them learn about the foreclosure through public notice. I want to tell them myself."

"You don't have," Tucker said. "I'll tell them."

Eli cleared his throat. "Let us do this, Willow. Let Audrey take you upstairs."

"No, it's my job, but I want the three of you to walk out with me." She held out her hand for Tucker's help.

Her husband obliged, and Willow leaned on her groom's arm as they walked out to meet their guests.

Audrey, with Eli beside her, followed close behind. She admired her friend's strength; not physical strength, but the inner strength that came only from a higher source and a woman of integrity.

The group walked to the front of the parlor where Willow and Tucker had pledged their love for each other just a short time ago. Now Tucker called for quiet, and the noisy celebration died down.

With head held high, Willow cleared her throat. Then she spoke softly, but with conviction. "It seems that Uncle Wallace took out a rather sizable note on this house five years ago. That note has now come due, and I'm unable to meet the payment. The constant rain has delayed the mortgage company from taking legal action, but they're here now, and I can't pay off the note. Judge Madison's home will be auctioned at noon tomorrow." Drawing a wavering breath, she added, "It would please me greatly if one of you would buy the house." Her eyes skimmed the interior. "It's a wonderful home. I shall miss it very much."

Murmurs of disbelief filled the room.

"The house was mortgaged?"

"How could the judge do that?"

"Why didn't someone say something earlier? Maybe we could've all pitched in and done something!"

"I'm sorry. I only learned of the note a few weeks ago." Willow quieted the whispers. "You're all good friends and neighbors. My husband reminded me earlier that we've faced many tribulations and come through. We'll do the same with this bump in the road."

Bump. Audrey would consider it a boulder.

People began to drift toward the door; a few approached Willow to offer their sympathy. Sully James walked up, holding out his hand. "I'm right sorry, Miss Madison . . . sorry, I mean Mrs. Gray. If there's anything I can do to help, you just tell me. I'll stop those men from taking your house, or my name ain't Sully James."

Willow smiled and patted his arm. "It's all right, Sully. Uncle Wallace owed the money, and I can't repay it, so they have a right to the house. I can't deny that."

"Well, it don't seem right. Putting you out on the street, and you been so sick and all."

Willow shook her head. "I'll be fine. My husband will take good care of me."

Sully nodded. "Now, that's the living truth. He'll surely do that, but just in case you need me, I want you to know all you have to do is ask. I ain't got no money, but there's always food on my table."

"I'll remember that." Willow leaned hard on Tucker's arm, and Audrey sensed she was near collapse.

"She needs to be in bed," she whispered to Eli.

Eli nodded. "Excuse us folks, but we need to get the bride upstairs and to her chambers." He nodded to Tucker, and Tucker picked up his bride and carried her to the stairway.

Eli went to help while Audrey returned to the kitchen, where she found Josh Redlin sitting at the table, downing a piece of wedding cake. Copper stood at the sink washing dishes, slamming pots and pans around. Audrey suspected the two had been at it again. From the looks Copper sent the ornery wagon master, it was pretty evident that she wanted him anywhere but where he was.

If Josh noticed her unseemly behavior, it didn't seem to bother him. Audrey told Copper what had happened, and Josh listened intently. When she finished the tale, he scraped the cake plate clean and pushed it aside. "That's a rotten wedding gift."

"Willow says Wallace did borrow the money and she can't pay it back. The men from the mortgage company are only doing their job." Audrey sighed. "But it is a rotten gift. It's not fair."

Josh shoved to his feet. "No one said life had to be fair."

Copper dropped the dishcloth in the pan and turned to confront him. "That's a very coldhearted thing to say."

"But it's basically the same thing Willow said," Audrey pointed out. "She just told the guests that the house will be auctioned off tomorrow at noon."

"Noon? On the Lord's Day?" Redlin lifted a skeptical brow. "That bank doesn't let any grass grow under its feet." He reached for his hat.

"Yes, they've acted very quickly. I honestly think they'll fail in their attempts to sell it. They can't move the ugly thing, and I really can't imagine anyone in this town wanting to buy it."

"It's nothing you need to worry about, Mr. Redlin." Copper stored cups in the cabinet. "You're about to move on."

"Yes ma'am. Anything to brighten your day." He grinned at her. "Well, duty calls. Plan to roll out early Monday morning. Be sure and stop by and wish me luck."

"In a pig's eye," Copper murmured.

"And a fine afternoon to you too, Miss . . . ?"

"You know my last name as well as you know your own." Copper slammed the cupboard door shut. "Now please leave."

Audrey winced.

Redlin left, and Copper turned to Audrey. "That is the most aggravating man on earth."

Audrey laughed. "But so appealing, don't you think?"

Copper's resulting look seared a hole in Audrey's dress.

"Or not," Audrey added.

Cordelia Padget sailed into the kitchen wearing her arm in a sling. "Thank goodness that vile illness has passed . . . oh there you are, Audrey. Where's Willow? I know you're all aflutter about the house, and I just wanted to tell Willow not to worry. Horace and I have had an eye on it for years, but Wallace refused to sell. We're going to buy it even if it will be on the Lord's Day. In a few months we'll have the best-looking house in town."

Audrey frowned. Willow was in need of a miracle but not this one, although a person was usually not well served to be picky about miracles.

Cordelia prattled on. "Yes, indeed. Of course we'll make suitable changes, and the first thing we'll do is change that horrible green color. But I'll make it a comfortable home, fitting for our community standing. I'll want to look it over carefully before we leave, but I feel safe in saying the house is as good as sold."

"The house will go up for auction," Audrey pointed out. "It will go to the highest bidder."

"Why, yes—which will be me. Who in Thunder Ridge could outbid us?" Cordelia smiled. "I mean, after all, Horace is the banker, and poor Silas is deceased now." She whirled and fluttered out like a hefty butterfly.

Audrey quenched the seething retort on her tongue. She supposed the good Lord had a reason for creating someone as galling as Cordelia Padget, but it was far beyond her understanding.

Copper's shoulders sagged. "I know I shouldn't feel this way, but I don't want Cordelia living here, in the judge's home."

"Nor do I," Audrey said. "But she's right. Now that's Silas is gone, no one in Thunder Ridge can outbid her."

"I know, but I don't have to like it."

Eli entered the kitchen. "Don't have to like what?"

"Cordelia and Horace buying this house."

He frowned. "They're planning to bid? Well, I guess they do need a place to live. Their house is gone."

Copper shook her head. "They need a bat cave."

"Well, sad as it is, we can't say who buys the house. It's whoever can outbid the other." He held out his hand to Audrey. "Care to take a walk?"

"I'd love it." She took his arm, grinning at Copper. Her friend put her hands on her hips. "What's this?"

"What?" Audrey asked in her most innocent tone.

"You." Her gaze swept Eli. "Him."

"Oh, him." Audrey's mischievous eyes met Eli's. "I'm waiting."

"For what?"

"One of those hard-sought miracles."

Copper rinsed out the dishcloth. "I'm glad you two finally opened your eyes. I wish I could be here for the auction, but I must leave early in the morning. I have lessons to prepare for the coming week, and I must attend a social tomorrow afternoon. One of the ladies in our congregation is turning ninety, and I offered to help serve. I won't be here when the house is sold."

"I'll write you right away and let you know who purchased it. I promise." Audrey glanced at Eli. "And nothing too exciting is going to happen right away."

She wouldn't exactly describe her and Eli's fragile involvement as imminently explosive, but she had a hunch it was going to quickly develop into fireworks.

If she had any say in the matter.

That night Audrey lay awake for a while, thinking about Willow and all the changes she'd had in her life. Now she had Tucker to lean on, and Copper had a school. Yvonne might be able to remain in Thunder Ridge, and the way Caleb treated her—well, when her grieving time was over, Audrey wouldn't be a bit surprised to see that woman win the other Gray's heart.

Audrey was up early, packing the parlor items Willow planned to take with her. Men were already loading the wagon with the judge's personal items to be stored in the barn at Tucker's place. Adele, Sadie, and Yvonne worked in the kitchen.

A knock on the door interrupted her work. She opened it to find Kirkland Burying, with his hat in his hand. "Good morning. I heard the judge's house is being auctioned off today and you're looking for a place to stay."

The question startled her. What was this? Kirkland making her an offer of . . . She met his gaze, perplexed.

His face brightened. "May I offer you the room behind the mortuary? It would be close to your work, so to speak."

"Work? What work?" She hadn't worked for Kirkland in a while, not since the illness abated.

He flushed. "I've been thinking about that. You're a young, single woman, I'm a single man, and perhaps the two of us could reach an arrangement?"

Audrey backed up a step.

"Uh . . . well, I'm indeed flattered, but since Willow's accident . . . You see, Kirkland, I'm replacing Willow. I'll be teaching here in Thunder Ridge. I won't be working at the parlor any longer."

"You prefer teaching to the funeral business?"

"Yes. I do." Ever so much.

He frowned. "That is surprising. I thought we'd make the perfect pair."

She managed a weak smile. Indeed. "Thank you so much for the offer."

"You're welcome." He tried to peer around her shoulder. "Is Copper available?"

"No, she left earlier this morning for Beeder's Cove." She glanced up. "She had community commitments this afternoon."

"Drats."

He turned and walked off.

"There's Yvonne—the new widow. She might be inter-ested in employment . . ." Kirkland didn't appear to hear her added response.

Indeed, she thought as she closed the door. Kirkland and her? The perfect match? She snickered out loud, picturing an even more unlikely scenario: Kirkland and Copper.

She chuckled all the way back to the parlor.

Toward noon, a crowd started to assemble. Seemed the entire town was present, but most were there out of curios-ity, because other than the Padgets, Audrey couldn't think of a man or woman in town with the funds necessary to pur-chase the judge's home. Earlier Tucker had taken Willow to his house; she did not want to watch the auction. Emptied of its contents, the house seemed to Audrey like an abandoned child sitting beside the road, waiting for someone to come along and claim it.

Noon sharp, the bidding began.

The black-mustached man lifted a hand. "Ladies and gentlemen. You've had a chance to look over the house and make your decision. Do I have an opening bid of twenty-five hundred dollars?"

Horace stood up and met the bid. The gathering mur-mured, even though it was exactly what they had expected.

Then another man spoke up. Audrey didn't recognize him, but she thought he might hail from Blackberry Hill or Beeder's Cove.

"Twenty-seven hundred," he countered.

"Twenty-seven hundred. I have a bid of twenty-seven hun-dred, do I hear three thousand?"

Horace took a step forward. "Three thousand."

Cordelia worked a fan, smiling.

"Three thousand. I have three thousand. Do I hear thirty-one hundred?"

"Thirty-one hundred."

Eyes switched to the stranger. He sat stone-faced, eyes fixed straight ahead.

"Thirty-one hundred! I've got thirty-one hundred; do I hear thirty-five? Thirty-five hundred?"

Silence fell over the gathering. Eli stepped closer to Audrey. "If I had the funds I'd buy it."

She slipped her hand into his. "Whatever for?"

He shrugged. "Can't tell when I'll need larger quarters." His gaze roamed the small yard. "It'd be a good place to raise young'uns."

"Indeed it would—fifteen rooms. A body could raise a lot of children here." Her hand nestled more tightly in his.

He gazed down at her. "You do realize that we are now officially courting?"

"I hadn't realized." This wasn't going to take nearly as long as she feared, but she was going to have to adjust to Eli Gray's rather confusing approach to love and matrimony. It made her head swim.

"You don't mind, do you?"

"Not in the least."

"Thirty-five. Do I hear thirty-five hundred, ladies and gentlemen? This fine home is a bargain at five thousand. Do I hear thirty-five hundred?"

Horace nodded.

"Thirty-five hundred. Do I hear four thousand? Four thousand?"

The stranger nodded.

Cordelia took a hankie out of her reticule and mopped her face. She leaned to speak to Horace. The couple exchanged animated whispers. Then Horace turned.

"Forty-one hundred."

"Forty-one! I have forty-one hundred. Forty-one, forty-one . . ."

A tall man parted the crowd. Josh Redlin appeared, dressed in rugged buckskin. "Sixty-five hundred dollars."

A collective gasp swept the onlookers. Cordelia swiveled to fix her eyes on the interloper.

Audrey leaned to whisper, "What's he doing here?"

"I don't know. I guess we'll see soon enough."

"Sixty-five hundred dollars! I've got sixty-five hundred, do I hear seven thousand!"

The stranger stood up, put on his hat, and left.

Cordelia yanked on Horace's jacket tail, but he shook her away. "We're not millionaires, Cordelia. Now hush up. We've been outbid."

"I don't have a home, you oaf!"

The banker firmly took his wife in hand and pulled her through the crowd. She was still berating him when he led her away.

Josh entered the small circle surrounding the auctioneer. "I assume cash will be sufficient."

The mustached man grinned. "Most sufficient. If you'll step this way, we'll conclude our business."

Audrey slowly turned to gape at Eli. "The wagon master bought the house? Whatever for?" She honestly believed that she had now witnessed every peculiarity this town had to offer.

Eli's hand tightened around hers, a slow grin starting at the corners of his mouth. "I want to be the one to tell Copper."

Copper. Oh my goodness. She would *swoon* when she heard the news. She matched Eli's grin when the enormity of Josh Redlin's purchase started to sink in. Why would Redlin want the house, unless he planned to move here and settle down?

Oh, Copper was going to love this. There was not nearly enough distance between Beeder's Cove and Thunder Ridge to prevent the clash that would result from those two dealing with each other on a regular basis. Thunder Ridge couldn't handle that upheaval.

Or could it? The following weeks should be mighty interesting.

Dear Reader,

Belles of Timber Creek has been one of my favorite series to write. The characters have remained in my head and my heart as I hope they have yours. As a Missourian who dealt with a great deal of rain this year, I sympathize with Thunder Ridge and its citizens. It is my hope that the theme of trust resonated with you throughout the stories. Trust—to step out blindly when there isn't a safety net. To expect with assurance. Tuck those words in your heart and carry them with you.

The year is flying by and I'm busy writing a new Christmas novella, *The Christmas Lamp*, to be published by Zondervan in 2009. It's a story about traditions, and how important they are in our lives. And watch for the final book of Belles of Timber Creek—Copper's story—in 2010. Also, I love to hear from readers through Avon Inspire or Zondervan Author Tracker found on my Web site, www.loricopeland.com. I love feedback, and if there's a particular subject you would like to read about, let me know.

Meanwhile, may God bless and keep you, and I leave you with the Scripture found in 2 Corinthians 4:16–18 (*The Message*):

So we're not giving up. How could we! Even though on the outside it often looks like things are falling apart on us, on the inside, where God is making new life, not a day goes by without his unfolding grace. These hard times are small potatoes compared to the coming good times, the lavish celebration prepared for us. There's far more here than meets the eye. The things we see now are here today, gone tomorrow. But the things we can't see now will last forever.

In His Name,

Lori

Discussion Questions

1. Audrey Pride came to Thunder Ridge with a job and a place to live. Then her plans crashed along with the water tower. Have you ever had life wreck your plans? How do you handle the resulting chaos?

2. Caleb was handsome, affable, and fun, but Audrey wanted Eli. Can we always explain why we are attracted to certain people? What qualities would you look for in a man?

3. Audrey took a job in the funeral home because she refused to be a burden to Willow. Do you think she had the right attitude, or was that a false pride?

4. Audrey, Copper, and Willow thought of one another as family, although they were not related. Do you have a friend who is as close as family? How far would you go to protect and preserve that relationship?

5. Willow planned to be married in her aunt's wedding dress. Would you want to wear someone else's wedding gown, or would you insist on one that was uniquely yours?

6. Audrey described Willow as a worrier. How would you describe yourself? Is worry all right, or is does it show a lack of trust?

7. Eli felt guilty because he was away at war when Genevieve died. Is it possible to let needless guilt prevent us from living life to the fullest? Do those feelings deprive us of God's blessings?

8. Copper liked to play matchmaker, although it upset Audrey. Is it fair to try to manipulate others?

9. Audrey lost her fear of the deceased when she tried to make her client beautiful for the woman's husband. Can you think of a time you did something good for someone who could do nothing for you in return? Have we really given anything when we expect payment of some sort?

10. Cordelia was afraid to help the people from the wagon train because they were sick and dying. What do you think? Does God expect us to put ourselves in danger in order to help others?

11. Caleb was attracted to Yvonne from the moment they met. Do you believe, from your own experience, that kind of instant attraction actually happens in real life?

12. During the terrible, dark days when Willow was sick, Tucker spent most of his time sitting beside her bed. Do you believe God is closer in the dark times, or is it harder to feel his presence when you are grieving?

13. Audrey was homeless and penniless in the end. Does trusting God automatically guarantee us a "happy ending" that fulfills all our desires?

One True Love

The next book in the Belles of Timber Creek series

by Lori Copeland

Coming soon from

AVON
INSPIRE

Copper Wilson scoured the chalkboard and imagined that she was wiping clean the past few months of her life, months cluttered with war and rain . . . lots and lots of rain. She stepped back, smiling at the clean surface. Her current existence was as bright as the piece of slate in the Beeder's Cove schoolhouse.

She heard the door open and turned to see school board president Benjamin Fowler enter the room. Swiftly removing his hat, he smiled. "Good morning, Miss Wilson."

She returned the greeting. "And a beautiful morning it is." Though not so beautiful for her best friend, Willow Gray. Noon yesterday they'd auctioned off Judge Madison's home, a place that had given Copper and others shelter those long weeks after they had arrived from Timber Creek. She'd worked to put the worrisome sale aside and focus on the future, but Willow's plight had been in the back of her mind since she opened her eyes that morning.

Mr. Fowler briskly rubbed his hands together. "I thought I would come by and check on the stove. Evenings are getting a mite cool lately."

"How thoughtful of you. I notice we have a sufficient stack of dry wood. Please extend my thanks to the person responsible."

Last week had been Copper's first on the job, and the time had proven difficult. She had tried to start a fire after school one afternoon, just to be sure she could do it. The old stove had smoked and the damp wood smoldered more than it had burned.

Finding dry wood had been difficult for the townspeople. Beeder's Cove hadn't received nearly the rain its sister community, Thunder Ridge, had experienced, but fall was upon them. Copper knew the children could wear their coats and mittens inside the classroom if necessary, but that was no way to start a school year. She suspected the old pipe might have gotten clogged over the summer, perhaps by some bird's nest-building activity.

"I will be glad to. We didn't get the heavy rains that plagued your area, but we got enough to make most of our firewood a little damp."

Damp. Mr. Fowler didn't know the meaning of the word. Copper's thoughts turned to all those weeks in Thunder Ridge, of standing puddles, wet clothing, and leaky roofs she had dealt with in the judge's old house. Frankly, though it broke her heart to think of Willow losing the judge's house, it would seem the foreclosure might be more blessing than curse. Now that Willow and Tucker were married, life might be easier for the young couple if they moved into Tucker's one-room cabin. Then when babies started to arrive Tucker could add rooms with the help of his cousins, Eli and Caleb, but then there was Audrey. Where would she stay? With strangers? Copper couldn't bear the thought but she had no answers.

She limped to the stove that sat in the corner of the room. It was a large black atrocity that looked capable of warming Hades had it been in good repair. The way it had smoked last week caused her to wonder about the history of the pot-bellied relic. The top hinge on the door was crooked and seemed weak. The left front leg was missing and had been replaced by an uneven block of wood. The pipe had a definite slant to it because the stove had not been placed directly underneath the hole where it went through the roof.

It seemed a little unsafe, and she had promised herself she would talk to one of the school board members about it, but she was too busy this morning to bring up the subject with Mr. Fowler.

Mr. Fowler focused on her limp. "Did you suffer an accident over the weekend?"

Copper glanced at the injured foot and shrugged. "Actually I injured the ankle a few weeks ago and it hasn't fully healed. These chilly mornings seem to aggravate the condition."

"An accident, you say?"

"It's a long story, but my friend Audrey and I were carrying ice one night to help another friend's high fever. She had received a blow to the head that left her unconscious for days. She almost died." Sadness washed over Copper when she thought how close she'd come to losing her friend. "Those were dark times. We thought she might not survive the injury, but our prayers were answered."

"I trust she's doing well now?"

"Very well." She smiled. "She married Tucker Gray this past Saturday."

"Ah yes. Tucker. Good man, as are his cousins, Eli and Caleb. We do business with the mill."

She bent to carefully place wood into the stove. "Mornings are getting quite chilly."

"That they are." Fowler took a step back, and his gaze followed the stovepipe to where it jutted through the ceiling. "Better let me climb up there and take another look before we light a fire. The building's sat empty since the war started, and someone was supposed to clean the flue, but it's possible a bird or two has built a nest up there again. I'll go take a quick look."

She nodded, his observation only halfway registering. Truth was, the thoughts of Thunder Ridge brought back memories of Josh Redlin, the impossibly arrogant wagon master who had carelessly stopped his party on the outskirts of town when illness broke out. For weeks Thunder Ridge had been forced to care for the ill and dying. It was only a short while ago that they'd finally buried the last of the bodies that had been stored in the icehouse. With the incessant rain, they'd had no other choice but to store the deceased until the ground dried, but thank goodness that aggravating, hardheaded mule of a man was out of her life forever, on his merry way to eastern Colorado.

She stacked dry branches around logs in the stove and, in spite of Mr. Fowler's cautions, reached for a match. In seconds the dry tinder blazed. She watched the progress until she was satisfied the fire had caught. Glancing at her timepiece locket, she quickly rose and hobbled to her desk. Children would be arriving soon, and she had not yet had time to register their last test scores. Overhead, heavy footfalls sounded on the roof, and she assumed Mr. Fowler was still piddling around with the stovepipe.

A dull ache settled around the rim of her shoe, and she

winced. The ankle was truly acting up today. Must be a coming change in weather.

Fowler opened the front door and stuck his head in, all smiles. "I believe we're in business. The stove seems to be drawing fine."

Copper glanced up from the recording ledger. "Thank you, Mr. Fowler. The room is starting to warm nicely."

"Anything else I can do?"

"Can't think of anything. Thank you."

"Sure am glad to have you, Miss Wilson. It's even better to have school open again." With a tip of his hat, he closed the door.

Precisely at eight-thirty, Copper rang the large brass bell that hung on the outside wall above the small porch. The sound carried nicely, signaling that class was about to begin. She had thirteen pupils ranging from six to fifteen years of age. The two youngest belonged to the Matthews family. Their grandfather was reportedly financially well-off. Others came from various parts of the area. She dropped the cord and took her stance at the front door.

"Good morning, Miss Wilson."

"Good morning, Sarah. Pete."

And so it went as the children filed by swinging their dinner pails. Coats were hung on the pegs in the short hallway, and dinner pails were stored beneath the desks. By eight forty-five, class was in session. The two youngest pupils, Emily and Mac Matthews (or Mackey he was called), sat in the front row, fidgeting.

"Today," Copper began, "we're going to talk about American history and the Revolutionary War." War was a subject she knew only too well. She, Copper, and Audrey had been forced to fight off marauding Yankees in the recent Civil War when their hometown of Timber Creek had been invaded. The town had been nearly annihilated by the Northerners. Copper, Willow, and Audrey managed to escape unharmed, but only because they stood their ground and fought. Afterward troops continued to ride through periodically, but the women, along with the town drunkard, Asa Jeeters, had managed to survive.

She forced her mind back to the lesson and picked up her ruler. "Now. Warren Brown." She knew full well the younger children needed to settle down before she addressed their study, but she had already noted that Warren had a tendency to forget his homework assignments, and she thought he might improve if she made his slackness obvious to the other students. "One of the most famous quotations from the Revolutionary War period is, 'I only regret that I have but one life to lose for my country.' The words, spoken as British authorities executed him for spying, were spoken by whom?"

Something in the stove made a loud *pop*, and in the silence, it brought a startled sound from little Emily. Someone else giggled.

Copper glanced at the stove and then scowled at the giggler. Silence returned. "You have all heard sounds like that from a stove. Now settle down.

"Now, was the quote spoken by Benedict Arnold, Patrick Henry, Nathan Hale, or Paul Revere?"

She had just posed the question to Warren when a loud crash turned everyone's attention toward the front door. Before Copper could form a thought concerning the cause of the racket, a large yellow tomcat streaked down the aisle toward her, followed by two large hound dogs, both barking at the top of their lungs. Evidently the front door had been left slightly ajar and the cat had dashed through. With typical canine enthusiasm the dogs had slammed into the door and continued the chase into the classroom.

The cat, openly desperate to find a perch above the yapping jaws, jumped onto the stove but immediately leaped back to the floor on the other side. Skidding to a halt, the lead dog slammed into the stove and knocked it off the block of wood. The stove tipped over, causing the door to fly open and burning logs to spill out onto the floor.

The feline reversed direction and headed back toward the door. This time it jumped up and dug its claws into a jacket hanging from a peg, and then climbed up onto a shelf that ran the length of the coat-hanging area above the pegs.

There it turned and faced the lunging, howling dogs, adding its own vocalizations of screams and hisses. The entire front hallway was full of lunging, barking, frothing animals.

The episode took only scant seconds, and Copper hadn't had time to comprehend any of it when someone cried out, "The floor's on fire."

She turned to look and was immediately grabbed by a terror she could not have described, even if she had been given the opportunity. A schoolteacher's greatest fear is a burning schoolhouse with the children still inside, and this was exactly what she was facing. To make matters worse, the doorway out of the building was blocked by the warring animals.

Instinctively the children flocked to her, and without instruction or thought they moved in a huddle to the side of the room opposite the stove as the stovepipe that had been dangling from the ceiling fell with a loud bang and soot flew out to mix with the smoke. With incredible speed, the fire expanded in a semicircle along the floor.

One of the children started crying, then another joined in. She knelt down and wrapped her arms around the weeping ones. "It's going to be all right," she cooed. She hoped she sounded more confident than she felt.

Glancing to the windows on the clear side of the building with the idea of maybe escaping through one of them, she called to a fifteen-year-old, "Harold, try to open a window. Hurry."

He tried the closest one, then another and then another. None would budge. Later it would be noted that they had been painted during the summer as part of the school cleanup project and were stuck.

"Never mind," she shouted. "See if you can do anything with that cat so the dogs will get out of here through the doorway."

Harold moved to the back of the room where the age-old battle between feline and canine was still in full progress. When he got close to the nearest hound, it turned and bared its teeth and growled at the boy. He hesitated and looked back at Copper, clearly undecided what to do next.

"Grab the cat and throw it out the door," Copper shouted. "Now!"

Plunging into the fray, he reached up on the shelf and grabbed at the cat. It immediately scratched him several times, and Copper had a fleeting thought that the tabby might jump on his head. He leaped back and glanced at Copper.

She assessed the fire's movement along the floor. It had almost reached the front-row seats and looked as if it might soon start to climb up the wall. Suddenly she had an idea. "Harold, put on some gloves and grab that cat."

Harold took a pair of gloves from the nearest jacket, grabbed the cat, ran over to the door, and threw it outside. The dogs nearly knocked him down as they rushed through the doorway.

By now the smoke had filled the room.

"Now children, quickly, everybody outside." Copper tried to get the traumatized children to hurry, without causing them to panic. It seemed an eternity before they reached the door and exited into the clear air.

"Keep moving. Don't stop. Get away from the building," she called. When she felt they were safe, she turned and looked back. By now smoke was boiling out of the front door. It was not until that moment that she had a fleeting thought of the long-term consequences of the fire. How would she be able to support herself if they could not have school in Beeder's Cove? What would she do for money?

Then, just as quickly, her thoughts returned to the immediate situation. She counted the children. Ten, eleven, twe— Count again. Ten, eleven . . . A thought more horrific than death hit her. There were two children missing.

She turned to Harold. "Harold, count the children. How many are here?"

Confusion, then comprehension, flashed across the boy's face. He reached out and touched each head as he counted. "There are only eleven, Miss Copper."

No, dear God. Please no. Please.

Whirling, Copper ran back up the two steps onto the porch and through the door. The smoke was so thick she couldn't see more than two feet in front of her. She immediately started coughing and her eyes began to water. *Please, God. Please. Please. Please.*

As she moved past the hanging coats, she stumbled over something. Reaching down, she encountered a handful of curly hair. She knelt down and reached out to grab the child, and her hand hit another small neck. Both of them! They were huddled together on the floor. How had she reached the outside without them? Which two was it? It didn't matter! She had them both.

All three of them were coughing and gagging as she crawled toward the door, dragging the children with her. *Don't let go of either one of them*, flashed over and over in her mind. *You'll never find them again*.

It seemed an eternity, but it was actually only a minute before they reached the porch. She tried to get the children to stand up and go down the steps ahead of her. As she started to take the first step down she fell against the railing, and it collapsed. The last thing she remembered was a fiery pain shooting through her ankle into her leg and then the sensation of falling.

Lori Copeland

LORI COPELAND is the author of more than ninety titles, including both historical and contemporary fiction. Lori began her writing career in 1982, writing for the secular book market. In 1998, after many years of writing, Lori sensed that God was calling her to use her gift of writing to honor Him. It was at that time Lori began writing for the Christian book market.

In 2000, Lori was inducted into the Missouri Writers Hall of Fame and in 2007 was a finalist for the Christy Award. She lives in the beautiful Ozarks with her husband, Lance, their three children, and five grandchildren. Lance and Lori are very involved in their church and active in supporting mission work in Mali, West Africa.